THE BLOOD RED SUN

Wu Kejing was born in 1954 in Fufeng County, Baoji, Shaanxi Province, not far from the ancient Famen Buddhist Temple. Originally a carpenter by training, he graduated from the Department of Chinese Literature at Northwest University, and has been described by Jia Pingwa as a "late bloomer."

A prolific essayist, story-writer and calligrapher of note, he has served as Vice Chairman of the Shaanxi Writers Association and Chairman of the Xi'an Writers Association. His novellas include *Five Maidens of the River Wei*, *Five Flavours Crossroad* and *The Handcuffs with Blue Flowers* (winner of the Lu Xun Prize). Wu Kejing's novel *The First Marriage* was adapted for television to great acclaim in 2018.

This book is part of *Shaanxi Stories*, a series of translated works by acclaimed authors from the Shaanxi province of China, produced by Valley Press in collaboration with Northwest University, Xi'an. The series editors are Hu Zongfeng and Robin Gilbank. Books in the series so far include:

#1   MOUNTAIN STORIES, YE GUANGQIN
#2   HOW OLD DAN BECAME A TREE, YANG ZHENGGUANG
#3   THE EARTHEN GATE, JIA PINGWA
#4   THE HOWL OF THE WOLF, HONG KE
#5   THE BLOOD RED SUN, WU KEJING

The Blood Red Sun

Wu Kejing

Valley Press

First published in 2019 by Valley Press
Woodend, The Crescent, Scarborough, YO11 2PW
www.valleypressuk.com

ISBN 978-1-912436-17-0
Cat. no. VP0137

Copyright © Wu Kejing 2019

The right of Wu Kejing to be identified as the
author of this work has been asserted in accordance with
the Copyright, Designs and Patents Act 1988.

All rights reserved. No part of this publication may be
reproduced, stored in or introduced into a retrieval system,
or transmitted in any form, by any means (electronic,
mechanical, photocopying, recording or otherwise) without
prior written permission from the rights holders.

A CIP record for this book is available from the British Library.

Cover design by Jamie McGarry. Text design by Jo Haywood.

Contents

The Blood-Stained Dress — 7
The Phoenix Widow — 18
The Qiyang Widow — 34
Red Lantern — 65
The Blood Red Sun — 81
The Black Bean Field — 95
Tile — 104
The Well Head — 118
Cliff-slide — 129
The Champion Scholar Goat — 143

Notes on the text — 209
Endnotes — 212
Acknowledgements — 213

The Blood-Stained Dress

There is blood in a man's head.
There is water in a man's heart.
— A folk saying from the Western Plain

Naturally, Madame Spots was wearing a *qipao* dress the day she came to my hometown.

The villagers had no idea the dress she was wearing was called a *qipao*. They all stood along the street to watch the graceful Madame Spots pass by, too dazed by her appearance to offer even a word of greeting. Even the cockerels, who crowed every day till our ears buzzed, kept silent. Even the dogs, who barked till the Heavens shook, didn't make any noise. A sudden quietness fell on the small village. It was chokingly quiet.

Madame Spots rode in a carriage. She could have stayed on board until she reached the gate of Uncle Spots' grand residence; she could have stepped out, marched in and sat down in the mistress's grand chair to receive welcome greetings from relatives, maidservants and manual labourers. Uncle Spots had many labourers and servants.

He hadn't always been this grand though. A long time before, he organised a gang of bandits and became rich overnight. Then he bought 300 *mu* of farmland, built a big house with three layers of deep courtyards and wings, and hired workers and servants, plus a pack of armed guards. Their shadows roamed around the village day and night.

People in Little Castle might hate Uncle Spots with a passion, but they all showered him with flattery as if they owed their very lives to him. Why? Because most of the young people in the thirteen clans of the village had joined Uncle Spots' bandits, carrying with them the dream that one day they would end up just as rich. Others were tenants on his farmland.

Madame Spots, for her part, had long heard of the wealth and power of her husband's family, but, as a graduate from Ginling College, she had been exposed to ideas of democracy and equality and such things and would not – no, never! – want to make a show in front of the village folks. So, still one full *li* from town, she asked the carriage driver to stop, lifted the curtain herself and stepped down on the ground, landing light as a swallow.

It was April in the Western Plain when she arrived. The rape flowers were in full blossom and the green wheat farmlands stretched to the horizon. Madame Spots drank in the scene. Around her, bees were buzzing about and colourful butterflies were fluttering here and there. What a charming pastoral scene! Madame Spots fell in love with the countryside on this, her first journey to her husband's hometown. She knew walking was not what Uncle Spots would do, but she had her own principles: she must be humble and respectful before the village folk.

Uncle Spots was stubborn and ambitious, rarely following other people's advice. But, strangely, he acted upon whatever Madame Spots said. Uncle Spots admired nobody but his wife. So, on that day, he also got down from his horse and walked into the village with her, arm in arm with an air of deep affection.

The dress Madame Spots was wearing was a *qipao* made of black silk brocade. It wrapped around her tightly and made her body look perfectly curved. Starting from her fair neck, a red fabric arc line glided over her chest like a shooting star. Running along it were evenly spaced chrysanthemum-shaped traditional Chinese fabric buttons, glittering like moonbeams. And small red flowers bloomed on the black background of the dress. As Madame Spots walked along with elegance and nobility, the villagers were struck by their own inferiority and unworthy lives and felt pain in their hearts.

Madame Spots smiled kindly at the people huddling on the side of the street. She acknowledged them with nods, but no one responded. Instead, they greeted Uncle Spots shyly. What a pity that Madame Spots did not realise the locals actually admired her most that day; a fact that was confirmed in folk stories passed down in later years.

After the event, everyone remembered that Madame Spots' *qipao* was made of black silk brocade. However, they disagreed on other details. The front opening, the piped edges, the fabric buttons and the flowers on the black silk became the subjects of much controversy. Everyone had their own views. As for the shape of the buttons, some said they were dragonfly-shaped, frog-shaped, bee-shaped, butterfly-shaped and swallow-shaped. Some said they were *pipa*-shaped, seven-stringed-zither-shaped and bud-shaped. Some even said they were chrysanthemum-shaped, orchid-shaped, peach blossom-shaped and kapok-shaped. But they were of one voice about one thing, without any dispute, namely, their judgement of Madame Spots.

To this day, they recall: "Madame Spots was somewhat unusual. She was different from us, not a bit different, too different!" What I heard in their various voices was an undertone of admiration, but also jealousy and a measure of hatred.

Uncle Spots had no spots on his face. His face was dark, chiselled and typical of the firmness and courage of men in the Western Plain. Uncle Spots' surname was not Spots. Actually, no one else was named Spots in the thirteen clans of his village. Where did his name come from? Either out of respect or mockery, he was called Uncle Spots – and it was completely due to his wife.

A short time before Madame Spots arrived in the village, a major event happened. The Japanese army broke into Shanghai. The whistle of cannons pierced the air and the roar of planes shook the earth. Both ripped the nerves of Nanjing City, the capital of the Nationalist Party. Generalissimo Chiang Kai-shek was at a loss about what to do next. He gathered his high-ranking military counsellors and generals and set a test to gauge their countermeasures. The question was: "The Japanese Army has come, what should we do next?" All weighed their words and wrote their ideas carefully. Uncle Spots responded to the question without hesitation. He took his writing brush and wrote "FIGHT" in big letters on the paper.

The instant he left the meeting hall, Uncle Spots, as Division Commander, felt his left eye twitching for no good reason at all. According to the saying, a twitching left eye foretells good luck while the right eye means bad luck. What good luck would befall him? His eye had been twitching for a few days without any explanation. Then, the officers from the government announced that he was being promoted to Major General.

A lady came with the officers. She was wearing a *qipao*. She had long legs and a slender waist. It came as a pleasant surprise to hear her say she had been appointed by the government as his confidential secretary. This is how Madame Spots entered the story.

Uncle Spots was grateful for the trust shown by the government from the bottom of his heart.

"Good," was his response.

He was a man of humble birth and few words. To many things, he reacted with one word: on the test set by the Generalissimo, he answered "Fight"; to his secretary, he replied "Good". He said "Good" chiefly because the secretary's *qipao* caught his eye. That *qipao*, made of bright pink mixed charmeuse, was as smooth as water. It opened at the front on the right side with lute-shaped Chinese fabric buttons. Its design was modish, with an air of simplicity. A plum blossom was embroidered on the part of her chest that protruded the most, giving a stereoscopic impression. This *qipao*, styled with elegance and decency, brightness and nobility, framed the secretary's body perfectly. Owing to two big slits up the sides, the lower part of the dress would float up slightly when she walked, producing a tantalising scene for Uncle Spots.

In the days that followed, when Uncle Spots saw the secretary walking past with her high-heeled shoes and *qipao* with the side slash openings, he would lose his head and say automatically: "Good."

It was really good. A few days passed. One night, the secretary turned back the bed for Uncle Spots, then unbuttoned her bright pink mixed charmeuse *qipao* and lay down next to him, amorously.

In the morning, they had to get up. The secretary washed away all the makeup from her face. Then, a few minor blemishes spots showed up. Uncle Spots collected her in his arms and licked every spot tenderly. Her body shivered with passion as a result of Uncle Spots' caress. She admired him, saying: "The Generalissimo said that your answer 'Fight' was written carelessly, but your answer was good. It was right. To the Japanese army, we have only one thing to say: Fight!"

The details of Uncle Spots and his secretary's everyday life spread around the Western Plain. My folks envied them. To them, Uncle Spots looked humble, illiterate and reckless; he had organised the bandits and killed many people. He had a bad – even worse – reputation in my hometown.

He brought his secretary back to his own village. In his hometown, she was not the secretary, but the wife of Uncle Spots.

Madame Spots never left my hometown after she came to the Western Plain, but Uncle Spots did not warm the adobe *kang* at all. He immediately left on his horse for the Anti-Japanese War. Bidding goodbye to Uncle Spots at the entrance of the village, Madame Spots touched his face gently, saying: "There is blood in a man's head." Madame Spots then pressed her hand upon her chest, saying: "There is water in his heart."

The villagers heard about her words. They did not understand them but liked the way they sounded. A few repeated them: *there is blood in a man's head; there is water in a man's heart.*

Madame Spots, in the eyes of the village folk, did not understand country life. Her 300 *mu* of wheat fields were on the east side of the village. The wheat was lush, as thick as the sea. When the wind arose, it stirred up tides of wheat. If the wheat had been left to grow for longer, it would have been a fine harvest. However, Madame Spots asked some villagers to level the wheat. They carried bricks, tiles, lime and sand. They brought a red flag and set off firecrackers before starting the building work. The time limit set for them was quite short and pressing. The brick kilns far away were baking bricks and tiles day and night but could not meet the needs of her plan. So, Madame Spots ordered her guards to lead all the manual labourers on the building site to demolish the temples and theatres of the thirteen clans in the village to meet the urgent needs of her new plan. The demolition of the temples and theatres outraged some people. They banded together and fought, using their tools and hoes as weapons. They were courageous but helpless without guns. *Bang, Bang!* Madame Spots' retainers fired rifles into the sky. The antagonists withdrew, knowing they could not win.

Madame Spots went to the building site to make her inspections wearing a *qipao*. She had so many *qipao* – a different one for each day. When she was wandering and inspecting the building site in her *qipao*, the workmen laboured even harder. With sweating faces and toiling hands, they also seized every opportunity to stare at Madame Spots. She obviously knew how to construct buildings. She gave advice here and made signs there. The whole plan was completed quickly. Eventually, everyone understood that Madame Spots was setting up a new school. A sign on the school gate was adorned with calligraphy by Yu Youren, the doyen of the Republic of China: *Free School of the New China*.

Madame Spots moved into the school. On a high platform, she worked, rested and ate in a house resplendent with the charms of a waterside town in the South of China. The villagers could see Madame Spots in her *qipao* pacing with grace and ease on the platform in the glow of sunrise and sunset. On the platform, she sat on a stool carved from a hollowed out red stump of mahogany. A woman attending her gave Madame Spots a celadon teacup with a lid. Then, she passed a vertical flute with two red tassels. Madame Spots placed it on her lower lip and played tunes that the people of the Western Plain had never heard. Naturally, the tunes were quite congenial. In contrast to the popular Shaanxi Opera of the Western Plain, her tunes were gentler and lovelier. Her tunes were favoured by people in the Western Plain. Her tunes made the sky bluer and birds of all kinds – magpies, turtle-doves and swallows – flutter in the clouds.

The first group of students came to school from our provincial capital, Xi'an. Some teachers with Chinese-style robes arrived as well. On the school opening day, Uncle Spots rushed back. He was the honorary headmaster but Madame Spots was the acting principal. All the students lined up on the playground for the opening ceremony. Then, Uncle Spots asked Madame Spots to make a speech. She did not give way to him but stepped forward from Uncle Spots' side and started to speak with elegance and ease. She had only spoken a few words when suddenly Uncle Spots shouted loudly at the students: "Open your legs!"

Madame Spots understood Uncle Spots' dialect. She looked back at him and smiled, then turned back, bowed to the students to apologise and said: "At ease, please."

"Open your legs" became a joke for Uncle Spots. People wondered why Uncle Spots did not know the words "at ease" or "halt" but insisted instead on the indelicate "open your legs." When it happened that first time, it soon became clear that the village folks admired Madame Spots and the way she handled the situation.

Everyone knew that the students in the school came from the occupied regions in the Northeast and North of China. Many of their homes had been burned down. They did not know whether their families were still alive. Madame Spots also encouraged local children to study in the school. If their family was rich, they could donate to the school; if not, they could study for free.

At the opening ceremony, Madame Spots wore a beautiful, dark red velvet *qipao*. Its buttons, like pinpricks of light, were as dazzling as gold. This *qipao* had long sleeves and a stand-up collar. Its cuffs and neckline were embellished with rabbit fur. A fire dragon as golden as the buttons was embroidered on the dark red fabric. The dragon's head was on Madame Spots' chest, its whiskers on her shoulders, its paws sticking to her belly and waist, its shining body and tail clinging to her delicate waistline and plump buttocks. The dragon came to life slinking around her. It was the soul and eternal beauty of the Chinese dragon. On that bright and sunny morning, she looked quite beautiful and charming.

Madame Spots had planned to wear this particular *qipao* for the ceremony. She had asked Uncle Spots to order it for her in

Xi'an. What she aimed to tell the students in the school was that the Chinese dragon would never die. The spirit of the Chinese dragon would last forever!

The last event of the opening ceremony was a basketball game. No one in the village had ever watched one before, including Uncle Spots. Seeing ten players running after a ball, Uncle Spots lost his temper with Madame Spots, saying: "If we can afford a free school, we can afford more balls. Buy one ball for each student and let him play by himself." Before he finished, Madame Spots started laughing and explained that basketball is played this way, with one ball.

Soon after, Uncle Spots had to leave. Again, Madame Spots saw him off at the entrance of the village and touched his face, saying: "There is water in a man's heart." Uncle Spots left. After a while, he turned around and shouted to Madame Spots: "There is blood in a man's head."

Madame Spots managed the school dutifully. A cohort of students matriculated, and then a new one was admitted. Most of them came from the occupied regions, but naturally, native children were welcome too. Madame Spots went from household to household to persuade some parents to support her in holding literacy classes for girls. Girls were being educated for the first time in the long history of the Western Plain.

Madame Spots paid all the costs; the students' accommodation and school equipment and the teachers' salaries. In the beginning, she made ends meet with money Uncle Spots mailed from afar, together with his local property. The villagers could still see Madame Spots pacing in her *qipao* on her platform in the glow of the sunrise and sunset, but now they rarely saw her smile, sip tea or play her flute.

It was at the same time as the Japanese surrendered that she was extremely happy for the whole year. Her *qipao* and her smiling face were the most brilliantly vibrant spots in the village. In the villagers' memory, Madame Spots wore a scarlet silk *qipao* with dark peony flowers that made her face look particularly young and fresh. Some folks clearly remembered that Madame Spots wore this *qipao* just for one day; the day the Japanese surrendered.

After that, Madame Spots wore different *qipao* dresses. One day, a yellowish silk *qipao*, the next day, a *qipao* stamped with the Chinese character for "happiness", and on another day, a green one with squares. All the different colours and styles made Madame Spots conspicuous in the village in the Western Plain, but she felt she had good reason. Uncle Spots had given her the *qipao* and it made her happy to wear his gifts. She changed them frequently so she could be freed from loneliness, sadness, grief and melancholy. She missed Uncle Spots greatly and craved his homecoming, or just a message. But Uncle Spots was like a drop of water evaporating in the intense heat of the sun. He neither returned nor sent messages.

People were guessing about his whereabouts. Some thought he had lost his life; some said that he was being punished by the Generalissimo Chiang Kai-shek because he supported the Communist Party; and some wondered if Uncle Spots had actually beaten the Communist Party on behalf of the Generalissimo. There were many guesses but no one was certain of his whereabouts. The day of the school opening ceremony was the last day he was seen in his village.

The cost of the school was now a serious problem, especially as there was no news from Uncle Spots. Madame Spots' savings were gone. As a result, she had to let go some of the servants and guards. The land rent was no longer paid to her, instead all the grains and land rents were handed directly to the school.

Then, the Second Chinese Civil War broke out.

The school had a hard time remaining open, and finally closed after the Liberation Army fought battles in Fufeng County and Mei County. Madame Spots did not leave the school. On the contrary, she still lived in her house on the high platform, built in the style of a waterside town in the South of China. Every day, she put on a different *qipao* and paced with grace in the glow of the sunrise and sunset. The time came, however, when the work team for land reform came to the village. Madame Spots was taken out of her house, paraded through the streets and then tyrannised.

The site chosen for her persecution was the playground where Madame Spots had made her opening ceremony speech. She was put on trial. Folks from the thirteen clans of the village and people from outside flooded in to watch. The large playground became a sea of faces. People even climbed into the high treetops or stood on the top of walls to watch. Madame Spots was still exceptional and attractive. In the Western Plain, all the women, old and young, wore home-woven, home-dyed black or indigo garments. Madame Spots was the exception; she had colourful *qipao*s and a rich knowledge.

Two armed gunmen escorted Madame Spots onto a platform. They pressed her head down over and over again, but she raised her head up over and over again.

While she was held captive on the playground, a man searched her home. Opening up her three mahogany wardrobes, he was amazed to find one *qipao* after another, each as delicate and exquisite as the next. He also found a box of jewellery. There were pearls, blue jades, all to match her *qipao*s. Her accessories matched so perfectly that nobody had noticed before. It stemmed from the type of education she had. Women without her education might wear silver and golden ornaments, but they could never have known how to wear pearls and blue jades like Madame Spots did.

Madame Spots still wore her *qipao* as she was tortured mercilessly on the platform. It was lily-white dotted with red baby's-breath. Madame Spots had deliberately worn it in a bid to identify herself as an advocate of the people's government. When she was in this *qipao*, a feeling welled up in her heart that the red stars were infusing her body and blazing forth. Her heart, trembling with excitement, felt aflame. What a flame of new hope for the future! Madame Spots had dreamed her life could prove as miraculous as the breath of a newborn infant, that she could be a conduit of hope, the harbinger of a brilliant future.

However, people in the Western Plain could not bear the fact that Madame Spots might have new ideas. She was labelled as the mistress of a reactionary warlord and the wife of a despotic landlord. The newly empowered villagers shouted slogans, rushed towards Madame Spots and started to hit and kick her to the ground. The first group that rushed forward was the women of the Western Plain. They kicked her, boxed her and spat on her. Their spittle, sticky as a hail of bullets, shot at Madame Spots' head, face and *qipao*. Someone twisted a brick from the wall of the school and smashed her head. Her skull was broken and bright red blood flowed out through her hair like a purling spring.

Madame Spots was dead. The pure white fabric of her baby's-breath silk *qipao* was stained with her blood, the vibrant red combining perfectly with the baby's-breath. The *qipao* was now a blood-stained dress.

On the day she died, the Special Commissioner of the newly established People's Government of the county rushed to the scene and made an embarrassing announcement: Madame Spots was an enlightened democrat.

Madame Spots was buried in the backyard of her school by the new people's government. Before the Cultural Revolution, I had the good fortune to be accepted by the renamed school and saw her tomb covered with winter jasmine. I fantasised that the numerous winter jasmines became a *qipao* for Madame Spots, which would not wither as time went by. However, some time later, the ghostly wind of the Cultural Revolution began to blow more violently. The young students with their red sleeve emblems used hoes and shovels to scrape the winter jasmine off the tomb and planed it smooth. The tablet, set up for Madame Spots by the new people's government, was overthrown in the Tomb-Planning Movement and broken into two pieces.

Now, if you have a chance to go to the Western Plain in Guanzhong, all you can see that remains of Madame Spots is her high platform. However, people who knew her still remember her words: "There is blood in a man's head. There is water in a man's heart."

The Phoenix Widow

Red skinned radish and purple garlic crown,
An able wife looks up, her husband bows down.
  — A folk saying from the Western Plain

She was not the only widow in Phoenix Town, nor was she the only widow who enjoyed wealth and fame.

Yet she alone garnered a reputation and prestige which extended far and wide, lasting for decades. It was unusual for the town where she lived to be appended to the name of a widow. However, she was indeed qualified to bear the epithet and she alone had the capacity to justify it. The title was fully deserved.

It was the will of the Heavens, or so the people said, that she was able to conjure up a fortune out of nothing.

There is, for instance, the story of how a pottery crock filled with gold was excavated from a clay pit north of the town. One spring in the last century, the Phoenix Widow hired two labourers to make adobe bricks in her pit. They were both tender hands, not seasoned enough to be driven too hard. The lads were told to come over to her house very early in the morning with their tools – including stone hammers, wooden moulds and iron shovels – and head home when the stars began to twinkle in the evening sky.

The Phoenix Widow rustled up three meals a day for them and had their food sent to the pit in a bamboo basket. She knew that if they weren't properly fed they wouldn't apply themselves. What is more, she liked the way they ate. One swallowed like a wolf and the other gulped like a tiger. The spread was nothing grander than steamed buns, dough ball soup and noodles. Each could polish off six buns and two bowls of soup per meal. If noodles were on offer, each finished two bowls without soup and two with soup. Once they were done, they put down the bowls and chopsticks and resumed their graft.

The two brick-makers did a decent job. If you were to stand and monitor what they were doing, you would soon find that each adobe brick was made in a very orderly way. To be specific, this craft required two people working as a team: one to hammer the clay, remove the bricks from the wooden frame and put them away; and another to make the preparations, such as cleaning the dust from the stone, adjusting the wooden frame, scattering a handful of plant ash in its cells and shovelling fine soil onto the plant ash. After these provisional jobs had been done, the hammer man would leap onto the stone hammer and then onto the soil to tread it down and make it as firm and solid as possible. When the brick was cast and ready, he would slip it out of the frame and pile it up with the other finished ones. The whole process of making an adobe brick could be executed in the time it took for you to catch your breath. The stone hammer swung up and down, producing an echo as if it was ricocheting off a mountain cliff. This could be heard three *li* away and became the enchanting and moving rhythm that redounded within the Phoenix Widow's heart.

The adobe brick-makers were adolescents and mischievous by nature. It was noon by the time the widow came with lunch. She was middle-aged but possessed delicate white skin. She hobbled over to them on her bound feet, leaving a pair of small but pretty footprints. They intentionally left them undisturbed, not breaking up the earth decorated by her footprints in order to make a brick. Perhaps they were captivated by her tender lotus feet. Or perhaps this served as a kind of spiritual stimulus, spurring on their productivity? They didn't have the heart to desecrate the footprints. Maybe they just wanted to play a joke on the widow, keeping her footprints intact so she would be stunned when she brought them the next meal? In that case, she might smile and complain sweetly, cajoling them to work more merrily and even harder on her behalf.

Frankly, the two young hands did this without a hint of malice or ill will. They carefully sidestepped the small footprints so that they stood out prominently on the terrain of the field.

Along came the widow, sashaying all the way from remote Phoenix Town. In the midst of that sunny afternoon, the basket hanging on her arm became a stage prop which picked out the paleness and delicacy of her complexion.

She walked over to the two brick-makers.

The widow knew nothing about the footprints and took no notice of how both the young men were squinting at her with mischievous but gentle smiles on their faces.

As usual, she shouted: "Come take a rest and eat."

The brick-makers didn't stop working until they finished another two adobe bricks with regimented hammering and treading. Nobody could tell whether they were really conscientious labourers anxious to work overtime or just pretending to be working diligently. After several rounds of shouting from the widow, they finally stopped and came to the bamboo basket, taking out bowls and chopsticks to eat the buns and drink soup at their usual pace. The widow, however, felt something was amiss.

What was wrong? The two labourers' uncertain eyes revealed the secret they had guarded carefully for the whole afternoon.

While tucking into their meal, the boys glanced at the widow's feet but could not see a thing as they remained concealed beneath her black satin embroidered skirt. People are sometimes strangely eager to see what they cannot. Those two pairs of eyes almost bulged out.

The Phoenix Widow, with a nature of an orchid flower, chaste and decent, knew their secret in no time. She glimpsed how her little footprints had been preserved deliberately in the earth. She knew at once they were hers.

As the boys had expected, the widow suddenly became flushed on seeing how they had left her marks undisturbed. She smiled gently, exposing her jade-like teeth, and accused them coquettishly.

"A pair of living treasures! Why did you keep those footprints? Can they be eaten or drunk?"

The young men laughed heartily.

The widow moved closer to the footprints, which had been preserved all afternoon, hitched up her skirt and compared her feet to them before wiping the marks flat.

The way she daintily rubbed her small yet pretty feet generated a shock: "There's treasure down there!"

Perhaps she should have felt grateful for the way embarrassment brought colour to her cheeks, otherwise, upon spying the bounty, she would have become flushed with intense excitement, betraying the secret of the gold to the two young men. Fortunately, the rouge on her face covered everything up.

There was neither pleasant surprise, nor panic.

When recalling that moment years later, she was proud of her consummate calm. She also still chuckled and expressed concern, kindness and care towards the brick-makers.

At the time, she asked: "Are you tired? If so, stop and take a rest."

Fumbling out two copper coins from her bosom, she handed them over.

"There will be an opera performance in the town tonight. Both of you should go along and watch it."

At first, they wanted to decline her kindness. However, the widow commandeered and confiscated their stone hammer, the wooden frame and shovel, urging and exhorting them to climb out of the pit and go to town for the evening show.

To the sound of gongs and drums, she dug out the treasure from beneath the small footprints kept by her labourers.

It was a jar of ingots, round as cakes fashioned from gold.

The pieces were indeed like hot deep-fried dough cakes lifted freshly out of a pot of oil. One, two, three; when she took the gold out of the container, her hands were trembling as though handling hot cakes. How many ingots were in there? Only the widow knew. How much did they weigh? Only the widow knew.

She had made a fortune overnight.

The widow had moved to the town after her marriage and, in truth, was not actually a widow. She still had a husband, though he was gravely ill. After years of him ploughing her body, they produced both a son and a daughter. Following that, he sprawled out sick on the bed, leaving his wife to deal with all chores both within and without the household.

People are seldom inspired by anything but money. The morning after she struck gold, her husband rose, all his diseases disappearing without a trace. The malingerer left behind his sickbed and set about assisting his able wife in certain tasks.

Phoenix Town on the Western Plain was an ancient place with a history of more than one thousand years. A small fair was held every other day and a large one every ten. Shops along the main streets conducted business of every kind. There were theatres, temples for monks, ancestral temples and schools, which made the spot flourish. It teemed and thronged with people coming from far and near. Nevertheless, some shops still closed down if too little profit was gleaned.

The proprietor of Jia's grocery store hailed from Qi County in neighbouring Shanxi Province. Several generations of his family, including himself, had done business in Phoenix Town.

One day, a notice was pasted on his door stating he had something urgent to handle back home and was keen to sell his store.

The instant the Phoenix Widow beheld the black and white characters on the sheet she went in the shop without consulting anyone else. Positioning herself before the red wood table in the counting room, she sat upright as she negotiated how much the owner might be prepared to accept.

"You're in urgent need of cash?"

"Why else would I be selling up?"

"Something urgent happened?"

The boss admitted: "Yes."

"What happened?" The widow pushed further.

Very painfully he responded: "Don't ask."

"I'd like to know," she insisted.

The man sputtered out desperately: "Kidnapping."

The worried widow went on: "Offer me a price then."

The price proposed by the storekeeper was less than the real worth of the business. She knew this and refused to accept. Instead, she whipped out a gold ingot, which together with two silver coins far exceeded the value of the shop. The owner was moved greatly by her generosity. The townspeople, on learning about the transaction, paid her extravagant compliments, deciding she was a generous woman rather than a simple-minded one.

Their responses served as a fine advertisement for Jia's grocery store. After changing hands and having minor repairs, it reopened for business and, as expected, had a far better turnover.

Taking the successful running of the grocery store as a springboard, the widow adopted "Prosperity" as her trademark. She acquired a clothing store, a grain merchant, a restaurant and an inn. Shops with the moniker "Prosperity" could be seen every few steps along the streets.

The widow began to walk with her head held high as she patronised the streets of the town. A smile or a movement of her hands would draw diverse reactions. Those around her laughed when she laughed; her gentle smile was met with an enthusiastic laugh from others. Her gesticulations – perhaps just a gentle swing of her hands – would make people dive away to the roadside tea shop and come back with a hot towel and a fully-loaded teapot. In a word, the widow had become the lynchpin in the community, well-known and respected. Clerks from the town hall secretly contacted local merchants in a bid to promote her to Chair of the Municipal Chamber of Commerce.

The general consensus became more and more favourable towards the widow. An aged scholar penned two lines in tribute, mentioning two local crops:

Red skinned radish and purple garlic crown,
An able wife looks up, her husband bows down.

Although the story has been circulating around the Western Plain for some 70 or even 80 years, there is disagreement over whether two products with such a spicy tang are fitting to describe a widow. But, after hearing the couplet for the first time, its subject visited the scholar in person with gifts. Speculation over the substance of their conversation was rife, but since they kept their own counsel, no definite answer has ever been found. All we can know for certain is that the widow chose to remain tight-lipped, and so did the man of letters. One thing that is clear is that from then on whenever the widow found she had time to spare, she would meet with him and bring along munificent gifts.

Accidents of various different kinds caused the Phoenix Widow one headache after another. Most dire of all was the widespread drought that struck the Western Plain in the eighteenth year of the Republic of China period, namely 1930. This was accompanied by a small blaze in the clothing store, incurring minor losses, and some pilfering at the grain merchant. Although the damage was not heinous, alarm bells rang, telling the shrewd widow to be vigilant and take precautions.

The most terrible thing of all happened in that dry, cold winter.

The widow's fourteen-year-old son was kidnapped.

Who was the culprit? She asked around among the gangs of bandits in the countryside and was told that none of them was responsible and none capable of such an act, particularly since the widow had agreed before the kidnapping took place that she would regularly give them a certain amount of money. A scrap of a note was delivered two days later, informing the mother that the kidnapping had been instigated by refugees who had fled from famine and were now living in the town.

The widow was relieved.

But her husband, so grievously shocked and discomfited by this incident, experienced a terrible relapse. He didn't eat or drink for two days, his mouth murmuring not the name of his kidnapped child, but that of his son and heir, who was in his twenties. After breathing his last, he fell stone dead.

From then on, she was a widow both in name and in fact.

Since she knew who the kidnappers were, she was in no great hurry to retrieve her son. Instead, she first summoned a troupe of musicians along with the temple monks in honour of the death of her husband. In the seven days before his entombment, all the restaurants that traded under the "Prosperity" banner were opened to fill the stomachs of the famine refugees for free. The widow also hired some hands to carry pots of food and steamed buns onto the streets and distribute them among those who were in greatest need of food.

Despite occurring in a year of famine, the funeral of her old man was transformed into a joyous and happy event by the widow. This much could be gauged by the smiling, sated, satisfied faces of those who had previously gone hungry.

The widow's man was thus buried.

Her son also came back home after the funeral.

The widow didn't shed one tear after her husband's death. Now, looking at her son, unhurt and undamaged, she approached him and slapped his tender cheek. Welts instantly appeared. She then embraced him and rubbed the marks with her hand, tears now pouring forth. A sorrowful and mournful atmosphere enveloped Phoenix Town in those days of hunger.

After the calamities of losing her husband and her son's kidnapping, would the widow still raise her head as high as she used to do? Anyone else might show some restraint. But she did not.

The widow would not have been true to herself if she shrank back and lowered her head. Her resolve surpassed normal expectations and no disaster was bad enough to make her curl up at home in floods of tears, lamenting the harshness of fate and the impermanence of the world. She would not.

Wiping the tears from her son's face and then from her own, it dawned on her what she should do in the aftermath of his kidnap and safe return.

The drought persisted. Famished people in the town, especially the frail seniors and the poorly young, succumbed in spite of the alms they received from the Phoenix Widow. Day and night, the streets bore witness to death. Weak as those who expired were, their death throes were nonetheless loud and harrowing.

Most anxious and concerned of all was the Phoenix Widow.

She stayed awake night after night, contemplating what she ought to do. One strong thought flashed though her mind and became viscid in her heart.

A road should be built!

Phoenix Town was 30 *li* away from the county town; not a huge distance, but three deep ditches – Dragon's Tail Ditch, Horse's Tail Ditch and Oxtail Ditch – marred the journey. As the plateau lay flat as a pancake, they could not be seen from a distance and were typically chanced upon by travellers whose path seemed to simply disappear. Their sheer depth and narrowness made people worry about becoming stuck and being crushed to death by the walls on either side.

The widow, therefore, reasoned that a road should be built with three bridges to span the ditches and enough room for a three-horse-carriage to pass by smoothly.

As the idea took hold, she sprang into action.

She knew perfectly well that it was too tall an order for her to manage alone.

When the widow arrived at the town hall, the civil servants were preoccupied with the hunger issue. She was seen by many as their saviour. When they saw her, they escorted her to the refectory, served her a cup of tea and asked what had happened.

The officials had thought the widow was there to enquire about the progress in her son's kidnapping case. She had been instrumental in solving numerous dilemmas for them, so it was only right that they should take an interest in her tribulations.

The reality was that employees had been sent out covertly to discover the identity of the kidnapper, with the intention of capturing him and sending him to the widow.

The widow craned her head to look as the ceiling as she drank her tea.

Her counterparts, meanwhile, were flustered and said: "We are working hard on it."

The widow knew only too well what they were talking about, but asked deliberately: "Working on what?"

"The kidnappers. Whatever else?"

"My son has come back home. Who are you looking for?"

"Even if your son has been rescued, we still need to find out who they are. How dare they kidnap your son?"

Levelling her eyes, she went from gazing at the ceiling to glaring at the civil servants. She corrected them, insisting that she had not come on account of her son, but because she had a brainwave to share with them. Following a few pleasantries, she outlined her proposal for crossing the three ditches with a road.

At last, the widow concluded: "Every one of us needs to do our share."

What a fine thing that was! Her listeners were very excited to be privy to such a great scheme. They, as civil servants sustained by rations supplied by the state, had considered pursuing some course of action that might benefit the local population. But, regrettably, they lacked money and a firm goal. The road building scheme now presented them with a goal and the widow's subsidy, together with smaller sums donated by merchants, made it feasible. The enterprise would not only solve the problem of the ditches, but also alleviate the hunger of some of the refugees; a problem that currently wasn't being dealt with because, as the saying goes: "It is hard to find such a good thing even with a lantern to light the way."

The townsfolk elected the widow Chair of the Phoenix Town Chamber of Commerce. The new Chairwoman quickly raised enough money and provisions to initiate the building of the road and bridges.

The town hall mobilised the hungry population, telling them: "We will build a road and bridges between Phoenix Town and the county town. Our dream of whipping horses and riding carriages all the way to the county town rather than going on foot will become a reality. To date, the widow has taken the lead in personally raising money and food from her own pockets and from the merchants in the town. What is needed now is a labour force!

"Join us in building the road and you will be fed three meals a day with one thin staple – porridge – and two dry ones – steamed buns and noodles without soup. Ten days of road-building will also earn you half a *sheng* of wholemeal flour and a quarter *sheng* of plain wheat flour, which you can take home to feed your parents and children."

There was no need to address them in this way and rally them into action. They had already spontaneously formed road and bridge construction groups, with professional teams of stonemasons and carpenters as well as unskilled labourers.

The subsequent winter and spring saw hundreds of ravenous people hard at work. With the widow's financial aid and initiative, three bridges surmounted the three ditches, and a road was built, running from the outskirts of Phoenix Town all the way to the county town.

The day the construction work was finally finished, the widow invited some opera singers from the provincial capital to stage a performance in the town.

The opera company from Xi'an arrived in a succession of carriages which, one after another, sped along the newly-built road.

The actors sang wholeheartedly on the stage, entertaining the famished who listened offstage with joy. Three days and nights of performances with loud gongs and drums pleased the people to their heart's content.

The hungry masses were grateful to the widow. So deep was their admiration and love when they sang: "Red skinned radish and purple garlic crown. An able wife looks up, her husband bows down."

She was indeed extremely capable insofar as her idea of building a road was executed successfully and the hungry survived the winter and spring famine in the eighteenth year of the Republic of China era.

The three-day performance drew to an end. The wheat in the field prospered after a hefty winter snow and a late spring downpour. People's spirits were lifted during those three days of opera, and the wheat in the fields was evidently roused too. It grew optimistically in the sunshine and ripened quickly. The summer wind blew by, bringing with it a fragrance of wheat in the field.

It was indeed a fine enough harvest to make people ecstatic.

For two years, the widow's "Prosperity" shops – the old grocery store, the clothing store, the grain shop, and the newly-opened restaurants and inns in particular – were heading on the right track. Bolstered by convenient transport between the local town and the county town, the widow expanded her business into the latter, opening even more "Prosperity" shops. Within two years, the rapid mushrooming of the "Prosperity" brand meant that all branches of her business were operational in the county town.

Unfortunately, man is not as deft as the Heavens when it comes to fortune telling. Rolling out the businesses meant a thinning out of the dividends and a multiplication of the problems. The famine of 1930 was followed by a drought in 1933. The ground of the Western Plain became dry enough to kindle a fire. Save for scant droplets of rain following the odd spell of thunder and lightning, the summer days were uniformly scorching. Clouds were a rarity. The village pool stood dry, as did the wells. The water in the beds of the ditches became as sparse and lifeless as an old crone's weeping.

Come harvest time, the farmers reaped nothing.

Barely had the Western Plain recovered from the famine than people were plunged again into the abyss of hunger. Hungry folks without anything to eat poured into towns where they might still cadge a bite of food.

Naturally, Phoenix Town was not spared. The famished descended from the villages around the town. They joined in the road building and rescue activities organised by the widow during the famine in the eighteenth year of the Republic of China era. They still recalled how the widow helped lift the people out of trouble during that hardship and sincerely hoped she could stand up again and enjoin them to combat deprivation, thus becoming their saviour.

What else could be done since the road had been built?

The widow was mulling over the selfsame thing. She would not stand by and watch the hungry die without doing something about it.

What could be done? Cooking porridge and provisions was not a long-term solution to the problem of food scarcity.

What could be done? The head of the town hall turned to her for assistance too.

What else could she do? After many days of anxiety, she hatched a plan to organise the hungry to renovate the main streets of the town, offering them food and drink and a necessary reward.

Fantastic! For nearly a century, the town centre had consisted of only two streets which met at a crossroads. These became muddy when it rained and dusty and insanitary when it was sunny. These conditions were not conducive to the development of trade. But the situation would be improved greatly if the bare lanes were tamped flat and paved with flagstones.

The head of the town hall welcomed this blueprint. As with the previous road construction project, the response was immediate, with cooperation from merchants and starving refugees alike.

For this unprecedented makeover, the widow donated a more substantial sum. Her financial support injected vigour and vitality. Tasks like quarrying stone, transportation, chiselling and laying were assigned to specific craftsmen. The widow and the town hall officer, meanwhile, walked around inspecting the quality of their work and estimated how the project was progressing. Experienced as they were from their previous road building, this time every step was taken efficiently and the whole operation wound on smoothly. The streets in the town were changed remarkably. Pedestrians were elated to mount the solid tiger-coloured flagstones. Their feet were content, as were their hearts.

Everyone thought to themselves: "The town should have been like this years ago."

Unfortunately, the drought continued. Paving the streets of the town did not alter the mind of the Heavens. No merciful rainwater was granted to ensure the farmers a harvest.

No rain landed on the ground. The town was seared by the sun. The hungry had been paving the streets for three months, during which time their bellies had been fed until they were round. The empty stomachs of their families were filled too. Now, construction was over, what were they to do in the days to come?

What work could furnish them with a livelihood?

The widow fretted about them too. When would the drought come to an end?

There was no end. Famine victims were buried in mass graves without funerals. Worse still, those who were spared no longer had the strength to dig pits to bury the dead. Some extremely poor households were wiped out, leaving not one relative in the world.

The widow didn't have the heart to step out of her house, since groups of starving farmers gathered outside, kneeling on the ground, yelling out that they wanted a hand up. The merchants in the town could not be counted on to establish a new welfare project. Most of them ran small businesses and also suffered from the depression of the famine years. What is more, donating what they could to the first two welfare projects had bled them dry. Another welfare project would drag them into bankruptcy.

The lives of merchants were hardly easy either.

It seemed that the widow had reached her wits' end. Maybe it was time for her to solve the situation alone. What was she to do?

How about building a mansion?

To grow her business, she had visited many places in provinces like Shanxi, Sichuan, Gansu and Qinghai. What interested her most were the stately residences in Shanxi Province, which were well-designed and grandly built. She was determined to have a mansion of her own constructed in the same style. She brought home an architectural sketch from a business partner in Shanxi. Successive famines had prevented her from fulfilling her ambition. The famine of 1930 had been followed by the famine of 1933. To save hungry people from trial by fire and water, the widow had shelved her home construction plans in order to engineer the two welfare projects. The famine relief and welfare schemes had found favour during the years of hardships. Would they now support her idea to build a mansion? How would they react? Would they scold her because of it? The widow ruminated over these concerns before telling them her plan.

There was no alternative to the mansion construction scheme. Her unease and dread of being scolded by others did not figure, giving way to her determination. She made up her mind to start building her "Prosperity Mansion" in the twenty-second year of the Republic of China era (1934).

Mountain stones were in great demand, so were green bricks. The stonemasons, carpenters and plasterers, who formerly participated in the road construction and the town streets renovation, comprised the main labour force this time. The untrained were spread about the construction site, grinding and polishing bricks to make them as clean as mirrors. The sound of bricks being ground was heard continuously for the next two years. The water people used to grind bricks flowed in a rivulet along the earth, giving off the pleasant aroma of bricks day and night.

The "Prosperity" project thus rescued the hungry from another year of want.

But the project was not complete and must continue.

Three years later, the main work was essentially done and beam-lifting ceremonies were held in rooms in different courtyards. The next two years were spent laying out back gardens with rockeries, fishponds, lotus ponds and other features. A traditional castle-like house, superb and grand, appeared and stood majestically in Phoenix Town, becoming the focal point of the ancient settlement.

The residence sat to the north and faced southwards, from which aspect it could embrace the sunshine. Each building within was higher than the next. Inside the mansion, tens of thousands of stones, bricks, animal-shaped roof ridges, sparrow braces, architraves, plinths and window lattices were exquisitely carved by craftsmen.

The construction of the "Prosperity Mansion" raised a group of artisans including stonemasons, carpenters, bricklayers, gardeners and painters. After the Liberation in 1949, groups of village craftsmen were recruited to Beijing to participate in the construction of the Ten Landmark Buildings in China, in particular the Great Hall of the People, the Museum of History and the Military Museum.

The widow's son and daughter left the town to pursue their studies. After they graduated, one elected to live and work in the US and the other in Hong Kong. She lived in the mansion, alone and forlorn. So, she decided to donate it to the government as the "Phoenix Primary School". The rooms were converted into classrooms and the rear garden into playgrounds. Since there was no longer anything that needed her intervention in the town, the widow gained approval to unite with her daughter in Hong Kong and never returned.

Stories about her were always on the lips of the townspeople. She was duly elevated into a figure of legend.

The Qiyang Widow

A family that chases lucre will surely wane;
A househole that cherishes virtue will always remain.
— A folk saying from the Western Plain

On the Western Plain, the widow from Qiyang was equal in fame to her counterpart from Phoenix Town. For a time, she even surpassed her in reputation.

Like the Phoenix Widow, the Qiyang Widow was widowed halfway through life. In common with the Phoenix Widow, the Qiyang Widow's family had possessed abundant property since the time of her forefathers. From an early age, she was sent to study at an old-style private school. As well as being able to read and write, she was skilled at strumming the seven-stringed zither, besting others at the game of *Go* and painting. What is more, she was familiar with the division rules of the abacus and plied its beads as deftly as a lion playing with an embroidered ball. She truly lived up to her reputation as one of the most gifted, peerless beauties of her generation.

Her husband was well-educated too and a dab hand with a writing brush. After the brush, with its bamboo stem and tip made from wolf's hair, was fully saturated with Chinese ink, he allowed his wrist to float above the rice paper. His *qi*, generated from the zone below his navel known as the "Cinnabar Field", surged all the way through his intestines and lungs, becoming concentrated at his fingertips. Suddenly, the brush swooped down, flying like a dragon and dancing like a phoenix. A remarkable piece of calligraphy, which was replete with both forceful and gentle strokes and bones and sinew, emulating characteristic inscriptions from tablets of the Northern Dynasties (385-581AD), appeared before people's eyes. How could any spectator fail to applaud? Could anybody refrain from gasping in admiration? Her husband had a further masterstroke – when it came to prose and poetry he was touched by the muse. If he gazed at the moon for any length of time, he would extemporise a verse; if he studied the flowers, another composition would be chanted out. His poems belonged to the new style, in marked contrast to the classical style. Take as an example, "When the Lotus Blossoms":

> *At nightfall, the cicadas have stopped chirping.*
> *In my dream I can hear that*
> *In the moon-lit pond outside the window*
> *A lotus*
> *Is blossoming.*
> *The next morning, the tourists and I*
> *All stare hurriedly at the surface of the lake.*
> *Everyone claims to have spied the red flower.*
> *Everyone wants to pluck it.*
> *But no one can succeed.*

They were such a well-matched couple. They lived in idleness for several years, complementing each other harmoniously like a seven-stringed zither might accompany its counterpart with twenty-five strings. Together they played *Go* and listened to zither music; together they painted and practised calligraphy. No one is certain what became of the *Go* set and the instrument the pair played, though one or two specimens of their oil paintings and calligraphy can still be seen in the homes of connoisseurs on the Western Plain.

Meanwhile, the county museums in Fufeng, Qishan and Fengxiang all have their own examples on display. I (the author) have had the good fortune to appreciate several of these and was struck by their profound artistic skill. One watercolour, entitled *Two Playful Butterflies*, is remarkably fresh and lifelike, depicting two chromatic butterflies graciously flapping over a cluster of blue chrysanthemums on a field ridge in the countryside; a gosling-yellow one is weaving about the wild flowers. The picture is not large, but a lively sense of artistic conception and an interest in life have been condensed into its frame. Judging from the epigrams, it was likely the handiwork of the newlywed Qiyang Widow, though her husband – the true calligrapher – added two short lines with a flourish of the brush in the margin:

The wild chrysanthemums were self-coloured and unadorned.
Where the butterflies hovered and the honey bees swarmed.

Her husband was a born poet. A poet's heart is romantic, as is his disposition. No one could say he withheld his love from his woman. Although he must have questioned his heart, he adored her so deeply that his flesh often ached. He also had three daughters, who were the apple of his eye. He understood what agony his departure would bring them. Of course, there were still his parents too. They were all tethered to his gut and his heart and to his very breath. But he couldn't bring himself under control. His heart had flown away. If his body was to tarry at Qiyang, he would be surrendering himself to self-delusion and deceiving his parents and wife and daughters as well.

So, one warm spring day when the flowers were in full bloom, he strode out of the door with his hands hidden in his sleeves, heading for who-knows-where. After a year or two, someone declared that they had spotted him at an ancient picture market in Xi'an. After another year or two, someone announced that he had bumped into him at an inn in Luoyang. Another year or two after that, someone was adamant that they had run into him in a teahouse in Nanjing.

Why did her husband leave home and wander to the ends of the world? Even his parents couldn't fathom it. They stared at the Qiyang Widow with bitterness written all over their faces, wanting to decipher an answer from her expression. All they saw was another face as bitter as their own. They could only wait in a bitter mood for him to change his mind and reappear before his family one bright beautiful morning or one sunny evening.

But his parents, his wife and his daughters were destined to be disappointed.

In his disappointment, his aged father passed away.

In her disappointment, his aged mother departed this world.

The Qiyang Widow and her three daughters found continued disappointment of their own with every passing day. But she couldn't allow herself to be enslaved by it. Not only did she refuse to be a prisoner to her emotions, but she was also determined to snap out of her misery, wipe away her tears and shoulder the burdens of the family. But what a heavy burden it was. The businesses left behind by their ancestors occupied half the street in Qiyang Town. They included an oil mill, a vinegar distillery, a liquor distillery, a draper, a grain merchant, a grocery, a salt merchant, a tavern, an eatery. So many going concerns really were a headache for the Qiyang Widow to manage. When the elders of the household were still alive, she had nothing to do with the businesses. She didn't need to and, what is more, was too indolent to worry about them. She preferred to remain carefree, playing *Go* and flexing her zither, practising her calligraphy and painting pictures. What about her man? When it came to business affairs, the elders all counted on him and so did she. But her husband was not a born businessman. He opened the account books when the old folks browbeat him to do so. But one glimpse at the cramped figures made him groggy. Another glance gave him a headache and a third look caused him heartache.

He knew that his heart was not in conducting business. It was in the mountains, in the clouds, along the waterside, out on the seas and in his leisurely and aimless wanderings.

He left without informing his family.

The Qiyang Widow wanted to cry her heart out but didn't. She didn't shed a single tear or release one sob. She yielded to her fate. Everything was predestined. She was born to shoulder the burden of her family. She could only carry it bravely. She learned how to check the account books and how to ply the abacus. The fingers that had formerly played *Go* and flexed the zither, practised calligraphy and painted now plucked at the balls of the abacus. She felt a little rusty to start with, though gradually that rust flaked away. The division rules for the abacus were so abstruse. It was such a challenge for "the lion to play with the embroidered ball". But she soon mastered the apparatus and people's admiration was as fulsome for this as it had been for her other skills. When the underbosses who managed the mills, businesses and shops came to the account room to submit their books, they were startled by the proficiency with which she flicked the pitter-pattering abacus beads. She earned their plaudits.

The underbosses hired by the Qiyang Widow's family were all prudent fellows and each had special skills in his respective fields. When the elders were still alive, trade in each of the businesses was brisk. They would all submit accounts and hand in the profits on time. Now the Qiyang Widow wore the apron. She studied as well as tested them. They still submitted their accounts on time but, compared with before, the profits handed in by some soared while others dwindled until they were almost in the red.

A case in point was the liquor distillery. It produced a kind of hard spirit called Flying Phoenix, which was widely-acclaimed not only on the Western Plain but also in the five northwestern provinces. It sold so well the jars frequently didn't last a whole night in the cellar. Customers and merchants even came from beyond the Shanhai Pass – that is to say, the provinces of Liaoning, Jilin and Heilongjiang – to place orders. The business prospered but the accounts submitted by the underboss went from bad to worse. Like gusts of wind and flurries of rain, gossip reached the owner. Smelling a rat, she always fired off supplementary questions whenever the winery underboss came to submit his accounts.

"The customers and merchants are satisfied with our stuff?"

"Yep." The underboss took on a swollen appearance as he gave his answer. "They can't complain," he added.

"Good. Then my heart is set at ease."

"I am here," the underboss cackled. "My coming over here should be enough to put your heart at ease."

She smiled. But her smile was not without undertones. The sly underboss began to panic, his heart picking up pace and the better part of his pudding face flushing red as if he had necked a hefty draught of the Flying Phoenix distilled under his supervision.

Who was the Qiyang Widow? The reddened face of the underboss revealed to her the phantom in the depths of his heart. His blush was a sure sign of conscience and a redeemable character. She wanted to save him. A distillery needed a man like him – a person of skill who knew the management ropes.

Pushing all the account books that had been submitted during the months she held sway towards him, she asked him for a clear explanation.

The underboss was in a testing position. The figures that should have been as dead as doornails now all seemed animated. With their blood-red eyes wide open, they grilled the underboss's already crimson face like flames.

He didn't dare look the widow in the eye, nor did he scan the figures in the account books. With his head lowered, he bleated for half a day as if his throat was gagged with a ball of cotton wadding.

"My mother died. She'd been floored by disease for years."

While he was making his incoherent confession, a young man who was tall and thin like a ripe sorghum stem entered the accounts room. After coming in, he first shot a glance at the swollen, red-faced distillery underboss and then turned to stare at the Qiyang Widow.

He was in very old clothes. His upper garments and trousers, made from black homespun cloth, had been patched and repatched. Repeated washing had faded the blackness to white. Their pallor matched the look of malnutrition he wore on his face. By contrast, his jet black eyes exhibited a stream of extraordinary alertness and smartness in the midst of that sallowness.

The Qiyang Widow did a double-take and started to like the young man a little.

He sensed that she was studying him.

"I am the bookkeeper at the distillery," he said. "My name is Lin Maosheng.

"Yes, the gaffer's old mother passed away seven days ago. Struck down by disease for a few years. I know everything about the profits and losses in the account books as well as why we made a profit and why we suffered a loss. I shall go through the figures that record the income and out-goings for the past few months, here and now."

In the serene accounts room belonging to the Qiyang Widow, Lin Maosheng had just introduced himself with a protracted one-man show.

The Qiyang Widow listened patiently, not wriggling to allay the stiffness in her buttocks until he stopped talking and stood to one side gazing at her with longing in his eyes. Allowing herself to relax a little, she sent an appreciative smile in his direction.

"Good," she replied. "I am all ears."

The confident young man took two steps forward and drew closer to her quaint redwood accounts table. Itemising each entry on his fingers, he sped through the accounts as if he was enumerating neat rows of cowpeas and aubergines. Sorghum, garden peas, rice grain, millet, barley. How much of each cereal was needed to distil liquor every year? From where were they bought? In which season? What was the price of the sorghum? And what were the prices for the garden peas, rice, millet and barley? There was also the dry firewood used to fuel the cauldrons, the crocks used to keep the spirits in store and the pots used to hold it. Each item was kept in his mind. The strings of figures were like the rice kernels he consumed every day – he knew abundantly well when he was hungry and when he was full. Finally, he drew attention to the records pertaining to the principal material used to make liquor – sorghum. At present, it was the end of autumn, the best season to purchase sorghum in bulk. One year's worth of the most significant material used by the plant should be bought within these two or three months – consequently, the expenditure would be huge for the time being and the profit small. After this season, the profits in the account books would rocket up.

He talked until he was a little thirsty. The Qiyang Widow stood up and poured him a cup of water. After taking a sip, he carried on talking.

"Please forgive my prattling," he said. "But the accounts of the winery should not be done month-by-month. They should be audited year-by-year."

When you listen to someone talking, you should pay attention to their overtones; when you hear the bray of the gong and the beat of the drum, you should try to catch the quality of the tone. From the words the young man was using, the Qiyang Widow had already figured out the tenor of his criticism. But the advice was absolutely beneficial and necessary. When the burdens of this large clan had fallen all of a sudden on her, what she was most in want of was well-grounded, sincere and candid criticism. This kind of feedback could replenish her mind, enabling her in turn to become intimately acquainted with the economic reality of all the businesses and to enlarge her family property.

Standing nearby in embarrassment, the underboss of the distillery was acutely indebted to the young Lin Maosheng. His timely arrival had dealt him a great favour and rescued him from his predicament. His superior skill at distilling had been the reason behind his rise to the top, but the purchasing and selling were all in the hands of Lin. His junior had reported the data piece-by-piece to him, but he could not fix them in his memory even if his life depended on it.

The crimson hue of the underboss's face gradually dissipated. Taking advantage of this, he confessed to the Qiyang Widow that several times he had taken the liberty of borrowing some money from the account.

Lin Maosheng also verified this from nearby, saying that each sum of money had an IOU and was recorded on the respective page.

He emphasised that the man's mother had been disease-stricken for a long time, that she had passed away only recently and that the widowed mother had faced great hardship in raising her son alone.

Lin's words moved the Qiyang Widow a little. Out of sympathy, she instructed the young man that no matter how much the underboss had borrowed, it should all be wiped clean with a swish of the writing brush.

"It's good for a man to be filial," she commented, following it up with a rhetorical question. "A man who displays no filial affection towards his parents cannot be expected to be kind to others. Not even the threat of a knife to my neck could force me to say otherwise," she concluded.

Apparently, she was praising the underboss for his filial dedication, which indicated that he was earnest and reliable. She had such a heavy load of business to manage. If she didn't have a team of people prepared to sweat and take responsibility on her behalf, the whole thing would be impossible.

She learned much from this incident. To be frank, none of the businesses should be expected to yield profit in a linear, constant manner. The fluctuation of the seasons and matters specific to each one caused boom times and periods of relative slackness. Moreover, a business magnate could not afford to fixate on what was right under his nose. Longer term plans had to be engineered. And yes, of course, the political climate influenced trade inordinately. They should open their eyes wide, investigate carefully and make timely decisions. In a word, doing business was like pursuing knowledge. There was simply too much to learn.

Luckily, she had discovered the young man Lin Maosheng. She perceived some of the businessperson's tricks. But when she talked with him, she discovered that his perception was more profound and his ideas were also more down-to-earth.

She came to set great store by the young man.

She wanted to transfer him out from the distillery to be her personal assistant and help her with all of the businesses. But she still wanted to test him once more.

One night as she was dreaming, she had a flash of inspiration.

After waking up, a method for testing him came to her in an instant. Despite always being in a foul mood after having been forced to take charge, she now couldn't help but smile wryly. She felt proud and cocksure.

Rising early in the morning, she ground an ink stick against the slab to get the liquid flowing. She spread out paper to write one letter of invitation after another. She then dispatched hands to deliver the invites to the underbosses and bookkeepers of the businesses. She wanted them to share dinner at her house.

Once the letters of invitation were sent out, she and the hired menial hands started to busy themselves. Some went to the street to buy meat and vegetables and some kneaded dough and prepared other materials at home. It may have seemed like something of a melee, but the work was carried out in an intense and orderly manner. When the sun had set behind the western mountains, the underbosses and bookkeepers of all the businesses shut their gates, locked them, changed into long gowns and mandarin jackets and came to her compound one on the heels of another for dinner.

This was indeed a special dinner. It was neither a festival nor Chinese New Year, so why lay on a banquet? The former master had thrown a banquet to entertain guests at Chinese New Year and on festivals, but never at his own home. He had a restaurant out on the street. How much trouble could he save by putting on a spread there? The Qiyang Widow had assumed the household reins with an untested hand. There must have been something behind her choice of venue. But what was it? Nobody could figure it out. They couldn't help making assumptions along the lines of: she is a woman and a woman is different from a man. Banqueting at home could mean she wanted to appear more thoughtful and amiable. With this in mind, they all felt more relaxed. Not caring if it was a festival or Chinese New Year or not, they each wore a hearty smile. When the dishes were put on the table, they dug their chopsticks in; when liquor was served, they drained their cups.

The last main course was dumplings in sour broth.

The broth was plentiful and the oil was profuse in the flowery fine china bowls produced in the capital of porcelain Jingdezhen. A layer of coriander and hotbed chives floated on top. The dumplings, each crystalline like a jade fish, were hiding in the mouthwatering sour broth swimming in red oil.

The Qiyang Widow was in a good mood.

As she was having guests over, she hunted out a small, bright pink brocade jacket from the bottom of a chest to wear with an embroidered and pleated dark red silk dress. That outfit made her look both beautiful and demure. She again dabbed on a little powder. A slight, knowing smile was now brimming up on her lightly made-up face.

She beckoned the others to wine and dine to their hearts' content. Raising her chopsticks, she also took a bite of the food; raising her cup, she also took a sip of wine. But any repast she took was tiny and purely symbolic. Observing how the others set to work on the food and wine with relish, she felt gladdened. The slight smile on her face deepened a little and, seeing that the others were contented, she raised her voice.

"The wine is weak and the dishes are simple. Please help yourselves. A man shouldn't have a guilty conscience. He shouldn't let his mouth down either. All of you have a clear conscience, but I'm afraid I've disappointed your mouths. Please, unwind and eat and drink."

The liquor course drew to an end as she was speaking. Dumplings in oily sour broth were now laid before each guest.

"I prepared the fillings myself. Please savour them carefully and see if the flavour is to your liking or not."

Swish, swish, slurp, slurp, tut, tut – a cacophony of delectation resounded throughout the dining hall of the Qiyang Widow's compound. Disturbed by the brouhaha, several swallows nestling on the ridgepole chirped and joined the clamour of the dumplings being savoured. Some found a copper coin in their dumpling and crowed heartily, while others excavated an ancient coin, leading to a bout of loud exclamations and low cackles. Those who failed to find anything auspicious were envious, and their congratulations were tinged with a hint of sneer.

Chatting and laughing in a raucous din, they dined on the dumplings. Some finished quickly.

"Scrumptious!" exclaimed the underboss of the distillery, having gorged himself on both dumplings and broth.

"Delicious!" concluded the underboss of the grocery as he did the same.

"Tasty!" was the comment from the underboss of the restaurant.

The underbosses and bookkeepers of the businesses demolished their dumplings, swilled them down with broth and were now mostly saying: "Wonderful."

But why wonderful? It went without saying that the broth was fresh and the dumplings fragrant, but was there any further reason? The Qiyang Widow always sported a smile. Now, her gaze shifted from one underboss or bookkeeper to another.

"Who can tell me how many dumplings he has managed?" she queried. "How many pork dumplings? How many mutton ones? And how many vegetable ones?"

She questioned every underboss and every bookkeeper with her eyes. No matter whose face her interrogating stare landed on, a swipe of honey glow would soar there and they all looked embarrassed. Apparently, they had all been single-mindedly feasting on the dumplings and looking for the coins, as they would in ordinary times. But they had neglected to count how many dumplings and of what kind they had consumed. Their faces could only blush in embarrassment because they had been remiss. Finally, the Qiyang Widow's eyes landed on Lin Maosheng's face. He neither blushed nor appeared embarrassed.

"I have eaten eighteen dumplings," he answered. "Six pork, four mutton and eight vegetable ones."

The Qiyang Widow nodded at Lin Maosheng, the smile on her face as brilliant as the peach blossoms in March.

"Maosheng, you are a scrupulous fellow," she reflected. "Come to my side and be my assistant."

The underbosses and bookkeepers all stared at Lin Maosheng. Not until now did they start to sense the true purpose of the wine banquet. The Qiyang Widow had thrown a banquet, but was this meant as a test rather than a show of hospitality? Had she intended to test how able they were and how dexterous? As in traditional theories of physiology, might it be that their hearts had wisdom and "many orifices" and could enlarge and adapt to whatever challenge was flung at them? What a pity they had simply dined and wined, wasting a prime opportunity. Only that lucky dog Lin Maosheng caught the bone. From being a bookkeeper at the distillery, he catapulted himself to being the widow's assistant, standing on the rung immediately below their mistress and above all the rest of them. From now on, they would have to be at his beck and call.

It was too hard a fact to accept.

They could not stomach it. But, in the end, would that matter? Would they not have to accept it since he had the support of their boss, the widow?

After a round of lukewarm applause, Lin Maosheng stood up. First, he bowed to the Qiyang Widow and then to the underbosses and the other bookkeepers. He didn't even feign modesty. While bowing once and then again, he assumed his post as the Qiyang Widow's assistant very confidently.

Two timeworn tales written in the annals of history spring to mind here. Liu Bang, the first emperor of the Han Dynasty, known by the posthumous title of the "Lofty Emperor", once went to Hongmen to attend a potentially perilous feast thrown by his foe, Xiang Yu. Zhao Kuangyin, the first emperor of the Song Dynasty, remembered as the "Founder Emperor", threw a banquet and removed his top generals from their military leadership. The Qiyang Widow laid on a liquor banquet to select a protégé through dumplings. On the lips of people on the Western Plain, this story was no less popular than those two great events hosted by Xiang Yu and Zhao Kuangyin. Locals waxed lyrical about the superhuman foresight and the legendary colours displayed by the hosts. The present author has heard tell of this ever since he was young. When I decided to write about the Qiyang Widow and went to Qiyang Town, no matter whom I talked to, they would relate this tale without hesitation.

The legend of selection through dumplings has come to be seen as a radiant treasure in the spiritual heritage of the Western Plain.

As assistant, Lin Maosheng did an excellent job.

Since she had Lin Maosheng's help, the Qiyang Widow seldom had to flick the balls of the abacus ever again. She now had time to tutor her three daughters, to play the occasional round of *Go*, to play the zither awhile, and to write and paint.

Her mind then wandered back to her lost love. Destiny had brought them together, yet she had suffered so much pain and still felt a sense of loss in the catacombs of her heart. She dug out his poems that had been scattered around the house, sniffed the remaining fragrance of the Chinese ink and started to retrace the man's rebellious and unruly spirit as preserved in his words. She first chanced upon *Stride Out*.

Stride out, you young man
With an umbrella aslant on your back,
Against the wind and frost and snow
Against –
Wild dogs and venomous snakes.
At dawn while going through
A strange river valley
And leaping over the stepping stones, suddenly
I bumped into a sika deer lapping water.
Fixing me and shaking her brows and eyes
She wanted to leave but did not.

The love who was her destiny had strode out. Strode out in search of his sika deer. Had he found it? The Qiyang Widow felt a barb of spite inside. She was looking forward to his return. She really was besotted with the rascal questing after a sika deer. She believed the deer he was looking for was her – she was his quarry. So, she would just wait. She was patient enough to wait for her beloved rascal to return.

Lovers who hold a grudge against each other are destined to be reunited. From then on, whenever she thought of her absent man, the Qiyang Widow couldn't help addressing that paramour as "you rascal" in her heart.

She was still reading through her rascal husband's poetry. She had recited *The Love between the Rivers Jing and Wei* so many times that every word and every meter had been committed to memory.

The wind from the Loess Plateau is fierce.
The gentleman is toughened into an agile rustic brave.
With a body-full of yellow earth and sand,
He looks like a prancing gold dragon.
The water from the Loess Plateau is sweet.
The lady is nurtured into a woman of beauty and grace.
With a string of crystalline dewdrops,
She looks like a hovering jade phoenix.
The River Wei gazes northwards and the Jing to the south.
With her eyebrows lowered, she is so bashful.
The jade phoenix plunges into the embrace of the gold dragon.
They brave their way to the great sea via the Yellow River.

Her beloved rascal had great facility with verse. She loved him from her deepest core. She sensed that his poems had crawled into people's bones and made the tips of their hearts shiver and the ends of their eyelashes bounce. Every time she recited one meter, it was accompanied by a single sigh. Her beloved rascal compared himself to a "Gold Dragon". She was willing to be his beloved "Jade Phoenix" and "brave the way to the great sea via the Yellow River" with him. However, the Gold Dragon had gone, leaving the Jade Phoenix behind in their hometown of Qiyang. The Jade Phoenix yearned for the great sea too! But she had no option. She had to guard the family property well for the Gold Dragon. Her only companions were her sighs.

The days passed by, one by one. Business rolled on, day by day.

With the assistance of Lin Maosheng, their trade spiralled. Having won them over, her underbosses in all the establishments took their responsibilities seriously and were content with their situation and behaved properly. But, when all was said and done, she was a woman. From time to time, kinsmen and acquaintances in Qiyang Town would spit out coarse words and bellyache about her. "Look," some said. "She seems able to clamber up into the skies and pick out the stars." Others muttered: "Her mind's eye is screwy – like a weasel's arsehole." Others complained: "Folks have been bullied into throwing in the towel. She wants to dupe people."

When these idle remarks first reached her ears, the Qiyang Widow didn't take them seriously. She thought, as time elapsed, everything would be swept clean as if a wind had blasted by. However, this was not the case. It seemed that the better she managed her family property, the more intense the idle gossip became. More rumour-mongers joined the fray with vicious sprays of saliva erupting from their mouths. It was enough to drown people.

High time to take some notice of the caustic remarks, she thought.

She planned to lay on a banquet at home to entertain some local VIPs. One folk saying sums this up: *A meal sweetens a man's mouth and a gift softens a man's hands.* After they had drunk and feasted and were given plenty of attention, the problem might be easily solved. It ought to be like splitting bamboo – as long as the blade made contact squarely with the tip, it should be easy to slice from end to end.

The dishes were delectable – all mountain produce and seafood cooked from raw materials which, ordinarily, they would only have heard tell of but never seen, let alone eaten. The liquor was top-notch, fermented from grain and not blended with anything else. Stored in the family distillery for thirty years, it was usually used as distiller's yeast. The tableware was very particular too, all fine chinaware manufactured in Jingdezhen and squirreled away at home to be used just once a year. The sizeable bowls and plates and dainty cups and spoons all had dignified floral designs and splendid gilded rims. Chief among the widow's accoutrements was a square, purple sandalwood dining table with legs that looked like a coiling dragon or a crouching tiger. It was burnished with gold leaf. Anyone who sat in the dining hall soon felt bedazzled and as though their eyes were prickling.

The dishes were devoured and the spirits gulped down. But then another problem reared its head. This time the unpleasant comments centred on the square, purple sandalwood table with its gold leaf finish.

The Qiyang Widow hadn't meant to parade her wealth by

putting the table to use. It was an heirloom passed down from her ancestors. In the past when they threw a banquet to entertain guests, they too had used this table. Back then, nobody was offended and nobody felt dissatisfied. More often than not, those who were invited to dine at the purple sandalwood table would use it as fodder for their later idle chatter and congratulate themselves on their luck. They would feel exceedingly glad.

Presently, the principle muck-spreader was her husband's eldest brother. His financial circumstances put him on an unsure footing, but he married an especially productive woman. Counting those "gourds" (the boys on the Western Plain were all bald) at the head of the *kang* one by one, there were six lads in total, each with a tiger's back and a bear's waist, standing as tall as a rifle tilted upright.

"One good turn deserves another," the eldest brother-in-law said to the others. "I should stand her a treat in return."

He was not jesting. On the seventh day after the Qiyang Widow's feast, a big red letter of invitation was delivered respectfully into her hands.

Should she go to the banquet? Certainly. How could she not? Though baseless chatter was being tipped into her ears, she still went along to her eldest brother-in-law's home in all her finery to share the liquor banquet on the appointed date.

She questioned herself seriously and found that at the bottom of her heart she still hoped that someone would invite her to dinner. She needed a stage on which to make a spectacle of herself. Her eldest brother-in-law's banquet offered just such a platform. So, she made herself up meticulously, precisely as she had done when she laid on a banquet to entertain others. She powdered her face, painted her eyebrows and eyes and applied lipstick. Her face – very pretty as it was to begin with – was thus embellished. She emptied out almost all of the clothes from her storage chests to pick and choose from, holding garments up against her body to see if they were suitable. Finally, she chose an embroidered aquamarine silk jacket and an embroidered matching dress. After dressing herself up, she stepped out of the door. Wearing her Sunday best made the Qiyang Widow feel happy and spirited. More than fifty years later when I (the author) visited Qiyang Town, people were still talking about the day she breezed along the high street, the sun paling in comparison with the mien she struck.

When the graceful Qiyang Widow reached the gate of her eldest brother-in-law, someone passed on the word. The host came out to welcome her like a blast of wind and escorted her into the ostensibly shabby living room. The relatives and friends who would keep her company had all settled down neatly around the big square dinner table. The seat of greatest honour at the head of the table was left unoccupied, waiting for her to assume it.

However, she wasn't allowed to sit down.

Four of her eldest brother-in-law's six sons each took hold of a table leg with both their hands and legs. Sitting under the table with their legs tucked up and their heads butting against the table surface, they didn't utter a sound.

What were they doing? The Qiyang Widow reached out a hand to haul up her nephews who were wrapped around the table legs to no avail. They all clung on stubbornly as if they had been soldered together.

"Take your seat," her eldest brother-in-law beckoned. "Take your seat, please. Take the seat of honour, please."

The Qiyang Widow was still unable to sit down. Her four nephews had put her in an awful bind.

"Take your seat." The close relatives and friends who came here to keep her company also invited her to sit down.

"Take your seat, please," they persuaded. "Take the seat of honour, please."

In a single moment, the awful bind untangled itself. She forced herself to think. "I was invited here with a big red invitation," she reasoned. "I should eat only what I should eat and drink what I should drink. Don't try to make a fool out of me. When all is said and done, who knows who will make a fool out of whom."

As she was thinking, the Qiyang Widow dropped herself steadily down on the seat that had been reserved for her.

What dishes had she eaten?

What wine had she drunk?

Afterwards she could remember nothing. She only knew she felt a splitting headache and was sick at heart. When she suddenly woke from her slumber and looked around, it was already pitch-black outside. She knew that she must have slid drunkenly under the table at her eldest brother-in-law's banquet. Throughout her life, this was the only time she had been inebriated.

How could she not get drunk? After waking up from her slumber, she was not able to fall asleep again. The liquor banquet once more sprang to life in her mind. Apparently, her eldest brother-in-law was pulling a trick on her. When she threw a banquet to entertain guests, she had used a square, purple sandalwood table with a gilded finish. Her husband's brother could not match her in wealth and finery, having no antique furniture. His one fig leaf was his six tiger-fierce sons. Not only were there two to wait on each guest, but the other four could be made to act as their masters' sentries, each clasping a leg of the table on which he dined. His intention could be deduced with only half an eye: he was taking advantage of his six sons to shame the widowed mother and her orphaned daughters!

The Qiyang Widow's eyes turned sour and a line of clear tears hung from her cheek.

Three days passed by. Three days that were neither protracted nor passed by quickly.

During those three days, the Qiyang Widow never once stepped foot out of her door. Nor did she allow anyone else to cross the threshold – not even her three daughters, despite them depending on each other for survival. What was on her mind during those three days? Nobody knows. Three days later, she summoned Lin Maosheng and told him from the other side of the door that she wanted to establish a school.

"A charity school," Her voice was low. "All the children who want to study can come." Her intention was resolute. "Please help me plan and prepare."

Lin Maosheng promised readily. For three days, the Qiyang Widow neither put in an appearance nor said a word. He felt very uneasy at heart. But her decision allowed his suspended heart to slot back into its proper place. He was pleased.

What should a person do with their money? Dig a cellar and stow it away? Purchase splendid clothes and flounce around in them? Buy delicious foodstuffs and pack them in their stomach? No. None of these solutions was any good. One way forward was to channel the money into something truly meaningful. Starting a charity school was certainly meaningful.

Lin Maosheng's mood, which had been gloomy, much like his mistress, suddenly brightened up thanks to the charity school.

"No man is a match for her!" he sighed in his heart. "A grand move! An absolutely grand move!"

Lin Maosheng threw himself into the plans and preparations. First, he purchased a plot of land lying idle at the entrance to the southern street of Qiyang Town that was ten *mu* in circumference. He then ran to the public school in the county city and took its layout as his blueprint. On the way, he poached a graduate from a Beijing university who had now come back to his hometown. They returned to Qiyang Town together.

The student late of Beijing happened to be descended from a large household in the Western Plain. His family name was Shi. The elder Shi sent his son to distant Beijing to study in the hope that he would rise through the ranks of officialdom. However, the younger man had a distaste for politics and a passion for learning. He aspired to introduce Western-style education to his native Western Plain and nurture a batch of talents who would later devote themselves to the country and the people. Working at the public school in the county town for two years, he had exerted himself yet failed to change the status quo even in the slightest. The public school kept its old ethos intact and continued to swing in the same operational orbit. He resigned his post feeling totally dejected and planned to go back to Beijing in search of further development. But luck brought him into contact with Lin Maosheng, who then recommended him to the Qiyang Widow.

Practically the moment she opened her mouth, the Qiyang Widow offered to employ the graduate, whose ideology was progressive, whose ideas were unique and who seemed to have given his undivided attention to the cause of educating the nation.

"Try as I might, I might never find a man of your ilk again," she said. "With you presiding over the Qiyang Charity School, my heart will be at ease. The school will cherish your blessings."

The engineering work on the charity school was overseen singlehandedly by Lin Maosheng.

The teaching staff was all hired by Mr Shi.

Both were key decisions in terms of the future and fate of the charity school. The Qiyang Widow didn't doubt someone in whom she had placed her trust and if she had any doubts about a person she would not place her trust in him again. She gave full latitude to Lin Maosheng and Mr Shi to undertake the great task of setting up the school. When she was in a good mood, she would go to the building site to see what was happening. She was never content just to sit on her hands. When she saw there were no bricks on the scaffold, she would help transport them. If she spotted that a menial labourer was dog-tired, she would hand him a bowl of water. On the building site, she appeared to take on tasks which ought to be beneath her. Never once did she wag her finger here or stamp her foot there and pass irresponsible remarks on the progress and quality of the engineering work. She certainly did not make carping comments on how Mr Shi hired the teaching staff.

Originally presuming that she was building a new residence, her fellow townspeople, including her eldest brother-in-law from the same family clan, all looked on from the street with cold stares. Gradually they understood that she was funding a charity school and their minds changed, knowing that her aspiration and theirs were never on a par. Slowly their gaze was not as cold and cranky and caustic as it had been before.

One year and eight months passed by before the charity school was complete and ready to recruit students.

Mr Shi wielded a writing brush to draft the recruitment notice in person. More than one hundred copies were then transcribed. Besides being hung in large numbers in the town centre, they were displayed in the nearby villages to broadcast the fact that the Qiyang Charity School had started to enrol students. Boys and girls ranging from eight to thirteen years of age could all come here to study. No tuition would be charged and a noon-day meal would be given for free.

What a piece of welcome news! But few school-aged children came forward to register.

Mr Shi scratched his head. Suspicious that his recruitment notice was not well-worded, he planned to revise it and dispatch hands to go to the streets in the town centre and to the villages to hang them up. The Qiyang Widow dissuaded him.

She appeared to know clearly what the situation was and felt very confident of how to handle it. She consoled Mr Shi, saying he need only prepare himself for teaching affairs. As for the students, she knew a way of recruiting them.

In those days, the populace had barely struggled through the spring famine. The climate was already balmy. A gaggle of peach and apricot trees in the town centre was already in full bloom. They provided shelter for young beggars whose legs were tired from running. The Qiyang Widow approached them. Four among the six or seven youngsters had been orphaned long ago. While scraping a living through begging at Qiyang Town, they frequently received alms from the Qiyang Widow. She stepped towards them, causing something of a commotion among the lads. Stroking their filthy heads, she asked them if they wanted to go to school.

Usually it was only children from well-heeled, respectable households who entertained the notion of going to school. But they were a gang of young beggars. Would they have such an extravagant dream?

They stared at the Qiyang Widow with their naïve, confused eyes. They didn't know how to answer her question.

"Whoever wants to go to school can follow me," the Qiyang Widow urged. "No matter who goes to school, I will take care of his meals," she enticed.

"Go to school?" the young beggars didn't know what had hit

them. "Meals on offer?" They lost their bearings.

"Go to school," she reiterated. "Meals included."

The four orphans became the first registered students at the Qiyang Charity School. Some other young beggars followed too, becoming students because "meals will be included if they go to school". The hard hearts of some of the people in Qiyang Town began to sway after they saw the orphans and beggars going to the charity school to receive schooling and recite from texts like: "When people are born, they are kind by nature. While their innate characters are similar to each other, it is learning that makes the difference."; and "Zhao, Qian, Sun, Li, Zhou, Wu, Zheng, Wang."[a] They all sent their children and younger brothers and sisters to the charity school one after another.

The charity school's enrollment was decent and the teaching routine followed the prescribed curriculum. The students learned not only how to read and write but how to line up to do physical exercises and how to sing and play games. Mr Shi proposed that an opening ceremony should be held.

The Qiyang Widow consented.

"I need such an opening ceremony," she thought.

On the day, at Mr Shi's suggestion, she put on a tailor-made black suit. It made her look especially solemn and respectful in front of the registered students and teaching staff. Her fair-skinned face turned a little red. No matter how she tried to mask it, she couldn't suppress the feverish excitement in her heart.

The townspeople enjoyed watching clamorous scenes. It was a foible of theirs. Those who could walk, paced over to the school; those who couldn't were pushed by their families in wheelchairs. It was a sea of heads, more animated than when a grand opera was staged in the town centre. The Qiyang Widow looked for one person in the crowd. That was her eldest brother-in-law. She searched until her eyes felt sore but still failed to locate even his shadow. Hadn't he come? She didn't believe it.

She raised her eyes and stared further afield. Finally, under a shadowy tree beyond the crowd, she spied him together with his six sons. Like cockerels with their necks outstretched, the father and sons were all transfixed by her. She was by then atop the tall speaker's platform for the opening ceremony.

She was gratified in her heart.

She had been craving just such a day and the chance to make just such an impact.

The repeating firecrackers started to detonate. One bang still swirled about the ground while another catapulted into the skies to explode. Repeating firecrackers were bursting and ordinary firecrackers were popping. In an instant, the opening ceremony of the charity school was entirely enveloped in loud, crisp bangs.

On the tall platform, a pair of students held up a roll of bright red gauze with two big fresh flowers attached. This was Mr Shi's idea. He called this the "ribbon-cutting", explaining that it was in vogue in Beijing. When a shop or restaurant began trading or a school or charity house started operating, a public figure was always invited to cut the ribbon. Hearing him out, the Qiyang Widow agreed. She thought it was really a good idea.

Moreover, she reasoned, it was similar to a local tradition. Whenever a shop or restaurant opened, the foundations of a new house were dug or the ridgepole erected on top of a new roof, people came with red sashes as gifts. They gave an air of solemnity and auspiciousness to the proceedings.

In the midst of the explosions and the popping of the big and small firecrackers, the Qiyang Widow took two steps forward. She halted in front of the red gauze draped between the two big flowers, raised her scissors high and snipped the gauze in half. All the students and teachers applauded warmly.

Later, I went to Qiyang Town to collect raw materials for my writing. When some elderly folk recalled the opening ceremony, they still exclaimed what a novelty it was. Everything the Qiyang Widow did was a novelty.

The old people's comments were correct. Cutting a ribbon, which is now such a common or garden event, was a complete novelty back then. But the greatest novelty was yet to come – namely, establishing the charity school and having Mr Shi teach the pupils according to a Western-influenced syllabus. No longer did they learn old hat like *One Hundred Family Names*, *Three Character Classic* and *The Classic for Girls* by rote. Instead, they digested the newly-compiled Chinese language and maths textbooks as well as learning painting, music and PE. A gang of children, much older than a present-day reception class, crowded around a basketball on the playground jumping, running and grappling – it was as novel as novel could be. The scene attracted many other local children, who hued and cried and demanded to go to the charity school to study.

Such spectacles delighted the Qiyang Widow.

From the mouth of a merchant who came from the South of China, she had learned that benefactors in some villages and communes down there had set up charity schools of their own. To ensure the charity schools run proficiently, one person chosen by consensus presided over the establishment of an organised charity federation with detailed rules.

An outstanding idea! The Qiyang Widow admired this type of arrangement.

Moved by admiration, she prepared to set up a charity federation in Qiyang Town. First, she hung out the flag by taking three per cent of the income from her business – whether it was high or low in each case – and handing it in to the charity federation. Following her lead, the other well-off households in Qiyang Town decided to participate too. Even those that were down-at-heel didn't want to fall behind the times and so contributed what they could muster. When it came to electing the chairperson to preside over the charity federation, all the federation members recommended in chorus the Qiyang Widow.

She didn't decline. Drawing herself up to her full height, she took the chairperson's seat. Lin Maosheng noted the instructions she gave and a system was devised for the Qiyang Town Charity Federation. The rules prescribed that the account books of the charity federation be accessible to all federation members who wished to inspect them, that the funds of the charity federation could be reinvested into business activities, for example to buy land for rent or to be loaned with interest charged to those in urgent need of support, that the funds of the charity federation could be used to provide free school places for children of impoverished households and to help orphans, widows, widowers and helpless minors.

The Qiyang Charity Federation rolled on like this. After the People's Republic of China was established in 1949, the nineteen-year-old establishment vanished. Probing this matter years later, I was told that during that turbulent age, the body had played a critical role in stabilising civil life, promoting a social ethos and developing the local economy.

What should be recorded in most detail was the contribution it made to the cause of local education. A few lines are not enough to clarify the whole matter. The former Qiyang Charity School has now been enlarged to become the modern-day Qiyang Junior High School, which is much larger than its predecessor. When I went to the Qiyang Junior High School to consult the data, I chanced upon the only extant copy of a register. This recorded all the names of the children who progressed from Qiyang Charity School with examination results that took them to the provincial or even to the national capital to study. A rough count showed there were sixty-three of them. Eight or nine out of ten came from destitute households. The financial help from the Qiyang Charity Federation gave them a chance to step out of town to continue their studies in the provincial or even the national capital.

The Qiyang Widow's eldest brother-in-law mopped his brow – according to the local saying, he had "ripped off his face and crammed it into his trousers pocket" – and went to see her. He would never have bowed to her if he were there purely on his own account. His six sons forced him over there. He had to edge his way to see her.

"Please let my children learn a few characters," he pleaded. "At least then they would have a scrap of pride. Don't be fussed about me – I'm on my last legs. My eye sockets are still here, but my eyeballs have all but been fretted away."

The rage that had been simmering inside the Qiyang Widow evaporated.

"This is what I like to hear. Children should be able to read," she replied. "Prepare schoolbags and tell them to go to the classroom tomorrow."

Her eldest brother-in-law's children were destined for great things. They all studied hard at the charity school. When they were about to graduate, their father was seized by an acute disease. The Qiyang Widow hurried over to see him. The herbal doctor who was attending to him told her to prepare his last affairs before putting away his medical kit and leaving in haste. She scooted out to catch up. Not until then did the herbal doctor tell her that it was obstructive intestinal fever. Not even an immortal deity would have the power to save him. However, the patient fought back for two days, refusing flatly to breathe his last. When she came to see him again, her stubborn eldest brother-in-law gazed at her awash with hot tears. His eyes were open wide like two bronze bells and he didn't blink even once.

"The children have all been entrusted to you," he muttered. "If they can make something of themselves, that will be all down to your blessings."

After speaking these words, his toes turned up and his bronze-bell-sized eyes closed tight.

As per the charter of the charity federation, the Qiyang Widow was the designated guardian of her six nephews, who proved adept at their studies. One by one they graduated from the charity school. If they were destined for the provincial capital to study further, she funded them; if they headed off to the national capital, she financed them too. I never had the chance to meet these six gentlemen but know that they all made it big – very big. I heard four toiled in their motherland as either university professors or elite members of scientific research institutions. Now, they are all in their seventies – few people lived past seventy in ancient China – and their fellow townspeople still uphold them as role models of education to their children and require them to gild the faces of their ancestors through learning from these six brothers.

I heard the townspeople say:

A family that chases lucre will surely wane;
A household that cherishes virtue will always remain.

This folk saying sums up the Qiyang Widow's life as well. It was said that she frequently repeated it when she was alive. As she oversaw the Qiyang Town Charity Federation, she needed to help children from poor households go to school and lend a hand to orphans, widows, widowers and hopeless people. She often felt the pinch if she depended on the charity federation's funds alone. When the income couldn't cover the expenditure, she turned to her own household. How much had she taken out? She didn't mention it, so how could others know? In a word, when the Western Plain was liberated and the 1947-52 Land Reform Movement enacted, the working team visited her home to divide up her movable property. Apart from the big compound with its three blocks and the furniture in the buildings, there was not a scrap of surplus moveable property. Lin Maosheng took care of the household for her. The working team checked the accounts he kept. They were startled to find that not only was there no surplus, there was also a modicum of debt.

But, of course, this story happened later on.

The Qiyang Widow died before the establishment of the PRC in 1949. She passed away out of the blue in the winter of 1948 when the Western Plain was liberated. It was said that she died a very easy death. She slipped into her own shroud and her corpse was laid out at home. Mr Shi led all the teachers and students from the Qiyang Charity School to bid farewell to her remains. Everyone sobbed. Her face was still ruddy and her eyes closed, but her calm and kind countenance seemed to be telling them that she was a little tired and that she needed to have a sleep and rest a good while.

Were there any among the Qiyang students who were still studying or already working in the distant provincial or national capital or elsewhere who had not benefited directly from her? After hearing tell of the grievous news, they hurried back one after another to say farewell.

The Qiyang Widow had no sons. Even so, countless people went to her bier to rip a length from the mourning cloth. How many people paid their respects? Nobody knows. They only knew that one roll of white mourning cloth on the filial son's shoulder proved not enough. Another roll had to be fetched. It was still not enough. A third roll had to be put on his shoulder and then a fourth. If the rolls were laid out end to end, they would have extended for half a *li*. On the day of the interment, the clear sky stretched out for 10,000 *li*. After she was lowered into the pit, a bank of cloud suddenly floated over and a flurry of snow fell. The drifting snowflakes dyed the lands of the Western Plain into a boundless white expanse – pure, clean and solemn.

Of the Qiyang students who came back to rip a length off the mourning cloth, some joined the Communist Party and some the rival Nationalist Party. They all walked out from the charity school run by the Qiyang Widow and gained their own patch of sky in the outside world. But they all returned to their hometown to mourn her death. They didn't linger for long. After ripping the cloth and seeing her off in silence, they quietly went their separate ways. They are not key players in this story but I would still like to share a little information with my readers: some among them followed Chiang Kai-shek's family into exile in Taiwan but some stayed in Mainland China to serve the New China.

In editing this story, I happened upon a news story about one son of Qiyang who came home after more than fifty years in Taiwan. He was accompanied by two contemporaries who stayed in Mainland China. The Taiwanese was a pursuer of the Three People's Principles[b] and senior cadre in the Nationalist Party. His companions pursued communism and were senior CPC members. They went back to Qiyang Town together to seek out any vestiges of the Qiyang Widow. But everything had changed. Her businesses had all gone … torn down. How refined those ancient buildings were, with their flying eaves, upturned corners and decorative animal figurines of the dragon, phoenix, lion, tiger, unicorn, heavenly steed, seahorse, fish, *xiezhi*,[c] *hou*[d] and the monkey. But they had all been demolished, leaving behind not even a trace. What replaced them were two parallel lines of one- or two-storey modern buildings constructed out of bricks and wood or concrete. These boasted not the least hint of native style and looked like stacked-up dens of predatory beasts.

The Qiyang Widow's tomb had disappeared too. Retracing the route from their memories of seeing her off, the three elders went to her tomb site to the south of the town centre. An expanse of cypresses used to stand in that spot, but not a vestige of them was left now. It was early autumn. The lush maize stalks were dark green. Fondled by a breeze, relentless green waves undulated. Their eyes became moist. They asked those they bumped into if they knew about the Qiyang Widow's tomb. Nobody knew them. No one could answer their questions clearly either.

One said: "Yeah. A tomb used to be there in that patch of maize. There were cypresses too – a lot of them."

Another asked in reply: "Tomb? Whose tomb? I don't know."

Still another replied: "It's been flattened. Levelled long ago. The dead shouldn't vie for the land with the living."

The elders who had come back to their hometown could only sigh for the vicissitudes of the past fifty years. Luckily, the Qiyang Charity School was still there. The original buildings had been torn down and rebuilt. Having been converted into the modern Qiyang Junior Middle School, the school didn't conform to its old appearance, but the campus was built on the site of the former charity school. The trio of seniors went over to have a group photo taken. Behind them a gang of students were on their way home from school, each young and bright and full of vitality. The three white-haired gentlemen provided a foil for them. The smiles on their faces could hardly cover up the wrinkles in their weather-beaten hearts.

Lin Maosheng the Assistant and Mr Shi the Headmaster were the most emotional over the Qiyang Widow's death. While they helped her daughters sort through their mother's legacy, they uncovered a collection of poetry edited, designed and bound together by the Qiyang Widow (this was verified by her daughters). It was made up of poems composed by her beloved rascal husband, which had been scattered around the house. She had gathered them together cautiously and the manuscript had never left her hand for a moment. What is more, this was the only copy in the world and was absolutely unique. Lin Maosheng and Mr Shi turned to a poem highlighted by a folded-down corner and took a look. The title of the poem was *Rural Festivities*. They read it carefully and another kind of sourness surged inexorably in their hearts:

A spring breeze can sweep across eight hundred miles in one night
And wake up
The accumulated snow on the Taibai Mountains
And the wild geese on the River Wei.
Lions are dancing in the eastern villages.
The hegemon-king's whips are cracking in the northern communes.
Stilt-walkers are pulling their stunts in the western hamlets.
Land-bound boats are performing in the southern towns.

So gladdened are those people in the seventy trades.
They vie against each other to lay a wine table in front of their doors.
When big bowlfuls of hard liquor have flooded their stomachs
The gongs and drums are more urgent and the dancers become merrier.

As one saying goes:
Rural festivities are organised in every village and commune
And everyone plays a role in the dramas.

Isn't that true? More than fifty years later, following the lead of Lin Maosheng and Mr Shi, the author finds himself feeling sour-hearted.

Reader, what role are you playing in the drama?

Red Lantern

Diligent girl weavers won't ever catch a chill.
Famines can be weathered if you watch how you till.
   — A folk saying from the Western Plain

RED LANTERN LOST her name.
At the very beginning, when she married into Tending Rites Village, she had a name. She didn't know how she came to lose it. Nobody could recall what her name was either. When she was asked about it, she replied that she too had forgotten, adding: "I am a lantern maker. Keep it in mind that my lanterns are fine and that is enough."

Red Lantern enjoyed her greatest fame as a lantern maker on the Western Plain of Guanzhong. This was a generally acknowledged fact. Nobody dared to try to be her rival. No one could pass muster. Later, people concluded she lost her name because her lanterns were so peerless that folks remembered them, while her name slipped their minds. So, it occurred to her, she should think only about the beauty of her creations and forget her own name.

Others therefore addressed her as "Red Lantern".

She also introduced herself that way.

But as I prepared to recount her story it occurred to me that there must be further reasons for the loss of her name. But what were they? I drew a blank.

By tracing her journey, the reasons might come to light.

When she married into Tending Rites Village, Red Lantern was a tender girl of only sixteen. Barely had she set foot over the threshold when her man was carried out of the door horizontally. That is to say, she had to doff her red bridal blouse and skirt and change into a suit of rough white mourning attire. She was forced to tearfully see off the soul of the departed before she could even figure out what her man looked like. Then, sitting in the empty chamber with a sob-streaked face, she became a young widow.

The guests left.

The neighbours left.

The raucous compound suddenly became cold and deserted – so cold and deserted that people broke out in goose pimples. Red Lantern wailed for days. After exhausting herself by crying, she huddled up at the head of the *kang*, closed her eyes and intended to sleep quietly awhile. But then she heard a light cough scarcely more audible than the buzz of a bee.

"Ma."

That buzz of a cough prickled her like a bee sting. She opened her eyes and spied four children of assorted sizes standing below the *kang*. They again called for her one after another.

"Ma."

"Ma."

Red Lantern knew that the four little ones were her man's flesh and blood. She married the widower to "fill in his house" – to act as a stepmother to them. She was still young yet knew full well the local custom. Before she came over, she had prepared herself mentally to make adjustments. Nevertheless, what transpired overrode everything. She must make adjustments to cope with the changes.

But what preparations could she make?

Temporarily unable to make head nor tail of it or to get her thoughts straight, she simplified matters by ceasing to rack her brains and ceasing to try to straighten her thoughts.

She hopped down from the *kang* and stroked the infants' heads one by one. The eldest was eight and was cradling the youngest – of one year and three months – in his arms. Red Lantern took the baby, clasped him to her breast and pursed her lips to give his small milky face a kiss. "Have you eaten?" she asked them.

"Let's go. Let's make something yummy to eat," she suggested.

This suggestion confirmed that she now held the reins and must draw the family cart. She had become the mother of the brood.

All manner of fortune and misfortune landed on the shoulders of the sixteen-year-old Red Lantern out of the blue like this. Her shoulders were still tender, but she had no option. She must carry the household on her tender shoulders in their onward trudge.

They should trudge onward.

But how?

Their family had several *mu* of fallow farmland. Not knowing how to farm, from then on she kept a diligent eye on her neighbours. When her neighbours neatened up their farmland, she followed suit. When her neighbours sowed seeds, she did likewise. Her farmland was neatened up and the seeds were sowed, but the harvest she brought back home was never as good as that gleaned by those around her. This was a thankless situation. She was too inexperienced at farming and in supporting a family. Night after night she racked her brains. Finally, she hit upon an idea – making lanterns.

Her mother at her maiden home was a good lantern maker. She had learned from her and the pupil had surpassed the teacher.

Her mother's lanterns had been made to be sold.

The moment Red Lantern started to fashion lanterns, her mother leaped into her mind. She recalled the parting words left with her by her mother:

Diligent girl weavers won't ever catch a chill.
Famines can be weathered if you watch how you till.

How pitiable her mother was. Barely had she shared that proverb, when she pushed her daughter in the direction of the matchmaker. A stomach-full of black liquid rained downwards from her body and a throat-full of black liquid spurted upwards out of her mouth. With a kick of her legs, mother breathed her last. She had only just stepped over her husband's threshold, when he too spewed black liquid up and down and kicked his legs out as he breathed his last.

When Red Lantern married into Tending Rites Village, this

lethal disease laid waste to all the villages and stockades on the Western Plain. Death visited them daily. In some households, one member died today and another tomorrow. Within a matter of days, the lot had been wiped out. Every village and stockade saw domestic tragedies like this. Doctors and herbalists were invited but they couldn't cure this disease. Necromancers and sorceresses were summoned, but they couldn't subdue this demon either.

People couldn't tell if it was a disease or a demon.

In mortal dread, they named the lethal affliction the "black water squits".

The bodily cavity of anyone struck down by the disease – be they men or women, old or young – would immediately become a vat of dye. The fine rice, pearly noodles, red meat and green vegetables they shoved into their mouths were all reduced to a fluid as black as Chinese ink and lacquer. After taking a tour around their stomachs and intestines, it erupted out of either their upper or lower orifices.

Back at her maiden home, Red Lantern's mother succumbed to the disease. Her new spouse died from the same thing. Her elder brother, sister-in-law, nephews and nieces and her man's parents and elder and younger sisters were lost too. In their desperation, the people beseeched the Heavens, but the Heavens didn't answer; they implored Mother Earth, but Mother Earth offered no promises. Precisely at this moment, the Western Plain saw its first flurry of snow following the arrival of winter.

Mixing with and being churned by the wind, the dancing, floating and sky-eclipsing snowflakes resembled the tears of a man who was so inconsolable that his intestines haemorrhaged. High in the skies, the snowflakes condensed into lumps as big as straw hats thrown to the ground as if hell-bent on blotting out the sky and submerging the earth. Mountains and hills were stained white. Farmland was stained white. Villages and houses were stained white. Most importantly of all, folks' desperate minds were stained white. During the heavy snowfall, the lethal "black water squits" vanished miraculously into the ether. No one else spewed black liquid upwards and spurted black liquid downwards and died in their boots.

The snowfall stopped. The winds died down.

The high and distant firmament also presented a rare spectacle. It became boundlessly crystalline, a transparently glossy pure blue that provided a perfect foil for the red wheel of the warm winter sun.

This was what the people had been craving.

When they fully realised the beauty of this round of winter snow, with a *whoosh* they all sped out of their doors and out of their villages and stockades that were as lifeless as lifeless could be and plunged onto the earth that was blanketed with quilt-like snow, turning and rolling and leaping and bounding in the limitless white world. Nobody knows who took the lead, but one and then everyone scooped up a lump of snow and crammed it into his or her mouth to munch on. The habit was infectious. They all started to gorge greedily on the snow like ravenous beasts.

On that winter day, the survivors of the "black water squits" all packed their stomachs full of the heaped snow.

How could the benevolence of that snow not become lodged in Red Lantern's mind?

To support the household and put food on the table, the stepmother bought wads and wads of sumptuous red tissue paper and started to fumble and fiddle to vouchsafe the family's survival. That red tissue paper was the raw material for lanterns. The paper was first cut up into the shape of a lantern and then pressed down into pads of small leaves, which were next glued to bamboo skeletons. A gaudy red lantern came into being in this way.

These lanterns boasted a healthy market when Spring Festival came around. Throughout the year, people could grin and bear grinding poverty, but not on New Year's Day. What family did not want to celebrate Spring Festival with auspicious bright crimson? The red lanterns thus became indispensable. Two were hung above the front gate and another two above the secondary gate. Whole compounds were livened up. Each claimed a sliver of joyous celebration, their portion of the blessings and a glimmer of expectation.

What is more, if a married daughter gave birth to a baby boy or girl, each maternal grandpa and grandma, uncle and aunt-in-law was required to send their grandson or granddaughter, nephew or niece a pair of lanterns. This was their custom – a custom prescribed by King Wen in the Zhou Dynasty and which to date had been popular on the Western Plain for several thousand years. Nobody was allowed to violate it. Those who did got their comeuppance. The elders – the grandpas and grandmas and uncles and aunts – did this in the expectation that when they passed away, sacrifices would be offered by their maternal grandsons and nephews. The sacrifices would be abundant. They would include a sheep's head, a pig's head, live chickens and ducks, lumps of steamed dough that had been twisted into all kinds of shapes and figures, and bowls of steamed dishes – too numerous to be counted. These would be put into food boxes and carried on the mourners' shoulders to be sent to their maternal grandpa and grandma and uncles and aunts-in-law, who by then were already in the Heavens. How were their gifts to be delivered smoothly if there were no dazzling red lanterns to illuminate their way?

In a similar vein, one of the folk songs in Northern Shaanxi went as follows:

In January it is the Chinese New Year.
Hang out the red lanterns, my dear.
The red lanterns look so great –
Hang them outside the gate.

The folk song confirmed that it was not only on the Western Plain where the custom of red New Year's lanterns was enjoyed. Northern Shaanxi had the bug too. Would other places be an exception? Would red lanterns not be hung there? Of course, the habit was universal.

Red Lantern had therefore taken the initiative to tap into a fertile market. It proved a masterstroke. She always kept the benevolence of that snowy spell embedded in her mind. Dipping a writing brush into the ready-prepared white paste, she painted snowflakes onto the red tissue paper.

She threw herself into her art. All the snowflakes were different, some with three petals, some with four, still some with five or six. There was one very special kind of snowflake that sprouted legs like vivid fat worms. Red Lantern had observed every variety of snowflake. They came from the same mould as those that dropped from the sky and followed the same template. She painted sundry snowflakes not found in nature. They all looked peculiar, some like pear blossoms, some like apricot blossoms and still others like wild chrysanthemums. But they were not pear blossoms, apricot blossoms or wild chrysanthemums. They were snowflakes true to the name – snowflakes which came from her imagination. All in all, copied from nature or imaginary, the snowflakes on the red tissue paper were all very pleasing to the eye and scintillating to the heart.

That was the effect she had been longing for.

Red Lantern dubbed her lanterns "Red Snowflakes". Her goods immediately caused a stir in the lantern market before the Spring Festival began. The lucky survivors all committed to memory the kindness of that round of snow. At first sight, every one of them fell in love with the meticulously designed and executed "Red Snowflake" lanterns. All the successful buyers were elated. Those who failed to lay their hands on the lanterns went to the maker's home to stand in line. Money was not a problem. Even if the price tripled or went up five-fold, they would still gladly dip their hands into their pockets.

The vendor could rest easy. The buyers were like cats on hot bricks. Red Lantern was already busier than a bee, but still her impatient customers were not satisfied. But they could keep their impatience to themselves. It was not her worry or concern. What she fretted about was that the lanterns might not be well made. As she had done at the very beginning, she kept painting snowflakes and working on the lanterns assiduously. She didn't allow one below par specimen to pass out of her hands.

The "Red Snowflake" lanterns garnered more than enough fame and fortune for her. They surpassed her expectations. Originally she only had the grace of the snowflakes in her mind. She had never set a target of how much money she should pocket, let alone contemplate fame and fortune. But now she was somebody, with a smidgen of money. She felt happy and contented.

During Chinese New Year, almost all the households hung "Red Snowflake" lanterns above their gates. This gratified and heartened her even more greatly. During the following year, "Red Snowflake" lanterns formed the most splendid scenery across the lands of the Western Plain.

Now that her family had money to spare, Red Lantern thought of sending the children to school.

It is tough to be a stepmother when you remain ever-conscious that the children did not come from you and the children do not accept you as their biological mother. It is easy to be a stepmother if the contrary is the case. Red Lantern cherished the children. First, she sent the eldest to an old-style private school run by a clique of rich households in Tending Rites Village. He studied scrupulously and regularly received praise from his teacher. The teacher, who often wore a long black gown, sometimes bumped into Red Lantern on the street or in the lane. When he saw her, he didn't talk but only shot a quick glance at her. His eyes were full of praise and admiration. After studying at school for two years and already able to wade through cryptic articles, the eldest kid brought back home a sheet of writing paper from the long-gowned gentleman. Two lines were written on the beautiful paper with a writing brush. Red Lantern was illiterate. The eldest son read them out for her:

Trusting in education and doing good, mother knows how best to raise her brood.
She who nourishes nature and aspiration, warrants our filial gratitude.

What did this mean? Red Lantern couldn't understand it. The eldest son then explained it to her: "With the first line, my teacher is saluting your kind-heartedness. You are so good to us. Though you are our stepmother, you are better than the mother who gave birth to us." Red Lantern beamed. She knew that the explanation "better than the mother who gave birth to us" was the eldest son's embellishment. She then asked about the meaning of the next line. The eldest kid lowered his head and was unwilling to answer. She probed again. Not until then did he reply in a low voice: "I will study hard and repay your kindness after I have grown up." With these words, he knelt down and banged his head before her in two loud kowtows.

She hurriedly hauled him up and patted the dirt from his knees, but her eyes couldn't help being clouded with a film of watery tears.

She didn't know why she wanted to cry so much – to cry her heart out without any scruples just for once. The aged long-gowned gentleman's praises moved her and so did the eldest son's attention to her feelings. Deep down, how could she not yearn after such a thing? But was such a result to be found so easily?

Never! Never so easily!

Red Lantern was still very young. When the eldest son knelt down and kowtowed voluntarily before her, she was only nineteen. That meant that she had stayed in Tending Rites Village for only three years since her marriage. Those three years seemed like thirty to her though. What is more, she knew that hard times were awaiting her in the future. She still needed to negotiate them day by day. She was the stepmother to four children and must apply herself.

But then she started to get mysterious marriage proposals.

Could she get remarried?

She couldn't.

With great difficulty she refused all the matchmakers who darkened her door time and again.

Night wore on. Unable to fall asleep, she got up to scrape at the bamboo strips and wood chips. Bundles of bamboo strips and piles of wood chips were stacked up in her bedroom. She whittled away her days and nights working on them. The bamboo strips and wood chips were the raw materials utilised to make lanterns after the arrival of winter.

She could only make lanterns. She couldn't quit even if she wanted to. Many peddlers who travelled from one village to another to ply their businesses would descend on her to place orders for the Spring Festival. Her lanterns were simultaneously becoming more delicate and their variety, design and colours much richer in range. There were now animal-shaped lanterns, for example: rabbit lanterns, duck lanterns, pig lanterns, dog lanterns, dragon lanterns, phoenix lanterns. Every last one was vibrant and true to life.

There were plant-shaped lanterns: Chinese cabbage lanterns, pumpkin lanterns, pomegranate lanterns, lotus lanterns, Chinese herbaceous peony lanterns, peony lanterns. Fresh and beautiful, each was indistinguishable from their archetype. What is more, there were horse lanterns, which could rotate and revolve, and ones that called for more intricate craftsmanship. Their unique characteristics meant they captured people's fancy like no other. Take the rotating lanterns as an example. With their flying eaves and upturned corners, they looked like quaint pavilions with one white gauze shade pasted on the outside and one inside. What set these apart was that the interior gauze shade was painted with historical figures and illustrated their stories. Her repertoire included *Zhaojun Goes Beyond the Great Wall*, *Guifei Gets Drunk*, *Mulan Joins the Army* and *Su Hui Embroiders the Brocade*. When the lanterns were lit, the shades would start to revolve. As long as the candles inside didn't die down, the shades carried on turning. The belles in their ancient costumes flashed splendidly in front of onlookers' eyes, popping up one moment and dematerialising the next. They were so stimulating.

Unfortunately, life didn't wind on as smoothly as her lantern making. She could shoo away whoever pestered her, but it was too burdensome to give vent to the loneliness and perplexity that fogged her heart.

She was a married woman. But, for her, how was being married any different from being unmarried? She was still a virgin! At the same time, she knew she was the mother to a quartet of children.

The stirrings of love were so pernicious. Struggle as she might, she must withstand their attack; she gritted her teeth as she tried to resist.

Much discomfort had to be weathered. When all was said and done, she was a stepmother, so how could she be exempt from the tribulations experienced by all the other stepmothers in the world? The four children called her "Mother" sweetly. But children are children. There is always a time when they will become naughty and won't know any better. She laid down a few basic rules for them: they should be diligent and frugal; they should respect the old and love the young; they should be honest and never bully; they should be upright.

However, from the mouth of the victim she knew that her eldest son and several other children from the village had stolen an old lady's persimmons.

Some might think that because persimmon trees were no rarity in Tending Rites Village then pinching a few fruits was no big deal. But Red Lantern didn't agree. When the eldest son came home for lunch after school, she called him to a halt and asked: "You have stolen someone's persimmons?" The kid didn't answer. She then ordered him to kneel down outside the front gate. Kneeling there for quite a long while, the kid still didn't utter one sound. The other three younger ones all crowded around him and tried to haul him to his feet. He didn't get up. The three younger ones then knelt down together with their eldest brother. Not until Red Lantern had finished cooking and gone to the front gate to tell him to rise did the three younger ones follow him to stand up. No one talked during their meal, but Red Lantern already saw a kind of hatred in the eyes of the three younger ones. Still the eldest remained considerate. After lunch he went to school. Standing in front of Red Lantern, his clear eyes showed not the least little sign of complaint. "Mother," he said. "I won't walk to school with those other boys."

From the tone of his voice, Red Lantern discerned a clue. She made enquiries among many people and discovered that it was true that the children had stolen persimmons, but her eldest child was only passing by and didn't join in. Feeling uncomfortable, she asked him why he didn't defend himself. He explained: "Back then, Mother, you were in a towering rage. I didn't want to talk back and rile you up. Thinking it over, was it a big deal for me to kneel down for a while? I felt I should set an example to my younger sister and brothers. They mightn't misbehave then and take the wrong road."

It was easy for the eldest one to reason his way through matters and do the right thing when he was misunderstood. The three younger ones were not as broad-minded as he. From then on, they made a fair amount of trouble for Red Lantern, particularly the second, who was a girl. Whether something had truly happened or not, she would scoot over to her dead birth mother's tomb and turn on the waterworks pitifully.

Gossip ensued. Red Lantern was said to be too caustic towards the children. She was supposedly thinking about getting remarried. If the gossips were fond of chewing their tongues, they should help themselves; if they had a liking for cooking up stories, they should be her guest. Red Lantern was unwilling to pay them any attention. Even so, one event made her tune profoundly into the problems of being a stepmother.

After the "black water squits" passed by, many blended families appeared on the Western Plain and every village had its share of stepfathers and stepmothers. One stepmother in another household in Tending Rites Village poisoned her stepson with white arsenic. The tragedy shocked Red Lantern's stepchildren greatly. The day after the incident, in order to assuage any potential doubts, Red Lantern made a point of cooking a range of dishes, namely homely tofu, pork prepared with rice noodles and eggs stir-fried in pure lard. Looking amazing and tasting scrumptious, it was not hard to whet appetites. But the children, the eldest son included, didn't come over and crowd around the dishes to tuck in as they had done before. Once again, it was the second one – the girl – who lifted up the plates and sniffed at them one by one. Her facial expressions needed no explanation: have these fine, fragrant dishes been spiked with arsenic? Red Lantern's nose turned sour and two streams of clear tears spilled slowly out of her eyes.

But she wouldn't allow her tears to sluice down. Picking up a pair of chopsticks, she took a bite from each dish. While she was munching, her stepchildren all stared fixedly at her mouth. Before she had time to swallow the food, they had already ducked their heads and started to shovel in big mouthfuls. She took one look at them. Their tender, small faces were similarly streaked with burning hot tears.

The blood of Red Lantern and her children blended completely together in their tears. She was their mother.

After the eldest son graduated from the old-style private school, he went on to study at a senior high school in the county town. Among the three younger ones, the third followed him to the private school in the village. Originally, Red Lantern had wanted to send the second to school. But that was the old society. It wasn't the tradition to give girls an education in the countryside of the stuck-in-the-mud Western Plain. So, the second one stayed at home, lending her a helping hand and taking care of the fourth. When her hands were not occupied, she learned how to make lanterns. Later, the fourth child went to school as well. After the Liberation of China in 1949 when the second one was already fifteen, Red Lantern finally succeeded in sending her to school and fulfilled her long-cherished wish.

The four children all lived up to their mother's expectations and were good with their books, first at the village and then in the county town. Later, they all went to study at universities in the very distant Beijing and Nanjing. Those who made the biggest splash were the eldest and the third child. Dispatched by the government, they travelled across the seas to study abroad.

Red Lantern became a role model for all the other mothers on the Western Plain.

But she didn't cherish the limelight and continued to arrange her life according to her former schedule. When it was time to scrape the bamboo strips, she worked on the bamboo strips; when it was time to cut up the wood chips, she worked on the wood chips. Everything was done in neat order and in accordance with her prescribed routine as she prepared in advance for the lantern market at Spring Festival. She needed to raise money to cover her stepchildren's tuition and living expenses. She must work harder.

Mutual aid teams and agricultural producers' co-operatives were established in the village. The locals had set foot into the era of the people's commune. No longer was there any question of her maintaining the lantern business alone. The villagers all got together to engage in agricultural production; this was their principal business. At the same time, they engaged in the lantern business together; this was their subsidiary business. Red Lantern smiled at whatever life brought her. Believing that this was not bad, she gave her undivided attention to the collectivised lantern business. This was what the collective had been looking forward to. With her advice and guidance, their lantern business began to flourish, extending benefits to every last villager and making them all think well of her.

But the policies changed according to someone's say-so. Their collective lantern business was branded a form of capitalism and Red Lantern a leading capitalist roader. The commune organised a denunciation rally on an outdoor terrace. Two tiger-fierce men took hold of her arms and marched Red Lantern, who by then wore dishevelled hair, to the tall stage. Slogans resounded, wave after wave. So much so that the people didn't notice at first that a military Jeep had driven up and parked by the terrace. Three awe-inspiring soldiers got down and mounted the stage. One knelt in front of Red Lantern, banged his head in a kowtow and called out "Mother".

The turn of events was too sudden. The man who was presiding over the denunciation rally wanted to step forward to order them to halt. The other two soldiers had shown him a copy of something that bore the stamp of a big red seal. Red Lantern was then carefully helped over to the dark green Jeep. A door opened and she was helped in. Some sharp-eyed people had figured it out. The soldier who knelt before Red Lantern was her eldest stepson. It was said that after graduating from a university in Beijing, he had gone on to an advanced research institute concerned with national defence. What was his research orientation? It was rumoured that this was strictly confidential. He seldom came back. This was in stark contrast to the three other stepchildren; barely had one left when another came in their stead. They were so considerate towards their stepmother onlookers would be red-eyed with envy. But the eldest son's return this time meant Red Lantern was spirited away.

Her departure turned the hearts of the Tending Rites villagers sour. Why should she leave like this? How dare she leave a denunciation rally? She had been humiliated because she had tried to ensure there was money in the villagers' pockets. The villagers could never forget that. They always felt they had given her the short straw. Frequently, someone rambled: "She should come back just once. Why doesn't she come back?"

She did indeed come back.

Many years passed before she finally made her return. She came back to Tending Rites Village in a delicate, small wooden casket escorted by her stepchildren. Her stepchildren all had their own children now. A large gang of people turned up without warning in the village in eight or nine glossy limousines. All the villagers were surprised.

At the sight of the small wooden casket and at the thought of what Red Lantern had said and done in the village, those who knew her soiled the fronts of their shirts and blouses with their tears. The younger ones might never have seen her, but they had heard tell of her many charitable deeds and magnanimous acts. The sight of the box left them heartbroken and tears threatened their eyes.

Red Lantern was brought home to be buried in Tending Rites Village. The villagers felt it a great honour and agreed unanimously that she should be buried by the roadside at the entrance to the village. Her tomb was built out of black bricks. A stone tablet was planted at the head of the grave but inscribed with no words. The top of the stone tablet, which was a slab of brick-red granite, was carved into a big red lantern. Illuminated by the sun, it twinkled and shone.

When I was writing this account, I sometimes passed by the lantern tablet. Whenever I bumped into a Tending Rites villager, they would tell me proudly: "You know what? Red Lantern is at rest here!"

The Blood Red Sun

Pa promised me he would take me to the streets of Phoenix Town. I had never been to the streets before but assumed they must be the greatest place of all, teeming with attractions. Once, I pestered to be taken there but Pa objected on the grounds that the town centre was too far away, making it unreachable for a brat like me. When I was rebuffed by Pa, I wept. Eventually, however, Pa was prepared to take me.

He frequented the streets of the town.

Every time Pa set out for the streets, he always carried his head-shaving load on his shoulders. There was a basin and a furnace on one end of his carrying pole and a mirror and a stool on the other. A popular saying goes that "just one end of the head-shaving load is hot". At first, I was baffled about what this meant. Only when I caught sight of Pa's carrying pole did it dawn on me that the "hot end" referred to the furnace, which was far weightier than the equipment at the other end. Since heavy items would be hung from one end of the pole and light ones from the other, the carrier was compelled to adjust the levelling point along the staff accordingly. As Pa lurched forward with his pole swinging back and forth, he appeared to be treading water.

Pa would always leave home at dawn and come back at dusk with yet more items on his carrying pole: something to eat, something for fun, something to wear or something to use. Upon hearing Pa's footsteps, Ma would turn to me and yell: "Date Stone, your Pa is coming back from the streets. Go and greet him at the door."

It was a crying shame that I, with my underdeveloped build, couldn't support Pa's pole and the load upon it.

Before Pa had the chance to rest his load on the ground, I was ready to start searching along the rod. I foraged eagerly for anything delicious or lovely that Pa may have brought home. On such occasions, it never occurred to me that Pa might have felt fatigued from lugging a pole that weighed dozens of pounds and more for a distance of leagues and leagues.

Pa bought me pencils, erasers and notebooks. Ma sewed a patchwork schoolbag for me; a store for all these treasures. She cut a pile of red and green scraps into identical triangles before matching them up perfectly. After that, Ma stitched them together one by one using fine threads and a needle to fashion a series of squares. When the edges were stitched together, a patchwork schoolbag with an artistic flavour took shape. I was so fond of the bag Ma had created that I entertained the illusion that the brightly-coloured square blocks were actually tiny windows. But when I covered my head with the patchwork schoolbag like a hood, I was unable to see through it.

Even though the idea of going to school preyed upon me, I was never to be given the precious opportunity of attending school. Wasn't that bizarre?

All I knew was that I was soon to follow Pa out onto the streets.

At that moment, he was grinding his razor in the yard.

Pa used to grind his razor in the courtyard with a gentle and agile motion, producing a melodious and rhythmic rustling like some marvellous, matchless serenade. With the razor well-ground, he would go out onto the streets to conduct his trade, his carrying pole swaying and a shiny black cloth fluttering in front.

People unloaded the huge mirror from Pa's carrying pole, placing it against his neck and forcing him to join the parade of miscreants and hooligans the authorities had chosen to publicly humiliate. Others who were dragged onto the street parade included the tofu vendor Wang, the noodle peddler Zhang, the bean jelly seller Ms Bai and the kung-fu performer Ding. The charming-looking bean jelly seller hung her head for the duration of the ordeal, her shining black hair, long and loose, scattered by the wind. Rumour has it that once she got home she committed suicide by drowning herself in a well. After all, women are narrow-minded and incapable of bearing shame.

When he returned home from the parade, Pa took down the huge mirror from his neck pole and hung it on the screening wall directly opposite the door. Peering at his reflection in the mirror, he fixed his eyes on his image in the glass as if he was inspecting unclean patches on his face. He didn't realise that, out on the streets, nobody paid attention to your face, however foul.

Pa fell into utter silence.

Motionless, he continued to look into the mirror. He then burst into laughter and guffawed with tears overflowing from the corners of his eyes. His laughter sounded like weeping. All of a sudden, Pa straightened up and struck his head against the mirror in a firm and stiff manner. As the mirror shattered, blood appeared all over his face.

Terrified, I shrieked, "Pa! What's the – "

Ma rushed out and dragged him into the house. Pa and Ma talked all the night long.

Pa sighed, "What should we do?"

Ma soothed him by saying, "The sky won't crumble."

Ma urged him, "Sleep. The King of Hell may rob you of your life but not your slumber. Let's go to bed."

"I can't. You just sleep on your own." He finally resolved, "I have no choice but to take our kid out onto the streets. It seems that I have no other option."

Ma objected, "No, that won't work." She affirmed, "Believe me, it won't do."

Pa and Ma's conversation was way beyond my comprehension: since Pa had often gone to the streets, why couldn't I go when my turn came? Were there any open wells in the streets? Pa dismissed Ma's words, insisting on taking me to the streets. He accounted for this defiance by saying that one cannot sit by doing nothing and starve to death. He added that Ma was going to have another baby, a younger sister for me, and how fantastic it would be for me to be the elder brother.

The collective dining hall for our Production Brigade only provided coarse food and thin soup, which was never sufficient to stave off my hunger. Consequently, I always had a rumbling stomach. As Pa was being shamed on the streets, Ma and I dug potherbs and stripped the bark from the trees in the meadows. Each passing day found me thinner while Ma grew plumper with a swollen and yellow countenance. Her bulging feet did not fit into her shoes. With her waxing belly, glistering and transparent as a mature silkworm, and her winding guts resembling a mottled snake twisting and turning in the field, Ma struggled to recline back on the *kang*. Reluctant to become attached to her, I lay on Pa's warm chest at night and, in my drowsiness, overheard his sighing and muttering.

"I'm so tired. Tired to death."

Pa proceeded to grind his razor.

For the first time, I noticed it was considerably larger than the one he had previously employed in daily use. He was grinding this red rusty razor with tremendous and malicious effort, blue veins protruding from his forehead and his upper lips being gnawed at by his teeth. The coarse grains of grit on the grinding stone were peeled away layer after layer along with the blood-red rusty water.

Pa yelled at me, "Date Stone, come over here."

Feeling intimidated, I approached him with hesitation, enquiring, "What's up, Pa?"

He seized me and said, "I have something to tell you."

"Son, I won't eat you," he went on.

Pa sat on the stone stool beneath the old mulberry tree. Where was the lush green canopy of the tree? Ma had gathered all the leaves and used the lot to feed her and Pa. A couple of sparrows perched on the bare twigs of the tree, chirping and dancing animatedly. The enchanting sunshine cast its tender brilliance over the old mulberry tree and the tiny yard, which were so gentle and so warm. Placing me in his lap, Pa patted my head with his huge, rough, weather-beaten hands.

He asked, "Son, if your mum questions what I am doing, how will you reply?"

I answered him directly, "Busy grinding the razor."

He shook his head, "Nonsense."

"But you are sharpening the razor," I retorted.

"You're a good boy; you'll soon know how to answer your ma."

Beads of blood oozed from around Pa's eyeballs. As the hand that was holding the razor quivered, a ghastly, dazzling white beam fluttered in the air.

"Pa, I will repeat exactly what you tell me."

"That's my boy, you son of a dog."

Twitching the corners of his mouth, Pa appeared to be crying rather than laughing. He bellowed, "Listen, Date Stone. When your Ma asks you, just tell her that I am toughening your scalp." He continued, "As long as you have a tough scalp, you will never suffer from thirst and hunger. And then my carrying pole will never get cold."

"I see."

What did I see? I saw nothing. Instinctively, I dodged away from the razor in his hand for fear that he would slice off my ears.

Together with the trembling of Pa's hands, I felt the movement of the razor on the top of my head and noticed my black hair tumbling down like falling curtains. Initially, I experienced no pain. Suddenly, though, I sensed that something was wrong. Having not lifted the razor for several days, was his skill faltering? Or was it that the razor had not been perfectly sharpened?

I screamed, "Pa, it hurts!"

My head seemed about to split in two as though it had been lashed with a whip.

Pa said, "What is there to scream about?"

"Hold firm!" he urged me.

Pa handled my head like he was dealing with a fresh gourd.

Gritting my teeth and straightening my neck, I could feel my scalp becoming tense, hot and numb. All at once, an overwhelming sense of oppression caused it to thicken.

And then the bloodstained razor fell to the ground.

Pa cast a handful of loess on my head, rubbing it into fine dust before finally pressing down forcefully on the scalp. As a result, a stream of blood gushed through the yellow dust and trickled down my head. As the blood ran down my neck, an unbearable tickling sensation nearly made me burst into laughter.

When Pa placed the razor in my hand, I tossed it up and seized the handle, realising that my previous terror towards it had been ridiculous. Now, it was nothing more than a razor, and a run-of-the-mill one at that!

Pa asked, "Do you know how to explain this to your Ma?"

I simply uttered, "Toughening my scalp."

He then flung me an open-mouthed cloth sack.

Pa dragged me out onto the street by my hand. The cloth sack, which hung on my shoulder, was as tall as me.

Shadowing his strides, I rushed with brisk footsteps, eager to shout and sing as merriment overflowed from my heart. The streets in my imagination were wide and spacious, with numerous mansions and a panoply of delicacies, tools, toys and spectacles, all of which filled my heart with longing. My heart was like a bird in full plumage that was already flapping abroad into the streets.

Straight ahead, there was a high and steep ridge topped by a few sparse trees standing erect. Two were leafless elms. With the bark already peeled away, a peculiar skeleton as white as wax was exposed. Pa and I climbed along the ridge, wheezing heavily like pumping bellows. Oozing sweat made our clothes stick to our skin with such a sense of chill.

The further we climbed, the steeper the ridge became. I imagined that he and I were ascending a staircase to the heavens.

"Pa, I want to pee," I pleaded.

"Let's take a break and then go."

With his visage sallow and emitting a rough gasp, Pa said, "I've never taken a refreshment break before even when I've been out on the streets with my fully-loaded carrying pole on my shoulders."

The surging urine, like a sparkling gold chain, chased after an earthworm and dived into the ground with a *splash, splash, splash*. On the distant horizon, the sun rose after soaking itself in the ocean for a whole night, burning the sky and the earth with its zeal. As I was still peeing contentedly, the glittery urine suddenly changed dramatically and took on a blood red hue that instantly reminded me of the toughening of the scalp Pa had meted out to me.

Since my legs could not help trembling, the toughening of the scalp had clearly exacted a deep impression on me.

Pa's breath grew a little more relaxed.

After peeing, I squatted down beside him. As I took off my sandals, I discovered a succession of blisters on each of my toes. I massaged them without muttering a single word.

Pa too had his eyes fixed on the blisters and was flushed with satisfaction at my determination not to complain.

Numerous mounds jutted up in lines along the edge of the ridge. Some of them were clothed with green grass and wild flowers while others were naked, bearing the original colour of the soil as if they had only been formed yesterday. Touchpaper lay on the top and willow sticks were poking upwards.[e] The willow twigs had already become withered. With narrowing eyes, Pa fixed his gaze obsessively on the mounds.

Pa asked, "Date Stone, do you know what they are?"

"I've no idea."

Pa grumbled, "You know nothing. You will know soon enough."

With ease, Pa lifted me up and allowed me to touch his scalp.

Pa's crown was hairless, with scars swelling like earthworms or an expanse of ranges. Having not washed his head for a long time, the peaks and ridges glowed with splendour and the valleys and vales between the ranges were filled with filth and foul dirt, like a waste dump. I dared not touch it with outstretched hands. I knew that each scar represented a story, each valley a memory. And that each of them must be bloody stories and bloody memories.

Pa asked, "Did you inspect them all?"

"Of course."

"Have you figured out the reason?"

"Not yet," I answered.

"Later your head will be exactly the same as mine. This is the toughening of the scalp. Remember what I told you about your grandpa."

Grandpa earned a long list of notorious accolades, including "Scalp-breaker", "Mountain-breaker" and "the reckless one". A huge band of starving, poverty-stricken fellows in rags flocked around him. So reckless was he that he tested out sharp knives on his own skull. Thus he was hailed as the "Champ of the Beggars".

The kung-fu of toughening of the scalp that Pa applied to my head had been inherited from the hands of my grandpa, who kicked the bucket right after he had toughened my Pa's scalp.

Grandpa had once stretched out his begging hand in front of the blacksmith's forge in the street, with his dirty fingers crooked and trembling. The shopkeeper, who wore a pair of reading glasses, slid the abacus beads, totally oblivious to Grandpa's presence. So, he simply stretched out his hand stubbornly to ensure the proprietor noticed him. Each and every shopkeeper on the street always treated him with courtesy.

The shopkeeper wore a ghastly, solemn look as he raised his head and shot his vicious gaze through his spectacles. He probed Grandpa, saying: "Scalp-Breaker, I have never seen any blood shed from your skull."

Grandpa grinned with brilliant naivety and replied, "Watch carefully, I will do it for you right now."

Grandpa fumbled a razor from his bosom. It was the glistening one that was later to be ground by Pa for several days and now lay on his bosom. With the smile frozen on his face, Grandpa leaned towards the shopkeeper. Panic-stricken, the latter ducked backward, a green light of terror flickering in his shrewd eyes. Grandpa tossed the razor up in the air. This was the trick customarily performed by a beggar as a show of bravado before cutting his scalp. Grandpa caught the falling razor with the flesh of his head. The moment Grandpa heard the shopkeeper let out a scream was the same moment the snow-white razor made contact with his scalp. The cut, which was initially white, opened wide like a fish's mouth. Blood oozed from it and flowed into a stream. Grandpa tossed his head and the blood gushed down, staining an accounts book on the shopkeeper's counter.

Hastily, the shopkeeper fumbled in the drawer underneath and tossed a handful of coins in Grandpa's direction. As the official coins of various colours flew like sparrows before Grandpa, two silver dollars minted under Yuan Shikai rolled forward rapidly, giving off a clangorous, ear-pleasing melody. The shopkeeper muttered, "I was just pulling your leg, and you took it so seriously."

With a chuckle, Grandpa turned to chase the two coins into the far corner. As he nipped them between his fingers and tried to test their quality by blowing a puff of breath on them, the unsteadiness of his steps caused him to tumble down in front of a male bystander.

The one who caught Grandpa's body was an apprentice in the blacksmith's forge whose surname was Duan.

Duan had formerly hung around with the band of beggars for some time and was a sworn-brother to Grandpa. He had been keeping an eye on the shopkeeper and Grandpa. Distracted from his business, a bar of iron which had been glowing on the anvil gradually faded to black.

Grandpa closed his eyes at peace in the arms of Duan.

The shopkeeper said, "Was it worth it for a few humble coins?"

He was insensible to the cruel glance Duan cast at him. That night, Duan sneaked into the shopkeeper's bedchamber and slit his throat with the same razor used by Grandpa.

Later, under the cover of night, Duan fled from the forge and joined the guerrilla forces in the mountains.

Later still, Pa came to encounter Duan. After Grandpa's death, Pa bore the head-shaving pole that had been handed down from his ancestors and made a living on the streets. On one occasion, Pa stumbled upon Duan when he was undertaking some mission on the streets. He was totally unaware that he had already been promoted to the rank of captain in the guerrillas and was now conducting a reconnaissance with a view to launching an attack there. While Pa was shaving someone's head at the intersection of the streets, Duan approached him and handed him a big razor.

Dumbfounded, Pa cast a surprised glance at the handler of the razor and began to sense he was an acquaintance. When reminded of Grandpa, a sorrowful teardrop rolled along that razor, which was already besmirched with the bloodstain frozen into the rust. Pa couldn't tell how much of the dried bloodstain belonged to Grandpa and how much to the blacksmith.

It then dawned on Pa who the guy was who had handed him the razor. He could not help but exclaim, "Duan!" It was a pity that Pa only knew his family name. By the time he raised his head from looking at the razor, Duan had already vanished. Pa only remembered that Duan had a robust and muscular frame, heavy brows and huge eyes with the sign of a blood red crescent moon on his broad forehead.

After that, Pa often thought of Duan.

He recalled the blood red crescent moon on Duan's forehead.

Finally, we arrived on the streets.

It was late in the morning, the time when the street dwellers were taking their breakfast. With a faint smile on his face, Pa commented, "We have caught the right moment."

Along the road, the gutter was filthy with countless bubbles and some withered grass floating on the shallow foul-smelling water. A lean, aged sow stretched out and ploughed its cucumber-shaped snout into the sludgy ditch, stirring up whiffs of stench as malodorous as sheep shit. Pa scooped up a handful of dirty black mud and smeared it on his face, head and neck before carrying out the same procedure on me. Afterwards, I felt my hair had gone rusty and become matted together like a patch of woollen blanket. I felt a layer of scar tissue forming across my face as the filthy smell stung my flesh, transforming me into a heap of rotten, stinky sheep dung.

Quite satisfied with this makeover, Pa patted the back of my head intimately and urged, "Be clever once the show begins. Your tongue should be sweet and your voice should be sad. A sad appearance will win other people's pity."

He added, "We can't go home empty-handed today. Whatever happens, we cannot go empty-handed. Your mum is waiting for us at home."

The mention of Ma saddened me. Pa had not taught me how to look sad. His instructions amused rather than saddened me. What touched a chord in my heart was that my mother had grown too starved and too feeble to lie down on the *kang*.

I murmured, "Ma is waiting for us to bring the meal."

I sighed, "As long as we bring back something edible, Ma will be able to get back her strength."

My words were accompanied by a string of bitter teardrops which gushed from my eyes, and my throat felt like it was plugged with a bung of shabby cotton. It was quite natural that the words I spoke should be extremely melancholic.

Thus, we staggered across the street, directing our footsteps towards the places from where cooking smoke rose.

Breakfast passed by, as did lunch. Still, my cloth sack contained only two knots of cottonseed pulp from which the oil had been pounded and three green-headed radishes, all of which had been traded for with my hot tears. I saluted every one of these "uncles" and "aunties" and pleaded miserably that my Ma was too swollen to get to her feet and that she would be waiting for my return with eyes full of longing.

Pa and I begged for food separately. After a short while, we met up and he spoke highly of my pickings. As supper approached, we rendezvoused again. He had had nothing to eat all day.

I pressed, "Pa, let's go back home."

Pa echoed, "OK, let's go back."

We returned home in dismay, the shrivelled sack containing the radishes and cottonseed pulp dragging behind me, knocking against my legs. It suddenly dawned on me that I had been wandering the streets all day long without ever taking a serious look around me. I am sure they would have proved disappointing and depressing. There was nothing special there apart from a few shops, more houses and packs of people. It was neither pleasurable nor attractive to me, being nothing more than a huge village.

There was a big arch atop the gateway ahead with two stone lions crouching in front. As Pa and I passed the beasts with indifference, I casually patted an embroidered ball beneath the stone lion's claws. This part of the statue had become glossy and shiny from being constantly touched by passersby.

Having already gone through the gate, Pa turned and asked me, "Date Stone, are you afraid of government officials?"

That entire day's experience had made me brave. So, I blurted out, "Pa, there is nothing terrible about government officials. After all, officials are people too."

Pa stood still. A terrific idea flashed in his mind, "Let's go and meet the government officials." Isn't the district government a government of the people, by the people and for the people? Pondering this, Pa turned back and passed the stone lions again before stepping through the gate to the district government.

I followed suit and located the backyard from where smoke was rising. The smoke was coming from the dining hall of the district government. As it was suppertime, there was a cluster of officials all dressed in uniforms with four pockets. Each received a portion of soup and a steamed bun as they chitchatted in a circle.

We drew close to the circle before they became aware of us. My wailing, which I had practiced all day long, spontaneously erupted from the tip of my tongue. I began to plead, "Uncles …"

The circle of people abruptly dispersed before the words which still lingered on the tip of my tongue had chance to fully spring forth. They scattered swiftly like a knot of startled sparrows.

Only one of them stayed. He got to his feet holding a pitch-black steamed bun from which he had bitten a mouthful. His figure was towering and imposing and there was a blood red crescent moon on his dark forehead.

The blood red crescent moon caught Pa's eye.

Both fixed their eyes on each other. A dense puff of purple smoke descended from the ceiling of the dining hall and clouded their vision. The air between them seemed to freeze.

With his mouth wide open, Pa exclaimed in astonishment, "It's you, Duan."

The other nodded his head without speaking a word.

Then a voice bellowed from the front yard, addressing him as "District Mayor Duan" in an apparently flattering tone, informing him that somebody was expecting him.

Pa was unaware that this was a pretext the official was using to shepherd Duan away from trouble. The only thing he cared about was that Duan, his former benefactor, was now the District Mayor. Accordingly, an overwhelming sense of awe multiplied and swelled within his veins, so much so that he nearly got down on his knees and kowtowed to Duan.

Duan had exacted revenge for the sake of Grandpa. Moreover, he had risked his life running through fire and water and facing dauntless fights to establish a new government for the sake of the poverty-stricken masses. Even so, Pa was still begging on the streets, using his scalp-opening tricks. He had begged as far as the district government and was now begging in front of District Mayor Duan. Feeling ashamed, Pa wished there was a crevice at his feet so he could shrink and hide himself away from this awkward situation.

It was indeed a shame. Actually, Pa's behaviour had caused the District Mayor to lose face.

That shout from the front yard somehow gave Pa a sense of redemption. He mumbled, "I am fine, District Mayor Duan."

Pa proceeded, "You carry on with your work, District Mayor Duan. I really have nothing to bother you with, so I'll be getting home now."

After passing his bun to me, Duan summoned the dining hall administrator and whispered a few words in his ear. The latter took out a small basin of black bean flour and poured it into the cloth sack on my back. Pa tried to decline, saying repeatedly that there was no lack of food at home. Confronted with this tough resistance, the administrator no longer insisted. Duan took over the basin and started to pour the flour into the sack. Pa presented no further obstruction.

The white and blue bean flour, resembling a waterfall, splashed down into the mouth of the sack. The administrator, standing to one side, grumbled indistinctly, his round eyes akin to those of a dried fish.

What Pa and I failed to realise was that the small basin of black bean flour was District Mayor Duan's monthly ration.

Duan escorted us out of the government yard, pausing beside the stone lions. When patted me on the head with his massive hand, I felt a piercing ache in my heart from the stinging pain in my skull.

"I shall call on you in the village in a couple of days," Duan promised.

Pa replied, "No, you needn't bother."

The blazing setting sun, pressing against the distant peak of the western mountain, bathed the entire sky in its crimson glow and permeated the firmament with a thick carpet of blood. The streets, thus enveloped, appeared sublime and splendid.

Pa murmured, "Oh, Duan … Duan … Duan … "

Pa's murmur was low and beseeching as if it was bursting forth from his innermost soul. Was Pa calling out for a past dream?

Suddenly, Pa ceased his murmuring, his body becoming frozen to the spot. Then he ordered, "Date Stone, turn around."

Obediently, I turned around and caught sight of a crescent moon leaping up beyond the streets saturated in a brilliant solar glow.

Pa fished the razor from his bosom. After testing the sharp blade with his thumb, he tossed it high into the air and let it roll over like a bird gleaming brightly against the rosy clouds. Pa caught the falling razor with his head so, with the agile movement typical of a beggar performing his scalp-opening trick, a cut appeared. He then picked up the razor again and made another forceful slice.

Blood sprang forth like a surging tide, complete with white brains!

The Black Bean Field

It was Dad's idea to eat sticky cornmeal jelly on the day we harvested black beans. And his idea was an imperial edict in the eyes of Mum. By the time we were halfway through the farm chore, which involved tugging the plants from the soil and laying them out to dry until the pods loosened, our bellies had broken down two big bowlfuls of jelly into light soup. This became lodged in our guts, causing a bloated feeling that left us flustered.

Mum, who had gone without a meal, raised her head twice, unable to put up with her hunger any longer. With her heaving, dough-like breasts quaking and her hands tweaking at her waist, she seemed as riled up as a hare in jeopardy. Darting to the other side of the shady slope, she disappeared in a trice. Now, pressing their backs against each other, my crouching father and brother managed to lever themselves to their feet. The two men stood in stark contrast. Brother was tall and sturdy with a bold, round backside, whereas Dad, while strong, was bent and wizened. Together, they surveyed the sky, firing out almost in unison jets of urine, which glittered as they percolated through the dried yellow dirt.

Wormwood Seedling pawed at her sister-in-law and asked if she was ready to take a leak.

"Yes, let's go."

Just as Mum had done, they quit the black bean field for the far side of the shady slope. The field was irregular in shape and yet characteristically Shaanxi in style. The plain beneath the slope swept across 80,000 square *li* and the field on the slope was also the same width. Only the towering tableland, lofty and high, traversed between the east and west with patches of cultivated slopes. Nothing was left but weeds and bushes as far as the eye could see.

After relieving themselves, the girls quivered as though touched by a jolt of electricity, then relaxed and felt comfortable.

"We should sit down here for a while," Wormwood Seedling proposed.

"You dare?" Sister-in-Law asked.

"Why wouldn't I dare? Come on, lie down. The grass here is soft and springy. No worse than your marriage bed."

"You are what others say you are, after all. You have a sharp tongue. Who would be brave enough to marry you?"

Wormwood Seedling smiled, as did Sister-in-Law. They sat down in a familiar manner after exchanging nudges. The sun lay on top of the tableland, golden and gilded. The black bean field was caressed by its beams and became shrouded in curling vapour. They averted their eyes from the sky and stared at their breasts which bulged like pale jade hares. A burst of unspeakable pleasure brimmed within their hot veins, resulting in a sense of unutterable desire.

"How good is must be to be a man! Damn it. When I'm born again, I must bring a meat dagger with me into the next life."

"You beggar description. I'm going to tell your parents to get rid of you by marrying you off. Keeping a grown-up girl is a risky business."

Wormwood Seedling didn't pay attention to what Sister-in-Law said. She was still fixated on the idea of having a meat dagger in the next life and continued: "Men are streets ahead of us when it comes to pissing. They can just whip it out and take a slash anywhere. We're forced to hide ourselves away and feel uncomfortable. Having a thingummy is definitely more convenient."

While she was speaking, Wormwood Seedling cuddled Sister-in-Law and rubbed her breasts: "On your wedding night, my brother … did he rub you like this?"

"Wormwood Seedling, you're being mean. You will have a taste of it in the future.

"The future is one thing. Right now is another. Sister-in-Law."

Sister-in-Law knew what Wormwood Seedling was driving at, so she pretended to grow angry, asking "How come you have been calling me Sister-in-Law from the moment I stepped inside the home. We were classmates and friends. Aren't we still?"

"No more nonsense."

Wormwood Seedling didn't give a damn whether Sister-in-Law was annoyed or not, so went on cheekily: "I was frozen something rotten that night. The wind seemed to have teeth – biting and gnawing … just like my brother did!"

"Did you eavesdrop on us?" a surprised Sister-in-law asked.

"I did. My brother is a wolf. He bullied you and let you scream and moan. Sister-in-Law, why let yourself … suffer? Do you hate my brother? You must hate him."

Sister-in-Law smiled slightly and asked: "How could I hate your brother? The bitterness of that night is what made it so sweet. The more bitter it gets, the sweeter the result. The bitterness I suffered that night means I'll have so much more sweetness in the future."

The vague joy of the experience stole across her face and she added: "Women are all the same in this business."

A leisurely cloud passed over Sister-in-Law's head. It resembled a ball of cotton wool, which glided and metamorphosed from galloping horses one moment to a broom that brushed the blue sky clear the next.

Dad cried out from the black bean field: "Where are you?" His voice was rather overbearing and put the girls in mind of a house catching fire. "Get a move on! No more slacking off."

But there was an ill-disguised glee in his domineering voice. Day after day, he had surveyed the ripeness of the black beans: the pink blossoms appeared to have been blown away overnight; the watery, verdant leaves together with the stalks look as though they were dyed by the golden autumn sunlight; and the bronze complexion made people burst with joy. Even the black bean pods were plump and mellow, interwoven into the texture of this painting of the season, a poetic composition on autumn.

Dad – ever the trailblazer – plucked beans ahead of the rest.

After all, compared with the fuss of reaping wheat and having to grind it on the granary floor, tugging black beans felt like teasing a newlywed in January. Earnest farmers are inclined to treat chores as merry matters. Dad bent his frame fully, flexing like a longbow, and managed to clear ten paces in the blink of eye.

The older man was thin yet energetic, with the bearing of a persimmon trunk. He had tilled the land for half of his life, toiling and reaping. But he seemed inured to headaches and backaches and, being a born farmer, had never had to sip on herbal soup as medicine. Now his pointy, awl-like rear-end wriggled jauntily as a wound clock ready to spring forward.

Mum was quite different. Stout enough to envelop Dad entirely, she was still fearful of her husband. Even if he just sneezed, her flesh would tremble for some time. Mum reserved her strength to keep pace with her monkey-like spouse, but no matter how much effort she made, she still failed. She was conscious of the challenge and almost got her face poked out on the stalks. Beads of sweat sparkled on her nose and her broad bosom heaved with a little burst of pleasure.

"Black beans, black beans," Brother murmured. "Sowing black beans is all you know about."

Brother lifted himself up and stared with anger at Dad in front of him.

Sister-in-law laughed and asked: "What on earth are you talking about?" Her smile was like a bowlful of honeyed water, acting as a salve to her husband's anger.

She then barked: "Stop gawking. Keep pulling."

Sister-in-Law too resumed pulling black beans while she talked. In contrast to Dad and Mum, she did not so much bend her body as lean forward, her legs bolt upright. Her hands were thus free to catch hold of the stalks with ease. Sister-in-Law was a woman of sense. She knew there were plenty of gossips in the village and that complaints and aspersions were rife. Folks took an special interest in newly-wed brides. In her situation, Sister-in-Law didn't want to leave the slightest room for error, lest she become the nub of their tittle tattle.

It appeared that Brother was actually rather satisfied with his wife's behaviour. He slapped her tight posterior flirtatiously, then bowed his head to pull beans like her.

Wormwood Seedling wanted to laugh but dared not. Instead, she cursed herself a little inside and busied herself with the chore.

In an instant, the black bean field fell rather quiet. The family were scattered to the front and back, a model of industry. In their wake lay hillock-like bundles of bean stalks.

Elegant, fair-necked birds were flying in pairs a little distance away, sweeping up and down above the field, chirruping in joy. Waves of opera being sung locally rolled over from the other side of the slope, stirring everyone to their core:

> *Xu Cuilian is so ashamed*
> *Regrets doing needlework outside the gate*
> *That gentleman was seen entering my house*
> *Tongues are sure to wag*
> *No one listens to good deeds*
> *But bad ones spread a thousand li*
> *When my mother comes back*
> *I'll top myself as I tell the tale*

The song revealed vividly the ambivalent feelings of a girl in love. Wormwood Seedling grew rather obsessed with the singing, which aroused emotions in her ranging from obscure joy to vague sadness. She lifted her head and caught sight of Mum and Dad, forever giving each other a wide berth like a pair of adversaries. Brother and Sister-in-Law were different. They were apparently still overwhelmed by the tender sentiments of the wedding night, feeling not a jot of shame. They cleaved close to one another and lent a hand to whoever had fallen marginally behind. Certainly, Brother had a lot of chances. Every time they rubbed against each other, making contact with hands or shoulders for even a split second, Wormwood Seedling could see their eyes dripping with enviable waves. Brother and Sister-in-Law harvested black bean stalks in this way, turning a grinding toil into a pastime and a pleasant job. They didn't seem to be working, instead whispering sweet nothings to each other in the windy and aromatic field. Consequently, Wormwood Seedling happened to overhear them.

Brother said: "I'll tell you a joke. An absolutely hilarious one."

"I don't want you to," his missus replied. "Is your dirty mouth capable of telling a joke?

Sister-in-Law's reluctance actually served as a kind of catalyst. Breaking into a sly smile, he asked: "Have you tried mashed black beans? No, not yet?"

Sister-in-Law replied defiantly: "I haven't tried it but I've seen it. What's the good in that stuff?"

"No rush. There will be a time when you want it. We'll just have to wait. In two months, when you don't feel like your meals are sour or spicy, you'll be asking for mashed black beans."

Sister-in-Law turned around and gave him a dirty look: "I'm not eating simple fare just to save you more money. Although, I could save enough to buy your coffin."

A restless Brother gagged her with the palms of his hands, saying: "What do you understand about this? Dad said he grew heavy black beans the year he married Mum."

In a moment of silence, he withdrew his hands and they stood in stalemate, looking at each other. Wormwood Seedling found it hard to comprehend the amorous emotions in their eyes, which made her feel dumb and hurt.

"I'm not tricking you," Brother continued. "Why ever would I trick you? Dad really did grow a crop of heavy black beans. He said they were like the ones we are picking today."

Sister-in-Law freed herself from Brother's grip and thumped him on the chest in anger. But she couldn't help but cackle hilariously as she turned around. Her laugh was unrestrained and wild, drawing the attention of his parents who were in front of the couple. Brother chuckled as well, but unlike Sister-in-Law he did so in moderation.

Wormwood Seedling honestly did not understand the black bean anecdote and why it was so funny. But she did notice Mum's eye falling on Brother and Sister-in-Law as tenderly and as pacific as the noonday sun. The corners of her eyes were tinged with fondness and affection. In retrospect, there was also some jealousy and sorrow hidden there too.

Dad thought to himself: "Shame on your forefathers! When pulling out black beans, you should just get on with it. You can always laugh behind closed doors when you get back home, so why do it out here on the slope!" Dad's thin, dark face stiffened into the semblance of an unpolished iron plate. Two burst blood vessels on his cheeks quivered like purple worms. He swore in his heart that his son ought to man-up for no other reason that he had just gotten hitched and it was creating an awkward scene. He was ready to box his ears so hard that the wind might whistle through them.

Mum caught sight of the burst veins on Dad's cheeks and knew all too well that these were fuses rigged to dynamite. If they protruded any further, smoke would billow out and the family would have no peace. She grabbed him by the lapels and, as she trembled in a flurry, her meaty flesh seemed to be cut with a knife. Mum was abasing herself to plead with Dad for something, but was caught off guard by a shove from his stick-like arm. She stumbled one step back and planted her backside on a heap of black beans.

Dad couldn't stand it anymore and yelled: "Shame on your forefathers! Just pull the bean stalks."

Brother and Sister-in-Law stopped laughing straightaway. Their laughter had been cut dead with a knife and silence reigned again on the black bean field. Only a pair of white-necked birds flew back and forth across the tableland, chirping wildly. They landed on the harvested land, where they bounded about and hunted worms. Directly ahead, a couple of hares scurried out from the ground and headed towards the top of the slope like fired arrows.

Brother pressed forward to keep pace with Sister-in-Law. He knew that this was what Dad had been hoping to see.

But Brother didn't know that old men like his father worried about getting their sons a wife. He had found a wife for his son to love yet baulked at him parading his affections. He expected him to assume a poker face in front of the woman. The reason was simple: a poker face reveals a tender heart. That had been Dad and Mum's maxim in life and so they anticipated that their son would do the same, and that this habit would be handed down generation after generation. In moments like this, Brother ought to lock himself into that indissoluble cycle.

Having something on his mind, Brother tugged quickly. He planned to help his lagging wife catch up but, quite accidentally, surged ahead, overtaking Mum and drawing abreast with Dad. Wormwood Seedling observed this and thought: "If our stalwart Brother fought with Dad, Dad would be no match for him. He would be pulverised."

Sister-in-Law struck a balance between posturing and pulling out black beans. She found she couldn't keep pace with them and fell behind. Once in a while, she grinned and stiffened her back, peering up at the sun at the end of the tableland. It had taken on the appearance of a fireball scorching the black bean field. As the black bean stalks dried out, they became as firm as entwined barbed wire in the sight of the burning orb.

Sister-in-Law stared at the shadows of Brother and Dad. She was becoming angry. When she bent to pluck stalks again, she caught her hand on something and let out a scream. She spun around like a blind bee with her left hand covering her right hand.

Brother tossed aside the black bean plants he was holding and rushed back: "What's up?" he asked in a shaking voice. "What happened?"

Brother prized apart Sister-in-Law's hands and spied a couple of gory wounds with blood still oozing out, red and shiny.

"The pain is killing me. The pods sting so much."

Brother took it out on Sister-in-Law: "When you pick beans you should grip the stalks tight. If you hold them tight, they won't prick."

While blaming her, he took custody of her hand and began to suck at every wound. Hence, a bloody froth gathered around his lips. After sucking at the blood, he steered her hand towards a cluster of herbs and removed a leaf. He squeezed out some green juice and dropped it onto the wounds. Then he blew on them. His cool breath stilled her pain down and her shivering stopped.

"Does it hurt now? Tell me, if it hurts."

Mum was moved and kept watching Brother and Sister-in-Law as if something from the past was lingering in her mind. It made her feel sad and peevish. Abruptly, she turned back and fixed

Dad's face. It was still a dark, stiff visage. Dad was cursing with protruding veins: "Shame on your forefathers! Shame on your forefathers!" But Mum, who was always scared of Dad, showed no trace of fear when confronted with his thin, dark face. After glaring at him for a while, she rammed against his belly like a bull, knocking him down onto his backside.

It happened so fast, taking Dad by surprise as he had not been expecting such a furious blow. As he sat on the ground, he wanted to lurch up like a tiger and tear into Mum's meaty flesh. But he didn't because he had seen how two tracks of clear tears were brimming from the crinkled corners of her eyes.

Tile

Giving birth to a girl is a joy
Like making a tile
Giving birth to a boy is a joy
Like uncovering jade

TILE WAS BREWING cold tea under the ancient elm tree. The dense shade of the tree was unable to occlude the sunlight which slanted to the west. She narrowed her eyes and could see that the fields were thronging with people harvesting. Even the daughters-in-law, who seldom went outside, were joining in. Here a pile of straw, there a gang of gleaners. They were hard at it, but in high spirits. For villagers, there is nothing more exhilarating than harvesting crops for food.

Tile picked out several elm leaves that had fallen into the tea box and, as she reached for the last, her heart suddenly became nervous. She lifted the hair from her forehead, subconsciously glancing at a rusty-coloured trench to one side, and was surprised to find that huge white mushrooms had risen into the air, and that these rolling clouds were spreading so rapidly that they had blotted out the sun in the west. There then followed a shattering explosion, which made her ears buzz and the ground beneath her feet tremble with alarm.

Some people hurriedly shouted: "Pots are flying!"

Tile followed suit. After a moment's hesitation, her face turned from red to frosty white. She rammed the earthenware kettle filled with cold tea to the ground, smashing it to pieces. Treading on the broken rim of the pot, she jumped out from the shadow of the elm and rushed towards the exploding kiln.

蛊

The night moistened the vineyards little by little. Crystalline dewdrops shone on the heavy clusters of grapes. Tile lay on her stomach under a grape trellis, feeling that there had been no change in her either psychologically or physically. Three days ago, the man who smelled of tobacco and freshly-made tiles had ardently thrust himself inside her body. He was too rough and gave no intimation that he would ever stop. She was gripped with a sense of agony and fear.

Tile waved her hands in despair and pleaded: "Don't! Don't!"

Making no response, the man instead continued obstinately with his business. His body was heavy like a millstone bearing down on her so she thought she was dying. Now she lay in the vineyard, crying and plucking green grapes to eat. Her mouth and her stomach were flooded with sour and astringent juice. Her mind turned to the man who smelled of newly-made tiles. He had bought her from the hands of a human trafficker and ought to treat her gently, so her heart would be swayed and she would be prepared to live with him steadfastly. After all, shouldn't a wife follow her husband wherever he goes?

The *ding-dong* of a copper bell could be heard far and near. The sound was shrill and pleasing to the ear. The quiet night was roused and Tile with her muddled heart was roused too. She jumped out from the trellis and stood on the road facing the approaching mule team, whose mounts had their heads raised high.

"I want to go with you," Tile called out.

The mule team consisted of a pair of men – one old and the other young – seated aloft on the back of the beasts, looking down at her.

Tile softened her voice and repeated: "I want to go with you."

The old and young partners stared at each other without saying a word. The old man climbed down from the saddle, pulled out a cotton blanket and draped it over another mule's back. Then he assisted Tile in clambering onto the mule and they headed off together along the bumpy road. She reached the village where the two muleteers lived, dismounted and got onto the younger man's *kang*. He duly became her new man.

She accustomed herself to the situation. In very little time, she could grow accustomed to anything.

Later, Tile laughed whenever she thought of it. She would laugh to herself about how she, as a woman, could be afraid of what went on in bed. Anyhow, men are all the same. Just like a hungry dog, the more you refuse, the more emphatic he will become. You end up getting bitten until welts erupt all over your body. Her frame quaked with excitement. She was happy and hummed in response to this frenzied torment. Daring in spirit ever since he was a little boy, her man now traded cattle for a living and was away from home for ten days or a fortnight. She slept alone on the brick bed. Her heart was restless and she was thinking hard.

Who was she thinking about? Was she thinking about her present man? Yes, she was thinking about him, but she was also remembering the man who smelled of newly-made tiles. To buy her, he had wiped out many of years of family savings. She had let him squander a packet. Could he reconcile himself to that? Not even she could reconcile herself to it.

How did Old Ji manage to find this village? Tile did not know. When she first spied him, he and her new man were offering each other cigarettes and discussing the contract inside the rusty-coloured trench. Her face grew scarlet with fright and her heart was choked, so she could not catch her breath.

Was Old Ji the man who bought her from the human trafficker? The smell he emitted seemed similar to that fellow's odour.

That ancient elm tree, full of vitality, grew by the side of the trench. The leaves, which created a dense, shady canopy, flicked over on the breeze with a *kat-a-kat-a-kat-a* sound. As if impelled by some supernatural force, Tile had opened a small tea stand here, which also sold cigarettes, soap, washing powder and other perishables. From time to time, a shuttle bus destined for the town hall would pass by. It would stop for a brief spell. People would get on and off the vehicle, and some would buy tea from Tile, no matter whether it tasted good or bad. She fretted about the rusty-coloured trench behind her. It was about ten feet deep and the bright red inside transfixed the villagers with terror and awe. They thought it was very peculiar. All around the vast Weibei Plateau, they could see nothing save for opaque loess, so why was this dyke so red? They then became fearful that the hot crimson earth would consume the land they farmed to feed their families. Their forefathers, by collecting grain and money, had erected a temple on the verge of the trench. Now, however, the old lofts were no longer standing, leaving only an empty temple stage still majestically ensconced.

Old Ji dropped his luggage on the stage, chose somebody as his apprentice and set about the process of fashioning earthenware basins in the rusty-coloured trench. In Old Ji's experienced eyes, the red colloidal soil was the best raw material for the job. He had travelled widely across the country and had been to a lot of places but had never found soil so suitable for the firing of clay pots.

Old Ji's hustling and bustling brought the quiet, decadent rusty-coloured trench to life. There used to be a number of cave-houses on top of the trench. In the era of production brigades, they were commandeered as breeding stations. After the teams were disbanded, these were left deserted, only to be spruced up now. One was fitted with a rotating pallet used to "wake-up" the mud. This was known as the "proving kiln". Another cave – the "airing kiln" – was used to dry out and store freshly-thrown pots. The last hollow served as Old Ji's living quarters, fitted out with a few wooden planks which, once covered with blankets, became sleeping cots. Having no ready-made firing kilns at their disposal, temporary labourers were hired to hew away at the cliff. They worked both day and night in the red trench. The earth was stirred with sweat, staining both their hair and eyebrows red as if they had been daubed with a marker pen. Labourers and trench shared a single hue.

Tile's man used to buy and sell cattle to make a profit. Whether he earned a mite or a fortune, it all belonged to him. Now, he invited Old Ji to open the tile kiln and they signed a contract from which all the villagers would benefit. The villagers appreciated him, saying: "He has eyes in the back of his head."

"Let him be the Village Head," they rang out in chorus.

Subsequently, when elections for cadres were held at village level, Tile's husband was chosen as headman.

Kneading pots and basins is technical work and nobody but Old Ji had the knack. For a few days, he showed his apprentice how to dry out and crush the red earth. They planted three wooden stakes in the ground and hung up a copper-bottomed dredging basket to sift the earth. The red earth, as soft as sorghum flour, was then mixed with water and piled into a heap in the kiln to be "woken up". Old Ji didn't speak as he worked, though his apprentice, who did not know the size of things, kept on asking questions.

"What are the right proportions of earth and water? … What should I do if there's too much earth? … What should I do if there's too much water?"

Old Ji did not answer. The apprentice asked questions with great patience, while Old Ji kept poker-faced, his feet and hands never ceasing their work. But the apprentice finally cottoned on and understood that the first stage of production was "waking up the mud". The process could not be done in a slipshod fashion. The quality of the resulting pots would be determined by how ripe or pliable the clay was. A good kiln-worker takes great care with this step.

The mud was being woken up in the proving kiln. Three days later, Old Ji went inside to paddle it with his bare feet. His soles stamped down with a gurgle and gurgled once more when they were lifted. He trod through the mud, working it into a pile. It needed to be left to prove for a whole night before being paddled one more time. The mud, as red as blood, was very sticky and squelched up his leg. The mud stains climbed high up his shins but always trickled down when they got so far up. After three days of paddling, at the beginning of the seventh day of the process, he carried in a two-centimetre thick, one-and-a-half-metre long ribbed steel bar. He swung it up and began to hum, chopping obliquely at the mud pile. The steel bar was very tensile, so it was like cutting potatoes with a sharp knife. With one hack, a sliver was pared away. He hacked lengthwise with slashing sounds, and then sliced horizontally. He kept attacking the red clay until it became extremely pliable. Then he pounded it into a round hill, leaving it to prove once more under a grass gauze.

Tile watched from beneath the ancient elm tree. She felt great compassion towards him. She asked herself, "Does he think he is kneading noodles? Even kneading noodles is not so troublesome!"

Old Ji and his apprentice emerged from the proving kiln, their bare shoulders encumbered with red mud. Each seemed to be clad in a layer of clay, like a couple of excavated terracotta warriors.

The cicadas trilled loudly in the ancient elm. The noise irritated Tile and she cried out: "Come and drink some tea. Cold tea."

A bus with scratched paintwork stopped under the elm tree, heaving with catarrh and disturbing a thick mist of dust. A few droopily-spirited passengers alighted. They had no clue why Tile was yelling so loudly and wore daft expressions, perhaps because they had been on the road for so long. Tile was not aware she had made such a row.

She cried out again: "Come have some tea; cold tea."

Her yelling was full of urgency and charm, with a kind of cool, sweet taste.

Tile was actually hailing the workers firing wares in the rusty-coloured trench. As soon as the two men of clay came out of the kiln, they prostrated themselves beneath the sun. The apprentice scraped the mud from his body, while Old Ji was enticed by the sound of Tile and looked towards the ancient elm tree on the bank of the trench.

Tugged by the wind, several clusters of white cloud flicked over from the blue mountain summit to the elm tree over Tile's head.

The elm drew a cool breath. No longer noisy, the cicadas stuck their faces against its trunk and savoured a moment of refreshment. In and around the vertical-sided trench, there was a period of quiet. The atmosphere was as still as the red gelled clay.

Old Ji might have understood Tile's cry or he might indeed have needed the shade of the old elm tree. Presently, he stood up and walked to the bank of the trench. Tile had already sniffed the fragrance of the rusty-coloured ground. The closer Old Ji came to her, the headier the fragrance of the mud became.

Tile cried out intentionally: "Come have some tea; cold tea." She did not realise that her man would emerge suddenly from the ground, swipe the cold tea from her hand and give it eagerly to Old Ji.

Without ever losing the bearing of a smart Village Head, her man often showed too much respect and hospitality to Old Ji. This made other people feel that his kindness was forced.

Tile knew her man was too shrewd; he thought too much. She couldn't help worrying about Old Ji, hoping he could become as shrewd as her present man.

Tile's man asked: "Has the mud woken up?"

Old Ji replied: "Yes, it's already awake."

"So, the next step is to mould the prepped material?"

"Yes, we must mould it next."

The conversation between the two sounded rather warm and friendly, but it put Tile on edge and gave her an uncomfortable feeling. It seemed as though there was a thick layer of something intangible suspended between them. Tile sensed there would be no peace in the trench.

On the road by the ancient elm, the car horns shrieked sharply.

Spurred on by the force of Old Ji's feet, the potter's wheel on its mud-brick base span faster and faster. He dug out a knot of mud, stuck it in the centre of the wheel and clasped it with his wet hands. When the mud had been stabilised into a neat round, he poked his right index finger into the middle of the clod while his left hand protected the outer edge. In a flash, the knot of mud unfurled into a basin. Then, he grasped another knot of mud and, following the same procedure, threw a jar with ears. The apprentice was kept on his toes, carefully shifting the unfinished earthenware pieces to the drying kiln, as though he was the custodian of priceless porcelain.

The day the firing kiln was ready for use, a whole kiln's worth of pots and basins of mud was also ready.

At the same time, Old Ji's apprentice attempted to throw some pots too and was able to pinch out some decent-looking earthenware utensils. A number of the pots and basins in the firing kiln were his handiwork.

On the day the kiln was first fired, a lot of people came to the trench. Tile's man bought two strings of "one thousand sputter" firecrackers and swathed them down from the top of the kiln, so red and enthusiastic. When the kiln was fired up, he lit the firecrackers, so they crackled and spluttered and shocked the earth. One bottle of liquor was downed, and then another. Everybody was drinking, grinning and shouting. The flowing spirits and the ricocheting paper debris from the firecrackers made the rusty-coloured trench more excited and intensely red.

Tile did not come to the kiln.

Old Ji was fussy. On the day the kiln was first fired, women were not allowed to attend. The good labourers of the kiln were enjoined to do likewise and prohibited from even touching their own women at this crucial time. If the evil spirits of women were brought to the kiln, it may cause a disaster. An entire kiln-full of wares might be lost or it might cause the pots to fly out and hurt people.

Beneath the ancient elm tree, Tile could feel the heat of the kiln. Her heart was ablaze too, like a fire inside a furnace.

A hillock of wheat-straw lay on the kiln floor. The apprentice quickly brushed it into bunches and handed them over to Old Ji so he could feed the fire. The wheat-straw was consumed vigorously, with blasts of flame continuously licking the rusty-coloured trench so it appeared to be burning. The low-lying stagnant waters were scorching red, encouraging the frogs to *ribbet* louder. Dense smoke gathered on top of the kiln from time to time and then dispersed, rolling away like horses galloping on the prairie. The rarefied smell of the kiln pervaded the air.

Tile couldn't bear to watch and said to herself, "See how hot it is. Why doesn't he come up for a bowl of cold tea?"

She muttered away, knowing that Old Ji would not leave the kiln. Firing up the kiln is the critical stage, so how could he afford to come to the ancient elm tree to rest and sip tea? She couldn't deliver the tea to the kiln either; Old Ji would never let her go.

The fire in the kiln chamber was blanching white hot. Thin plumes of smoke rose from the top of the kiln. The wind made them soar into the blue sky. Old Ji studied the colour of the fire and smoke. He knew that the goods in the kiln would soon be ready and it should a good batch. He became intoxicated with the impending success.

Tile could not restrain herself any longer. The red kiln chamber was calling out to her eagerly like a brightly-coloured mouth. Old Ji and his apprentice were in desperate need of quenching tea.

Without a sound, Tile positioned herself behind Old Ji.

She scanned his naked back, dark and rough as it was. The skin was dry, like half-desiccated leaves. Tile's heart trembled softly, and so did the cold tea she held in her hand.

"Drink a cup of tea. It will refresh you."

This startled Old Ji, who was in a whirlpool of intoxication. The warm words of concern he heard were not being carried afar from under the elm tree but were being spoken directly into his ears. The muscles on his face twitched and his heart seemed to plunge into the water, becoming sweet and bitter again.

"Ruined!" Old Ji threw aside the fire fork in his hand and turned in the other direction. His round eyes were wide open and glistened with a fierce bloodshot light.

He growled: "Let the devil drink!"

He couldn't tolerate this turn of events. "Screw your ancestors. Let the devil drink!"

The cold tea splashed out of the bowl and wet Tile's skirt. She wanted to turn and walk away, but she could not lift her feet. Her legs were as heavy as lead. Tears swirled in her eyes and she was on the brink of crying out. She could not feel wronged. It was her fault. She had caused the trouble.

Tile turned and walked away. Old Ji took an unfired basin from his dried-up kiln and swiftly ran ahead of her, smashing the object violently under her feet. He then picked up a shard and gashed one of her fingers savagely with it. A dull pain crept into her heart as blood spurted out. It was so strange. How could a finger be sliced open with something made out of mud?

Tile. Why did her parents give her such a name? Later, she heard Old Ji repeat a proverb: *Giving birth to a girl is like making a tile*. By treating a woman in a really base fashion, he was trying to rescue the kiln. Old Ji wanted to drive away the bad luck and he could only do so with the help of Tile's blood. This is called "attacking poison with poison".

Tile paced around the kiln field as if putting on a public show in broad daylight. Each step she took was accompanied by a drip of blood, and the kiln field became speckled with peach blossom-like stains.

Peach blossom. Gorgeous peach blossom. Over the next few days, peach blossom – so fresh and gorgeous that it perfumed the whole world – regularly floated through Tile's consciousness as a vivid fantasy. Maybe as a consequence of Tile's bloodletting, each basin and pot that left the kiln was finer than the previous specimen. Every last one of them was round and smooth to the touch, with a celadon and shining blue glaze. Old Ji exclaimed with elation that he had never fired such pristine goods before. Other people placed orders, so that the next batch sold out while it was still in the furnace.

They fired another two kilns full of big, ancient-style urns to fulfill a contract that came from a nearby vinegar distillery. They persisted in using the traditional method, which required huge ceramic urns for fermentation. To expand the scale of production, they commissioned two large loads. Old Ji's kiln grew in renown. More and more peddlers came to the village, preparing to ply their trade. They became quarrelsome if they couldn't lay their hands on Old Ji's wares. His pots and jars were soon to become a fixture in restaurants in the provincial capital, the proprietors having also heard the positive word of mouth.

Tile's tea stall was replenished with pots and jars. Old Ji gave them as gifts. She was no fool and knew he was trying to make amends. She was willing to accept these presents for, in the eyes of country people, a brand new, quality, blue tea set is a token of trust that can be passed down from generation to generation. The pots and jars were never without cold tea, and it seemed more soothing and flavoursome than that brewed before. Tile was glad to restock her stand.

Old Ji also fired a tiger-head pillow for Tile's other half.

Her man was the Village Head, after all, and so Old Ji spent a copious amount of time kneading that pillow. Each side was crafted into tigers' heads, with open mouths and staring eyes. They struck the posture of roaring atop a mountain rock. The craftsmanship was detailed and exquisite. On hot summer days, water could be tipped in through the mouths – nothing compared with the experience of sleeping on such a cold headrest.

Tile's husband once said that whenever his head made contact with the pillow, he would have a dream. Every one of them was an augury of good fortune. Tile had doubts in her heart. She dared not looked at the majestic tiger pillow head-on, casting sideward glances at it instead. When she was at home alone, she would nestle the tigers' head tile pillow against her bosom, like she was caressing a domestic pet. She stroked it with tender love. Tile had banished from her mind every object in the house of the man who bought her as a wife. But she could still remember that a tiger-head pillow lay on the bed. The two tiger-head pillows were separated from each other in time and space, but felt like they were the offspring of the same tigress.

All night long, Tile's man murmured through his dreams, the tiger-head pillow resting under his head. On and off, when Tile listened she could catch the gist of what he was saying. Her man wanted to drive Old Ji away. In his dream, he ground his teeth as he talked: "My trench field, my money. How can I let other people get their hands on it? Screw splitting the profits! I won't give you one penny."

Filled with apprehension, Tile shoved her man awake. "Are you jealous?" she asked.

He rubbed his bleary eyes and replied: "What? Jealous of what?"

"Are you going to drive Old Ji away?"

"Drive away Old Ji? Who is going to drive him away? He has a contract in his hand, so who can do that?"

While talking, Tile's man flipped over and pressed himself against her body. The thing that should be done with tenderness and care was finished in a crude and barbarous way. This was the first time in their intimate life there had been such a bout of tyranny.

From dawn the next day, an evil rumour seemed to have sprouted wings and flown around the village. Many people, who found themselves unable to distinguish what was true from what was false, bought touchpaper and burned it on the temple stage by the rusty-coloured trench. Several old people and women showed up at the start then, a few days later, even young men arrived to make burnt offerings. Everyone worshipped the trench god, praying that he would shield them from misfortune. The peace of the whole village was about to be shattered.

Tile, who was behind the tea stand under the great elm tree, knew everything in her heart. She knew that it was her man who was behind this dirty trick. Her man was determined to drive Old Ji away.

Tile was running. Her feet felt cold. She found that the blown-up crumbling tiles were like a flock of flying flamingos, curling up in the afterglow of the setting sun. The tumult of the flying pots had passed and there was a deathly stillness around the rusty-coloured trench. Suddenly, frantic footsteps were heard together with bursts of shouting: "Ah! Quick! Quick!"

Tile's man ran out in front, as did Old Ji's apprentice. Footsteps came like a thunderstorm in the summer, arousing a confused red dust on the uneven dirt road.

Tile stumbled in fits and starts as she ran, asking herself, "How could this happen?"

Tears blurred her eyes and she asked in her heart, "Why is this happening?"

Tile ran to the kiln field, her face awash with mud and tears. Her man and the apprentice, who had learned some skills from Old Ji, were the first on the scene and had already utilised one of the blown-off kiln doors as a stretcher for the wounded Old Ji. They called on others to help bear him to the hospital. Tile clutched one corner of the door and followed the crowd. She looked at Old Ji without blinking. She saw a lump of flesh had been blown clean away and his right hand, which he used for fiddling out pots and jars, had lost three dexterous fingers.

However, hearsay, like a snake, wriggled out to pester the injured Old Ji: "Was the trench god so easily provoked?"

The snake spat out poisonous, hot fire: "Look, the trench god has shown himself!"

Tile was hauled out of the crowd by her man. She thought of the three fingers Old Ji had lost and went back to the carnage of the trench field to find them. She wondered how Old Ji, so adept in firing technology, could ever have made the pots fly. Even that time she caused a mishap, no catastrophe had ensued. After that, she had not caused another problem, so how could the pots fly? Conspiracy. It must be a conspiracy.

The fingers, now incinerated into charcoal, were finally recovered. She took out her handkerchief and wrapped them up before running into the crowd carrying Old Ji. Tile stood for a moment under the ancient elm. She looked back at the red earth trench. Once hot and noisy, it had abruptly turned miserable.

The unfinished pots and jars in the kiln were falling down, scattering all over the trenches. The red colour resembled coagulated blood. Was it Old Ji's blood?

Tile was scared to think about it. But deep inside she clearly recalled how Old Ji had so rudely gashed her finger to appease the kiln. The drops of blossom-like blood were mixed with the tiles strewn about the kiln floor. Before Tile's eyes, they had broken out into full blossom.

The Well Head

Beneath the Chinese honey locust tree at the eastern end of the village, there crouched a public well. This was the only one of its kind in Running Cow Plateau Village and the villagers depended on it for both drinking water and washing. A square brick well head surrounded the mouth. This was sodden all year round and the walls of the well were cloaked in soggy moss. The shaft measured about 36 *zhang* – almost 400 feet – deep; so deep, in fact, that when a brick was dropped down it, no noise could be heard at all. A full-sized windlass with a winch projected above the mouth with a bucket at either end of the rope for hauling water. As one pail plopped down, the other rose. The creaking of the windlass could be heard by half the village.

At dawn, after the cockerels had crowed three times, villagers would elbow their way to collect water with either a carrying pole or a partner to assist them. A thicket of poles then became visible from afar as the villagers helped each other unremittingly to wind the winch or pull up the well rope, talking, laughing and teasing in great harmony.

Despite being a public amenity, to the minds of the villagers the well did have an owner – Fa Maidui, who lived at the end of the village next to the Chinese honey locust tree.

Fa Maidui was fifty-four years old. Fifty-four years ago, his mother gave him an auspicious and superb name – meaning "Legal Wheat Stack" – in the hope that stacks of golden wheat might festoon her family lands. Now, Fa Maidui had four fully-grown sons, each of them valiant and strong. They formed an extended family with a successful business and ample wealth, giving them the courage to pipe up louder than others. Every year when work points were earned and something had to be done, small families were forced to take their cue from the Fa clan.

The public well was the selfsame well that Fa Maidui dug with the villagers when he served as the Chair of the Association of the Impoverished Families more than two decades ago. The opening of the well marked the end of generations being dependent on rainwater collected in pits dotted across Running Cow Plateau. For years, Fa Maidui had taken responsibility for cleaning the well and repairing the rope with his own hands. Although he was no longer chair of the village association, he still acted as the well's diligent retainer. Of all the achievements in his life, this was the one in which he took the greatest pride. As they drew water from the well head, the villagers would always spy Fa Maidui either standing in front of the gate tower or squatting beneath the Chinese honey locust tree with a coat slung over his shoulders. They were touched with gratitude and respect towards him.

In the villagers' hearts, Fa Maidui was the de facto owner of the well.

One spring day, the 36 *zhang*-long rope snapped unexpectedly.

The rope was decrepit. It had been wound around the windlass since the shaft was dug and had broken five times in the last two decades. This could be ascertained by counting the number of wheat-head knots which kept it fused together.

The people of Running Cow Plateau Village were never surprised to find themselves with nothing to eat for dinner. Yet, each family would sink into despair when not a drop of water was to be had. The old-style cellars which had been used for water storage were now almost all filled with dirt. Having been obsolete for so long, they were bone dry. In their desperation, every family had to tramp all the way over to Running Cow Valley Village to fetch refreshment from the creek. One round trip down the valleys and up the hillsides took at least half a day.

As they carried water from the valley, the residents all wished that the well owner, Fa Maidui, would repair the rope. A new one would cost only a little over 100 yuan, but, since the Production Brigade had been disbanded, who was going to foot the bill? Even though each household had set aside a little money in the past couple of years, nobody would volunteer to pay for it. If Fa

Maidui, the well owner, did not raise the topic first, the other villagers were unwilling to talk about it.

Without question, Fa Maidui was the publicly-acknowledged owner of the well. He took it as his own business once the rope was broken, even if no one told him to. The next day, when all the families filed past his door to fetch water from Running Cow Valley Village, he strode out from his courtyard with a new rightward-buttoned Chinese overcoat over his shoulders. "Damn it! If I dropped dead, you'd all die from thirst," he said after taking a quick glance at the empty well head with its coil of dried, old well ropes. Though it was a passing gripe, everyone could taste its flavour from his tone.

Someone followed that up by saying: "Absolutely! You have accumulated virtue through this well. Everyone knows you're the owner of the public well in Running Cow Plateau Village."

A singularly pleasant feeling spread through Fa Madui's body. He laughed out loud and commented: "Accumulated virtue? Oh, my goodness! I'd rather that no one cursed me behind my back." Then he turned around and made a beeline for two skillful men who knew how to lash the rope into wheat head hitches.

Small Spoon stumbled her way back from Running Cow Valley Village, balancing two buckets of water on her shoulder pole and rested herself bashfully beside the well head.

She was just forty-five years old, but had been widowed for twenty years. She looked fairly healthy and strong. Decked out in a nicely-fitted blue Chinese overcoat buttoned to the right and a pair of black trousers, not to mention having hair shorn above her ears, the impression she gave was one of neatness and dignity. Nevertheless, longstanding hardships had added four or five years to her face. It was not until she started to cultivate her own farmland a couple of years ago that some pink began to register on her yellow cheeks and her eyes filled with energy.

At that moment, she lay down her pole and rolled up her sleeves to wipe the sweat from her forehead while watching Fa Maidui and the rope-menders on the well head. However, those now busying themselves and their spectators did not notice her. For decades, the widow had not drawn anyone's attention. She languished like a little potato.

Small Spoon was not bothered. Instead, she inched a few steps closer and suggested in a slightly higher pitch: "Take a break and sup a little water. I had it in mind to share this with everyone."

No one drank her water. The two pails were more than half-full and had been hauled several miles by the widow! She had no son, only a daughter as white as the inside of a spring onion. The mother and daughter raised about 100 chickens and some goats and pigs, which demanded copious amounts to drink. Who would be so shameless as to deprive her of water? To everyone's astonishment, hadn't such a silent and passive woman just aired her thoughts in public? Seeing her blush, some guessed she was perhaps tired of being a widow and was angling after someone new? How could she flaunt such thoughts here?

Seeing how the villagers turned their heads in her direction, she redirected her face to Fa Maidui. He had a black cigarette pinched between his fingertips. Fa Maidui, although a bit on the old side, had a rather deft brain. Catching sight of the widow's strangely vivid eyes, he remembered that her husband had died for the sake of the public well. Twenty years had elapsed since the incident and yet he could still recall the miserable scene very clearly. Little Spoon, still a youthful-looking wife at the time, had wept desperately. Suddenly, Fa Maidui was gripped by such a sense of guilt that he realised he ought to have sent one of his hardy sons to carry four buckets of water for Small Spoon, just as he had done in the past. This time it had slipped his mind. More's the pity! How apologetic he now felt.

"The rope is simply too old," Small Spoon whispered in a sinking voice while staring at Fa Maidui.

Fa Maidui tingled inside. It was all about the well. Unwittingly, he said: "Yes, it is old."

"It should be replaced with a new one."

"Oh. That's right."

Little Spoon groped inside her waist pocket and said: "Brother Maidui, I … Here's one hundred yuan. Please take charge and get a new one." She then removed her hand from her waist pocket and waved a wad of cash in Fa Maidui's face.

Fa Maidui did not move. It was as if he were an unpainted clay idol in a temple. The skillful men fixing the rope and the spectating villagers were stunned. Every pair of eyes stared at Little Spoon, who lowered her head.

A flame of anger rose up from the bottom of Fa Maidui's heart: "You, Little Spoon, are prepared to cover a new rope? You want me, the owner of the well, to buy a new well rope with your money? Isn't that like bopping me with a bladder? It has been down to me to take care of the official well ever since it was dug. It ought to be me, Fa Maidui, who pays for the rope. I don't need your show of generosity here. Even if every family were prepared to cough up, it shouldn't fall on you!" Discomfort now swelled inside him; discomfort suffused with an indescribable sorrow. All sorts of people want to stand on his shoulders. What a thing! Tossing the half-smoked fag down at the roots of the old Chinese honey locust, he yelled with mounting anger at Little Spoon as if he were also speaking to the spectators: "Take your money and use it to build a water tower if you think you're rich enough!"

Little Spoon picked up her pole and carried her water buckets home with a heart so heavy it was as if a millstone were pressing on it. As he vented his deep outrage, Fa Maidui wore a fearsomely ugly expression. But why on earth was he so annoyed?

Little Spoon's gratitude to Brother Maidui was heartfelt. Her husband – short, thin and puny as he was – had gone to collect water in Running Cow Valley. While climbing up the narrow, sheep's intestine-like slope of the valley, he lost his footing and took a tumble together with his water pole. Fa Maidui, who was walking behind him, threw aside his pole and rushed towards the falling man, saving him from a fatal disaster. He saved his life. It was because of this mishap that Brother Maidui initiated the project of the public well in the village. The villagers of Running Cow Plateau gained a well from which they could drink.

Whoever could forget the kindness of Brother Maidui? Her own thin man volunteered at the outset of the well-digging project, but Fa Maidui tried to dissuade him from participating in such a gruelling job. By the time the well had reached a depth of 30 *zhang* and water started to gush, Little Spoon and her husband regretted not taking part. Digging the well was a good deed that would benefit future generations in Running Cow Plateau. How guilty he would feel if he did not put in any effort! A toad has four forces of strength and he had to try his best to help.

After considerable discussion, the couple descended on the well beneath the Chinese honey locust as everyone was enjoying their noontime nap. Little Spoon planned to haul up the dirt as her husband dug inside the well. Little did they know that the hole now reached so far beneath the ground that there was insufficient oxygen within. As soon as her husband landed at the bottom, he succumbed to asphyxiation. They had intended to lend a hand, but trouble ensued.

Brother Maidui, however, made sure that the lamentable one received full dues. Afterwards, it was entirely down to his warm-heartedness that the widow enjoyed the privilege of being taken care of in everyday life and in matters of finance. In Little Spoon's mind, Brother Maidui was the living Buddha of Running Cow Plateau.

Now, she was offering up her own savings to buy the rope because she wanted to shift the load off her mind. One hundred yuan was not a fortune, so how come it pierced the lungs of Brother Maidui?

The villagers' lips had been aquiver for years with talk of building a water tower. Nevertheless, the Production Brigade always found itself shelling out a fortune while reaping a pittance. People talked without taking action, so the water tower remained on the tip of their tongues. Now that Fai Maidui brought it up, Little Spoon found herself alive with excitement. But constructing a water tower was not the same as buying a well rope. Electricity and a deep-well aspirator were required. One thousand yuan would only scratch the surface in this situation. The total bill would run into thousands. Without money, it would just be a pipe dream. Little Spoon asked her daughter, who had matriculated from middle school, to make the calculations and, after some very careful thought and serious deliberations, finally straightened her ideas out.

"I didn't contribute to digging the well. For years, I've been a burden on my fellow villagers. Now, if I can put in more money and the other villagers give their fair share, the water tower will soon be built, won't it? As the saying goes, *when everybody adds fuel, the flames will rise high*. I am adamant about it."

She shared this thought with her daughter, who was preoccupied with the matter of her dowry. The mother and daughter warmed to the idea. The daughter, however, added: "It's okay to pay more, but I don't like Uncle Maidui's temper."

"Oh, my goodness. You can talk like that? Mightn't he have been feeling uneasy all these years?"

With a curl of her lip, the daughter reflected: "It's his mind that has not been at ease."

Little Spoon was heartbroken by her daughter's words. She cursed her and felt sorry for Brother Maidui. Fa Maidui returned with a new rope, which he bought for one hundred and three yuan. He could have used the walking tractor, but he did not, letting it go into town for business. Instead, he hiked all the way back to Running Cow Plateau with a huge and unwieldy coil of white rope spooled around his shoulder. The weight of his load forced him to take regular breaks. As he approached the village and spotted the flowering Chinese honey locust, he was already sweating and could not lift up his legs, both of which had gone numb. He had not exerted himself like this for years, yet it made him blissfully happy and excited to have spent his own money on the public wellbeing. In contrast to his former heartache, a triumphant pleasure now swamped his chest.

It was quarter past three in the afternoon and a group of villagers surrounded the well head. Spent, Fa Maidui sat on the bulging old root of the Chinese honey locust. He slid a long, machine-rolled cigarette from his chest pocket and started to draw in clouds and puff out mist, listening to the cordial comments and praise of the people without saying a word. He savoured the spiritual satisfaction that in days gone by he had tasted rather often, but had not done in the last couple of years. His spending of a hundred yuan triggered an argument at home with his son, who accused him of being a soft touch. "Bullshit!" was how he cursed the boy in his heart. "What would he know! Even if others are press-ganging us into action, we can't hush things up. True popularity cannot be bought; not with a thousand pieces of gold!"

Under the direction of the elders, a pair of young men set about replacing the old rope with the new one. Two strands of bitter, hot cigarette smoke spurted out from Fa Maidui's nostrils and his body was infused with a renewed strength of the sort he had enjoyed while in charge of the Poverty Alleviation Association. He cried out in a deep and resonant voice: "The rope should last for twenty years!" Then he clambered up and planted his hand on the fresh rope. It was at this moment that he caught sight of Little Spoon walking toward the well head with her daughter.

"Hey, hey, how timely." His eyes narrowed into slits.

Little Spoon was now at the well head and nobody noticed her except for Fa Maidui. She shuddered slightly on glimpsing the new coil of white rope. Swiftly, she deduced the import of Fa Maidui's stare. She bit her lip tensely, hesitating, and then lowered her head after exchanging a glance with her daughter. Fa Maidui was flooded with contentment, and then a kind of regret. How could a man make such a fuss about a widow? The new well rope was on show before the villagers. So, he generously greeted Little Spoon with: "I have bought the rope. Spoon, please rest assured that we'll no longer need to carry water from the valley."

Little Spoon raised her head to inspect the new rope and the villagers did not make a peep for quite a while. She was still deep in thought when she was pushed from behind by her smart, pretty and vigorous daughter. Finally, she spoke up sheepishly in front of Fa Maidui: "It's good to have the rope replaced. Brother Maidui, you are so kind generous. You were right the other day. Our village should build a water tower. We have been twisting the windlass for twenty years. Should we have to twist it for twenty more?"

"Then … you tell me … " Fa Maidui was lost for words. He

opened his eyes wide as if they were cowbells, clueless about what the widow wanted to do next.

Little Spoon was totally bewildered. How should she broach the subject? If she talked to him as she had planned with her daughter, it would stoke his rage and encourage him to blame her for doing things without consulting him. She could not pluck up enough courage to raise the matter, despite being poked and pushed by her daughter.

Her daughter could bear it no longer and launched herself in front of her mother. The young lady was not as hesitant: "I suggest we build a water tower so we can have running water like the people in the city!"

The daughter's words enervated Little Spoon and a rare glimmer of glory crept across her face. She pulled her hand out from where it had been hidden in her pocket. Clutching a pile of money, she announced: "Brother Maidui, you led the villagers to dig the well in the past; now please lead us to build the water tower. We'll pay for it. Here's our family's two thousand yuan."

"Ah … "

This was the last thing Fa Maidui had expected. A hush descended over the well head and the crowd was astounded, astonished and dumbstruck.

"My fellow villagers," Little Spoon explained. "I have discussed this with my daughter and we both agree. Over the last couple of years, we have saved some two thousand yuan, which we were planning to spend on my daughter's dowry. We need this money urgently. I am not showing off our wealth. Had this been two years earlier, I would have definitely given more. If each of us pays our small share, won't we be able to build the water tower?"

Full of hope, Little Spoon raised her face to fix Fa Maidui. She was anxious that he understand her heart's desire and take the money from her hands. "Brother Maidui, you can make this happen for us villagers in Running Cow Plateau."

Not hearing the rest of her words, Fa Maidui was searing with fury. Little Spoon came here with sincerity, but she had placed herself in an extremely embarrassing and unspeakable situation.

He wanted to bite back brutally, but could not find the right term of reproof. If he were too voluble, it would be he who lost face.

Indeed, the once peaceful well head had been transformed into a wok of boiling water. The peasants became red-faced with the heat of the argument. "Let's build a water tower and lay pipes so we can bring water to our homes. It's time that we farmers had modern courtyards. Was it our fate to be born to spin the windlass and hump water?"

"Maidui, you take the lead!"

"Uncle Maidui, let's do it!"

Fa Maidui gritted his teeth and did not say a word as the masses hollered. Ultimately, he produced a heavy snort of dissatisfaction and shoved his way resentfully out of the crowd. He picked up the now obsolete new roll of rope, grasping it tightly as he headed home, a bleak smile on his livid face.

The packed and noisy well head suddenly fell cold and dreary.

"Mum, let's go home!" The daughter insisted in an angry and tearful voice.

Little Spoon did not answer, nor did she move. It was a warm spring day, but she could feel a kind of inescapable chill. She took two steps back and leaned against the thick trunk of the Chinese honey locust, her wrinkled eyes staring at the omnipresent but inaccessible blue sky. As she closed her eyes, tears oozed out from beneath her lids.

"What's going on here? It's fine if the water tower doesn't get built. You can haul up water and carry water. So can I."

Little Spoon was knotted up inside, overcome with sorrow that Running Cow Plateau was not able to take one step forward. Two pearly tears trickled down and hung from her cheeks. She could not hold them back.

"Yes, we will build one! Who said we couldn't?"

The farmers called and shouted out loudly: "We shall build a superb tower and bring water to our wives' kitchen range."

"Really?" Little Spoon straightened herself up and looked around. To her disappointment, she could not find Brother Maidui, for whom she was searching.

"If Brother Maidui doesn't agree, who's going to take charge?"

"You must! You must take charge of it!"

"As time flows on, the leader must change. Spoon, you will be the new well-owner!"

"With your kindness, it is possible!"

Little Spoon peered at her daughter as the crowd cheered. Her daughter pushed her forward, thrilled. As her rattling heart calmed down, it generated an unprecedented power that colonised her body. Buoyed by such strength, she knew she could help her fellow villagers have a life with water on tap.

As she reached her decision, she pitied Brother Maidui. And yet, she knew she had no choice.

Cliff-slide

The land crumbled and the stones fissured. Li Yuan was in the throes of lovemaking when he finally realised he had been swallowed deep into the earth at Phoenix Mouth. Dan Dan, who was stark naked too, found herself buried with him. It had been Li Yuan's longstanding hope that someday they would be able to embrace and writhe together. The impromptu cliff-slide did nothing to horrify or disappoint him. Instead, he was stoked by a cathartic feeling of transcendence. The soil and gravel pressing down on his body became feathery and warm in texture.

Like the moon suspended on Phoenix Mouth, the happiness of death shone like an eternal smile.

Having no good man is just as bad
As taking a grave as your lifelong mate.
Having no good man is just as sad
As chopped chilli and garlic on the same plate.

That everlasting song echoed through the passionate embrace of Phoenix Mouth.

To Li Yuan, who grew up having to scale Phoenix Mouth, it was this song that had added fantasy and joy without measure to his childhood. At the same time, he was acutely aware of how paltry his lot was. While listening to the song, he would look ahead at the heavy shadow of Phoenix Mouth and ponder how small and insignificant his father – who trailed the hooves of the old yellow bull – actually was. The sun slid down; the moon rose again. The shadow of Phoenix Mouth swooped over once more so that his father melted into the grave. In that instant, he tasted unspeakable excitement and sorrow. He knew that one day he would fill his father's boots. His son would fill his boots too. He also knew that good women call for good men and the world needs good men.

Li Yuan hardly dared to believe that he could be a good man. After nightfall, he stalked out of his miserable, accursed mansion and found refuge in that impassioned dream of his.

Close as it was to the rapidly expanding Chuan County, the street where Li Yuan lived was still a work in process. How cruel he was to leave all this behind and clamber up to Phoenix Mouth to Dan Dan's house. It was she who made the old Phoenix Mouth amorous and mysterious. A mountain ridge with a thin sharp point poked down at the county. The dignified tableland to the south, like the wings of the phoenix's mouth, stretched and flowed freely, comforting and fondling every blade of grass and stone. These grasses and stones configured a never-ending dream sublimated by the crystal-clear, meandering River Wei. An arched stone bridge had been erected in Phoenix Mouth. Small as the bridge was, it nonetheless connected the county and the Mouth together like brother and sister.

The snowfall became heavier.

Climbing along the narrow, snowy slope, so slippery yet soft, and winding to the top of the tableland, Li Yuan felt as though he was stepping on the creamy body of Dan Dan.

Li Yuan had travelled to many places. Wherever he went, he sensed his feet were treading on Dan Dan's body. To him, even the foundations of his freshly-built home in the new village seemed to be laid on Dan Dan's body. In his spare time, he would drag an upholstered chair to his roomy balcony and brew a cup of tea, all the while gazing at the old, grim, damp cave houses in Phoenix Mouth. Then, his heart would be spiked with melancholy and pain.

But Dan was unable to move down from the mountain. Phoenix Mouth was designated as a hazardous area by the county because of the risk of landslides, so people gradually migrated to the new village, which they also called Phoenix Mouth.

Every time Li Yuan returned from the fields, he hastened to the old Phoenix Mouth to visit Dan Dan. If she was not there, he would head to the county town. The city authorities had allocated her three square metres of land at the corner of the farmers' market for a monthly rent of fifty yuan. Here she would hawk vegetables, hailing customers with a mellifluous voice, far sweeter than that of the sellers of cabbages, radishes, garlic sprouts and green onions. She was always surrounded by a clamour of people and would flash them a winsome smile even if not everyone was prepared to buy. Her voice itself was a delicacy and they thought it added to the flavour of their subsequent meal.

Phoenix Mouth was always prolific in producing vegetables, therefore there were many vegetable dealers, outnumbering even the donkeys. Try as they might, their business was never anything like as good as Dan Dan's. The vegetable plots along the banks of the River Wei had been inherited from their ancestors. They had no choice but to sell produce despite knowing it was no way to get rich.

A few years ago, even wild rocket was to be had on the river bank. It would begin to sprout in early spring while Phoenix Mouth was totally bare. When Li Yuan was a kid, he used to sit on the Mouth with intent eyes, scanning the vast tracts of rocket, which people would forage and share among themselves. Once steamed, this provided them with a lifeline in the face of spring famine.

Li Yuan had no idea at that time, but while he was staring at the green of the fields, Dan Dan's eyes, which shone like the wild rocket, were peering back at him. Dan Dan, who was the same age of Li Yuan, scratched a living with her grandpa Old Seven.

Nowadays, people were still planting wild rocket, but the bank looked more florid on account of the greenhouses assembled to provide a perpetual supply of tomatoes, cucumbers, juicy chilli and chives. Downtown residents could endure a day without grain but would not tolerate a dinner without vegetables.

Still, he hated that evil man of hers.

How could you leave such a good woman and choose to insanely gamble until the last minute of your life? You devil! Even Dan Dan's warm embrace couldn't make you stay.

After her man's death, Dan Dan started to sing the song of

Phoenix Mouth without any grudges and sorrow. It appeared as if she was strong enough to shoulder all the sufferings of that place. But as she came to the last part, her tone turned bitter and mournful:

Having no good man is just as sad
As chopped chilli and garlic on the same plate.
Wild chrysanthemums bloom on the upland
Ready for a good man to take.

Li Yuan heard the song as he mounted the slope and suddenly felt a thrill. How could he tread on Dan Dan's body and keep on walking? He had trodden between her legs, across her wrists and was approaching her bosom. He could feel the undulating contours of her plump breasts. He even could smell the fragrance that was unique to her trembling body and soul.

His peculiar passion bumped about in his chest and his muscles quivered crazily. When he opened his eyes, he saw a fire being lit in Phoenix Mouth. The flame from Dan Dan's cave was as potent as her youth. He felt that her pyrotechnical force could smelt him into being a good man. But …

Unconsciously, he turned back and looked in the direction of the new village. He saw a compact red building – his home.

The woman inside, like a bundle of wet wood without the merest spark, was unable to ignite the least enthusiasm or lust in him.

Now, Li Yuan ceased his hesitation and broke directly into the resplendent and magnificent cave house. The paraffin lamp flashed unsteadily, picking out the freshly-dug and neatly-cut vegetables that had been arranged evenly in two large baskets, ready to be sold at the dawn market. The grain that had been collected in the autumn and summer was placed on a piece of reed matting in the kiln, where the shovel, pickaxe, pitchfork, broom, clothes, brick cook-stoves and bowls were all stored in their respective places. Dan Dan was lazily reclining on the *kang* at the mouth of the kiln.

Both her son and daughter were away at boarding school.

Dan Dan – who he had been yearning for day and night – was

naked without a stitch of cover, and the splendour of the cave house lent her a halo of light. He was surprised. How could she sleep so comfortably naked and unshielded on a cold, snowy night like this?

Li Yuan pounced on Dan Dan.

Within the halo, Dan Dan lifted her head in a daze. Her face wore a charming and enchanting smile, and she stretched her arms out to cling tightly to his neck.

After human life has been smelted, inherited and refined over the course of tens of thousands of years, our original instinct still bears testimony better than anything else to the potency of our life force. Now, Li Yuan was holding his beloved woman tightly in his arms. He was a man; a good man. He pressed his hot lips against Dan Dan's soft mouth.

Life was completed in this instant.

Life was over in this instant.

A devastating black wind ransacked the cave, blasting away anything that lent colour to the place. A tremor struck Phoenix Mouth, catapulting Li Yuan and Dan Dan into the corner.

Li Yuan felt his head split as it collided with a shovel or some other hard implement. It fell without a sound like the broken red flesh of a watermelon landing on a waste heap. A swarm of voracious flies hummed with a deafening din. How infinitely small he was. The Phoenix Mouth that he had been trying to forget but could never put out his mind had swallowed him into the pit of its stomach with just the slightest of reflexes.

The sky outside must have still been passionate. The road through Phoenix Mouth must still have been as soft as the body of Dan Dan with her patient smile.

Li Yuan tried to raise his body, but he could not. There was silence all around. He found nothing except Dan Dan's eyes, as delectable as a wild rocket flower, revealing despair and resentment. Like a thorn, this made Li Yuan's heart bleed. His head was filled with the sound of the cliff-slide at Phoenix Mouth 20 years ago.

That year, Li Yuan was thirteen.

Phoenix Mouth still retained some legacies from ancient times;

the status, wealth and fame of a family could be clearly identified from the position of their cave houses. The blue-bloods lived on the lower tier while common people were relegated to the upper reaches. The different layers of caves were a hierarchical chain in which those at the bottom governed those at the top. Brothers would compete against each other for a space in the foothills. When they married and moved out of the family home, they craved these hollows because living at the top was unsafe and inconvenient. There the ceilings were low and the topsoil thin, so anybody making their home up above would have to surrender their fate to the Heavens. One happy family might be snuffed out before morning came and slumber eternally until they were excavated as fossil relics in the next century.

In that very distressing moment, it was very silly for Li Yuan to sleep like a log at night after indulging in the autumn rains for the whole day. He had no clue that Phoenix Mouth was about to be struck by a quake and that his life would be endangered.

In his sleep, someone brought him up sharp with a pointed hand tugging at his belly button. Five sharp thorns pierced his skin and nearly jagged his heart and lungs. It reminded him of a scene one winter's day when an eagle swooped down and impaled a chicken as it pecked in front of the door.

That hand hurled him into the deepest part of the cave, so he banged violently against the wall. At that moment, he opened his eyes and saw a black head and a pair of hands lifted in the air.

Whenever he brought to mind a cliff-slide, this image would immediately flash through his imagination: a black head and a pair of uplifted hands.

It was the portrait of a man. That man was his father.

Li Yuan always thought that his father's hands had not merely meant to throw him into the safety of the kiln. He must have been trying to hold steady the whole of Phoenix Mouth with his strong and powerful mitts. But he wasn't to make it.

Everything fell silent. Just like now, the moon, the universe, Phoenix Mouth and the River Wei seemed to be appreciating a natural masterpiece with mysteriously blindfolded eyes. The wind was meticulously blowing away at the hot debris and threads of rain without number were infusing the cracks.

Tightly surrounded by pan soil and gravel, Li Yuan trembled with fear. He was desperate to live.

Nothing was visible in the darkness. Li Yuan was dazed. His muscles ached and his breathing became more and more difficult. Not long afterwards, he felt a pain in his face. Raising his hand to slap it, he realised it was a hungry mouse. More ravenous than the mouse, he seized the panting rodent without any thought, tore it apart and swallowed it, flesh and bones.

Provided he could muster a little energy, he would desperately dig away at the soil. While digging, he wanted to figure out how much he had shifted already. As he reached out his hands to feel, tons of debris suddenly fell down and buried the sieve-sized mound he had accumulated. He had wanted to see the results of his own survival efforts. The boy's persistence and perseverance were completely crushed. Li Yuan began to cry inconsolably on the sunken heap.

Waves of wailing echoed about the enclosed space. In his despair, he pawed at the hard soil around him.

Exhausted, he bent over on the pile of debris as if reclining on his mother's breast.

He heard a girl's sobbing. *Dan Dan?* she cried plaintively, with tears sliding down her cheeks and onto Li Yuan's face.

Dozens of hands simultaneously grabbed hold of Li Yuan. Some pulled his arms and legs and some tugged his hair. He felt that his hair and scalp were about to be rent apart. His closed eyes detected powerful shafts of light – red, white, blue, green and yellow. These multicoloured beams were interwoven, preventing his eyes from opening and making him feel his head would crack open. He tried to beat his head but could not lift his fists.

He could detect someone gauging his breath.

Sleeping on a pile of hay, he felt warm, and there was a crackling fire. He nodded off quietly and couldn't believe that a miracle like this could happen. After the long roaring sound in his head had died down, his ears began to flinch.

"Li Yuan!"

"Li Yuan!"

"Li Yuan!"

Hearing people's calls, he felt two drops of something cool with a refreshing aroma moistening his throat.

Wild rocket oil!

He recognised the taste immediately. A great force impelled him to turn over, sit up and open his eyes. So many friendly and familiar faces were smiling at him – the folks from Phoenix Mouth!

Old Seven was holding out a chopstick and drizzling wild rocket oil from it.

Besides him was his granddaughter, Dan Dan, who was holding a crimson clay pot with several dirty dark stripes on her face. It was a clay pot for wild rocket oil.

After his body healed in hospital, Li Yuan returned with an intense feeling of loneliness to the new cave house prepared by the Production Brigade. In hospital, everyone had come to visit him, and Old Seven and his granddaughter, Dan Dan, stayed by his side for days. He had become emotionally dependent on both of them.

At nightfall, Dan Dan returned holding the jar again. After the catastrophe, there was nothing left in the cave house and Li Yuan was at the mercy of others for support. Dan Dan put the jar on the newly-built stove and said: "My grandpa let me bring it for you. Have a drop of it now and again. It'll help your recovery."

Li Yuan was choked and couldn't breathe a single word while looking at Dan Dan's hands.

Dan Dan put her hands behind her back.

Her hands were wrapped in gauze. During the five days and nights of the rescue, her fingernails had been worn out with digging.

For the sake of a man's life, all the locals participated in the operation. The workers, the students and the soldiers assembled to form a rescue team. At the beginning, each shift lasted for half an hour, then it was shortened to ten minutes as more and more people became involved. Modern bulldozers, excavators and earth-shifters were almost useless. Many people lost their fingernails like Dan Dan.

Li Yuan's life had been saved by good people digging tirelessly with their fingertips.

He went to see his old cave house. Not even the bare outline of it remained; only a few broken branches jutting out from a huge mound. The whole family was buried including his father, his mother and sister. The huge mound had become the grave of the three of them.

Li Yuan knelt down. He was grateful in that moment to his father for being so sober, sensible and for treasuring the duty of a father. Before he died, his first thought was for his son. Was it because little Li Yuan would be the man in Phoenix's Mouth?

Father: such a noble title was engraved in the heart of Li Yuan.

From then on, he bore the mission of two men on his shoulders.

Lying on the grave, his tears drained away. The dried-up wormwood in Phoenix Mouth swayed silently and a hare observantly munched seeds with its little triangular mouth. Whether it was seeking out Yuan or just wanted to take a short rest, nobody could tell. The creature squatted down on Phoenix Mouth as if to contemplate how precious and beautiful life was.

A flock of wild geese appeared, honking and wheeling in an orderly fashion over Li Yuan's head. Their flying formation was printed against the blue sky with striking clarity. In just a few days, Li Yuan had been able to search through the nooks and crannies of Phoenix Mouth. His sensitive nature made him take on the duties and responsibilities of a man and moulded him into an adult male in a flash. He visited all the folks who had assisted in saving his life and kowtowed to them as a sign of gratitude.

Li Yuan climbed to the top of Phoenix Mouth, feeling the autumn wind blowing against his thin chest. Quietly observing the River Wei and his parents' and sister's giant tomb, he solemnly declared: I shall spend the rest of my life being a good man for the sake of Phoenix Mouth!

Twenty years passed. Li Yuan became a man with a thick and generous chest as well as a brain full of intrigue and strategy, which had been shrouded in darkness in the cliff-slide twenty years ago, the suffocating darkness biting and chewing away at his flesh.

As it turned out, his iron foundry was not actually haunted. The plant was built in a warehouse yard with machine tools, a drilling machine and a milling range. A larger furnace of cast iron was set up in the open air. On the morning operations were to commence, he took a tumble by the edge of the lathe and knocked out a front tooth.

Dan Dan dragged her ghost-like man from the gambling den and entrusted him to Li Yuan.

The roar of the machine awakened Phoenix Mouth, which had been dreaming for thousands of years. Everyone grew green-eyed as they counted benefit after benefit Li Yuan earned. Their bowels became twisted and their teeth chattered.

Dan Dan's devil of a man directed all the slyness of a gambler into some stunning accounting. "The rich are rich, the poor are poor, and Li Yuan has seized all our money!" His terrible words denigrated the image of the plant with its modern machinery. They also incited a gang of idlers from Phoenix Mouth to torch the iron casting machines and stone-built workshop into ashes.

Li Yuan was distressed, frustrated, resentful and helpless.

Dan Dan came over with her head sore, feeling denuded of the courage to live. She blamed the arson attack on her devil of a man, who had just been slain at the gambling den. When his body was carried out, his accomplice's knife was poking out of his stomach.

It seemed only natural that Dan Dan should marry Li Yuan. But Old Seven died prematurely and his medical treatment consumed all the family's savings. How could she afford to bury her grandpa? Dan Dan cried lamentably. Faced with Dan Dan's tearful eyes, that tall and bulky man still couldn't fathom a way out. Poverty almost drove this hot-blooded man to hang himself.

Reluctantly, Dan Dan sent about a message: she would marry the man who could bury her grandpa.

What an irony. The devil man had been capable of burying Old Seven but now Dan Dan had to ask for help to bury her grandfather and the heap of meat who was her husband.

At the mention of the devil man and the burnt-out factory,

Li Yuan's eyes bled as he visualised the devil man dancing and rejoicing around the burning foundry with a gang of gamblers. Phoenix Mouth tilted to the sound of their roaring laughter so that only a pile of twisted scrap metal was left.

"Bury him? He deserves to rot away layer by layer!"

Li Yuan flew into rage like a roaring lion.

No one in Phoenix Mouth paid their respects to the dead body of the devil man. When he was a captain of the militiamen with a gun on his back, he cursed everything as if he were the kingpin in the community.

Once allocated land from the government, he did nothing but gamble and even bet his life away, leaving his woman and children to suffer.

Dan Dan turned her back and walked out quietly.

Li Yuan never forgot how Dan Dan had been forced to borrow salt, vinegar, chilli and matches almost every day after marrying that man. All her neighbours lived in dread of it. But she had never asked Li Yuan for help. After calming down, Li Yuan stared at Dan Dan's back and then rushed ahead of her to stop her.

Li Yuan knew Dan Dan. She had come to him because she trusted him. He gave all his money to Dan Dan to bury the devil man. Then, after slapping the dust from his back pockets, he left feeling relaxed as if he had paid off all his debts.

It was the first time he had gone out to make money. As a consequence, he didn't earn much. Even so, he still bought some new seeds and a few bags of imported fertiliser for Dan Dan.

"When I sold out of vegetables, I … "

Dan Dan accepted his help, but she had still not reconciled herself to the dreary and miserable life of a widow.

"Who wants you to pay them back?" Li Yuan thought of the crimson pot filled with wild rocket oil. He said: "We grew up together and offered to help each other. Do you need to pay?"

Dan Dan turned around and left.

She sang hysterically amid the vegetable plots of the River Wei. His eyes chased her, and he felt sad for her as he listened to her sing the never-ending song of Phoenix Mouth:

The wild chrysanthemum withers on its root.
From spring right through to fall,
A woman longs for a good man,
While there is none in the world at all.

On that late spring evening, Dan Dan sang as she climbed and Li Yuan stood by the river. The setting sun on top of the western tableland turned a ditch of the River Wei flame red. Mantled with rosy clouds, Dan Dan stood up from the vegetable plot, ready to head home. She looked sick or tired, vacillating and staggering as she walked like a drunkard to Phoenix Mouth. Suddenly he wondered: why didn't she start a new family? It would not be hard for her.

When he got home, he asked his wife, who looked like a bundle of wet firewood, what she thought. It was the first time he had spoken to her, so she felt extremely flattered and told him all she had seen and heard. In the end, she said: "Dan Dan has sworn to live alone in her later life."

Li Yuan didn't lift his head. He understood the real meaning of her oath.

As he put down his bowl, the scene of Dan Dan coming out of the vegetable plot and climbing up to Phoenix Mouth swirled about in his head. He tried to persuade her to remarry in his mind, but a vague inkling made him rejoice in secret. He even hoped Dan Dan would never remarry so would have to borrow money from him time and again.

A fleeting past thought intensified when Li Yuan was in anguish. Her looks always followed him no matter where he went.

Having her around, Li Yuan grew confident and motivated.

He earned a living with only a sack and his mouth. Even though it was not as easy as he expected, finally he had got his way. Like a lively ghost fish swimming in the blue sea, Li Yuan engaged in trading, taking scarce rice from Sichuan, transporting corncobs shaped like dog turds from Wei, hawking kiwi fruit from the Qinling Mountains and carrying apples to Qiao Hill. On the Qinling Mountains, there were tens of thousands of excavation workers with hungry mouths to feed. He always dared to do the things others were afraid to try.

In his graceful Western-style mansion, he could now have whatever he wanted: a TV set imported from Japan, a sofa bed, a floor lamp, air conditioning. He often stood on the balcony overlooking the new village of Phoenix Mouth. The rows of low bungalows gave him a sense of satisfaction and achievement. But these feelings were fleeting. Afterwards, he wanted to embrace the terraces, holding them fast to his bosom as he cried.

He was often aroused by the anguish of being misunderstood and powerless. Why did everyone stand together to oppose him? He had no idea.

Li Yuan felt frustrated about his poor relationships with others. In his despair, he missed Dan Dan. He knew he could be comforted by her alone.

He came after her but was buried in Phoenix Mouth by that sudden cliff-slide. He never expected to get out alive, believing his time had come.

He was clearly aware that he was not the same Li Yuan of twenty years ago. Back then, people had voluntarily gathered together to rescue him from death. But who would come to his aid now?

Dan Dan started to struggle against the pain, biting his shoulder as she moaned. Her bites awakened Li Yuan's responsibility as a man. He heard Dan Dan's groans of pain. She was calling out her son's name and mumbling about her daughter who would come home for steamed buns on Wednesday.

The air was becoming thinner. There was only the sound of desperate digging in the darkness of the cave.

Li Yuan woke up.

He rolled over and stood up, staring at everything in the cave house with eyes agog. He couldn't believe he was still alive and sitting in such a glorious house.

His wife was cradling Li Yuan awkwardly like a scared hare as beads of sweat dropped from his chin. She asked: "Are you sick?"

Li Yuan awoke completely from his dream. He could see blue light glistening on the electric clock embedded in the wall. The water-like moonlight flowed through the partially drawn curtain onto the wall, where it reflected against the desk.

"Put on your clothes."

Li Yuan never expected her voice could be so sweet and mild. He promptly got out of bed, dressed and walked out alone.

Walking towards the small stone bridge that spanned the River Wei, he looked out over Phoenix Mouth. The place was enveloped in warm moonlight and Dan Dan's cave house was being warmed among the vastness.

The smell in the dream again returned to his mind. He lit a cigarette and the heavy smoke, too dense and impassable, cast him asunder from Phoenix Mouth.

The Champion Scholar Goat

When Cadre Jiang stopped Feng Laicai in Head-of-the-Slope Village and told him, "This is your moment; don't doubt me on this!", his chubby visage bloomed like a flower at the good news. No offence to Cadre Jiang, but the face of every cadre who works in a township government alters in colour according to who he has before him. So, perhaps Cadre Jiang should not have worn such a flattering smile. This much is true: a shabby goatherd like Feng should warrant nothing but cold eyes, which would freeze his heart with only a single glance into a lump of ice.

After taking care of his paraplegic father, Feng Laicai shuffled out through the door and up along the ditch to tend his beloved goats. This was where he encountered Cadre Jiang. On taking in Jiang's words, he stood and asked him to what moment he was referring.

Instead of telling him, Jiang answered with a question: "Don't you know?"

"If I did, why would I bother asking you?" Feng Laicai replied.

Like an over-fed cat that has caught an undernourished mouse, Cadre Jiang was in a good mood. His shining face suggested he wouldn't miss a chance to tease Laicai. And it was always an amusing thing to have someone with whom to trifle. So, Cadre Jiang merely looked at him with a wide-open mouth. He was in no hurry to get anywhere.

Feng Laicai was thinking about his unattended goats on the slope and did not intend to natter, so he lowered his head to move on. Seeing this, Cadre Jiang piped up again.

"Is it true that your goats are fed on Chinese medicinal herbs and mineral water?"

This question killed the conversation. Feng Laicai strode ahead with his head down. But Cadre Jiang quickened his pace and barred the way. Left with no choice, Feng raised his head and stared at Cadre Jiang. With his stumpy arms and legs, Feng Laicai was "half a man". Of course, that's being vulgar; a more civil name would be "dwarf". Although much shorter than Cadre Jiang, his gaze was superior. Thus, Cadre Jiang's merry face turned to embarrassment.

Many people besides Cadre Jiang, his fellow Head-of-the-Slope villagers especially, wanted to know the answer. Feng Laicai was the only one who had responded to an appeal from the government to farm goats. At first, the attitude of Head-of-the-Slope villagers to Feng and his herd was that they believed he'd been fooled by the government and were happy to gloat over his failure. However, that failure never transpired; the beasts were getting stronger and the selling price higher. As expected, the villagers started to feel regret; regret that they lacked the guts to follow suit. Such thoughts brewed in their minds and burst out with a tang of jealousy. Every time they encountered him, some sour comments would inevitably ensue.

Two passing Head-of-the-Slope villagers managed to overhear the conversation and interposed excitedly.

One said: "What herbs? What water?"

The other said: "Easy, let's kill one of them and make a broth. Then all will become clear."

Feng Laicai had no interest in this hearsay and was also uncertain about the herbs and mineral water business. It sounded too much like bragging to him; he would never express such sentiments.

Who would have put it in those terms?

Magistrate Jiang! That was it. He was the only individual who sprang to mind. How could Magistrate Jiang, that well-educated, knowledge-equipped, scientifically-enlightened and research-primed chap, be wrong?

The goats, under Feng's watch, turned out plumper and sturdier by the day. As a result, his withered life exhibited some signs of recovery.

This was Feng Laicai's blessing; he had been blessed by the goats.

Magistrate Jiang came to Head-of-the-Slope village to promote a strong breed called Boer goat which he had introduced from Australia. With absolute sincerity, he went door-to-door setting forth the advantages of and reasons for choosing this strain. And yet, after his saliva had run dry and despite elaborating veritable valleys of speeches, not one household was moved. Their polite rejections sounded similar: "We are inexperienced; what if we fail?"; "That's disgraceful, Magistrate Jiang. We can't afford that."

Once Feng Laicai had agreed to sign the contract, the Magistrate set him up as an example who could work continuously to try and sway the villagers.

Unfortunately, even in the face of this supplementary rhetoric, the villagers still wouldn't embrace the idea: "We'd better wait and see. If Feng Laicai turns out to be successful, we will be sure to do the same. To pocket some extra income like this will save your reputation, Magistrate Jiang."

Lacking any other escape route, the Magistrate had to stake everything on Feng, the "half man".

Worried about Feng Laicai and the Boer goats, Magistrate Jiang would occasionally come to Head-of-the-Slope Village. He would follow Feng Laicai onto the slope where he herded the goats. While driving the herd from the rear, the Magistrate warily took note of the grass they were inclined to graze. The slope was fearfully large with corners giving way to more corners. The wide, deep slope was a haven for grasses – one hundred, nay, one thousand species of which surpassed the limits of Jiang's knowledge. Magistrate Jiang came across what Feng Laicai termed "the gentleman vine", "the crow pillow", "mouse food" and "ditch bud", the goats' favourites. The Magistrate was appointed by the provincial capital as subprefect in charge of science and technology. After weathering a few days there, he was sure to be promoted. That was the reason he was prepared to put up with all inconveniences by collecting grass samples and sending them to the provincial capital city for testing. And that is where the rumours came from: every grass is a form of traditional Chinese medicine.

This reminded Feng Laicai of a quip among his fellows: "No grass is midden in the land of Qin."

Whenever he came back to Head-of-the-Slope Village, Magistrate Jiang still tailed Feng Laicai as he herded goats. Replete with grass, the herd descended all the way down the slope, as did the Magistrate, who stumbled on behind the animals to the bottom of the ditch where Feng Laicai, the half man, had long since arrived. A clear brook, half-hidden among the grass, was silently flowing. The goats gathered along its bank, extending their necks to sip the water before thrusting their heads backwards to swallow. They would then extend their necks once more and again swallow the water; greedy yet unhurried. Delighted by this, Magistrate Jiang dipped an empty bottle into the brook and took it back to the city for analysis. He was then able to bring yet more news to Head-of-the-Slope Village: "That is indeed mineral-rich water in the ditch."

It crossed Feng's mind that villagers returning home from the innermost mountains had told him that the brook was fed by a highland spring.

Thinking of his herd, and of whether the goats were nourished with herbs and mineral water, Feng Laicai, the half man, stared at Cadre Jiang, sensing his guff and that of his fellow villagers. He'd become bored with this talk, so he said: "Believe it or not, that's been verified by Magistrate Jiang."

"How dare I doubt it?" Cadre Jiang became serious. "There is going to be a county-level goat competition. We've decided to send you. We want you to represent our town by competing."

"Competing for what?"

"For a prize!"

Feng Laicai sighed. "The prize is not for me for sure."

Failing to convince him, Cadre Jiang became a little impatient, speaking of Magistrate Jiang the way Feng Laicai had spoken of him: "Magistrate Jiang called. You still won't go?"

As he possessed no means of confirming that, Feng asked: "Did Magistrate Jiang really call?"

"How could I lie about this?" Cadre Jiang replied.

Feng Laicai had no reply. Now that Magistrate Jiang had called, he was obliged to go. Yes, he must go; Magistrate Jiang was like the burning sun which shone within Feng's heart. There could be no reason to refuse. Casting his mind back to Magistrate Jiang and the day they first came to know each other, Feng Laicai had a feeling of sweetness. He could not help but grin.

山羊

During those early days, Feng Laicai dared not stay at home. He had to hide from the cadres.

Who didn't? Every young adult in Head-of-the-Slope Village ducked away as far as they could, like they were avoiding the plague. In just a few days, that once boisterous Head-of-the-Slope Village, a community rippling with the bustle of people and the neighing of horses, a settlement busy with the harvesting of wheat and the planting of corn, suddenly fell silent. Only infirm old men and ignorant kids were left behind. *When the corn ripens and the wheat turns gold, even maidens leave their household.* Everyone, including the infirm old men and ignorant kids, became overwhelmed with farm work. And, when the wheat was harvested and corn had been planted, the elderly were exhausted and lay steadfastly on their beds. As for the kids, they had to carry their satchels to the village school to catch up on missed lessons.

Only the cadence of reading aloud hovered about the placid Head-of-the-Slope Village. Still, some vitality could be sensed.

Cadres vying for grains and tariffs arrived. Year in and year out, the cadres, who had learned from experience, would always swoop down on the village immediately after the harvested wheat had been put into storage. There were yells and cries. The noise lingered on. Not a single household was exempt. Speaking of the agricultural tax, however much they might struggle in their lives, the villagers never failed to submit theirs. Offering up agricultural tax was a custom adhered to by families for more than a thousand years. The villagers had the ability to tell right from wrong.

Even so, other levies demanded by the cadres had excessive numbers of articles, none of which were known by the villagers. Every article written in the cadres' notebooks naturally became the ultimate authority and the sums were arbitrary, depending on the will of the officers. Some cadres arrived one day asking for an additional education fee, a school buildings fee and a fee for private tuition; others arrived the next day requesting fines for violating the family planning rules, levies for promoting family planning, fees for sterilisation surgery. Each township cadre took charge of his own article and had his own titles. The titles had names such as the "popularising agricultural techniques fee", the "building countryside culture fee", the "township government-invested road maintenance fee" and others of that ilk.

Cadres surged into the village as though they were on a revolving whirligig. Those who came too early had to go to the granary to pilfer wheat. Those who came too late for wheat stole the tiles from the roofs of houses or drove cattle from the open fields. Their eyes all turned green when collecting fees, green like the eyes of a wolf gnawing at men's bones.

The villagers, in their terror, had no choice but to run.

Luckily, there were places for them to hide. Jumping onto random vehicles headed for the city, those who had relatives there knew they would find refuge. Others looked to fellows from their hometown for temporary jobs. Nowadays, cities are like fast-swelling monsters, with scaffolding and high buildings swarming all over the place. Villagers, for their part, are eager to take up the resulting low-paid jobs like being a porter or a tiler, which are in abundant supply. These suffice as long as they keep them away from the cadres for a while.

Feng Laicai would rather have moved to the city to work, but being born a half man, with stumpy arms and stumpy legs, was cause enough for discouragement. Who would be prepared to hire him? And for whom should he work? What was more, what would his only kin – a paralysed old man – rely on for survival?

His strong personality circumscribed by a feeble destiny, Feng Laicai had no other option but to stay idly at home.

Every time cadres arrived, Feng Laicai had to duck away. He was not worried about his old man. That ancient bone who lay in bed all day long thought nothing of the oncoming cadres, no matter how ferocious and violent they might be. What damage could they cause? Feng Laicai, on the other hand, was a wretch of no significance apt to elicit tears from others. Cadres demanding grains and tariffs showed him no mercy at all, let alone leave him undisturbed. Past experience, like a sharp-edged blade, incised his bloody heart with painful memories.

On account of outstanding tuition fees (hell only knows what tuition he could owe), Feng Laicai was arrested by the township government and thrown into a black detention cabin. Feng Laicai dared not move his feet inside the cell. It seemed that they were connected to a trigger and every time he twitched someone started to moan in the overcrowded space. With time, he grew accustomed to the darkness. The area alongside the bucket used for crapping was the one place where there was a little room for him to uncurl one of his legs, so he expended all his energy crawling over there.

Once he sat his posterior down, a blast of fetid air gushed into his nostrils and he almost fainted. He heard a cough. There was a woman sitting next to him. Not knowing what to do, he inched a little nearer to the bucket. As he was doing so, the woman exclaimed: "Where the hell are you going? We are not the only ones here, you and me." What a sweet voice.

Feng Laicai stopped. He moved neither towards the bucket nor towards the woman. Oh, those days in the cabin were so hard to endure. Men and women were penned in together and felt too embarrassed to take a shit or have a piss. Feng Laicai, like many others, became sick just days after being incarcerated. No one knew where the illness came from, but a few men who were infected with the malady began to experience fevers and to rave. In the end, this incident proved the very reason why Feng Laicai was released.

The moment Feng Laicai stepped outside, the sunlight caused him to scrunch his eyes tightly. This was not a ray of light, Feng thought, but a round of arrows, and every one of the shots pierced his eyeballs. He cried without any sound. Tears of turbid yellow hung like strings from his face.

Feng Laicai didn't have the balls to think about the black cabin again. It gave him goosebumps every time.

However, Feng was fond of the woman with whom he had been incarcerated. They were close and so had had ample chance to talk. The woman, named Ma Lala, was a pitiful widow who had been married to a sickly man and spent all their savings on medicines. Likewise, Ma Lala knew his name and, naturally, knew that he, like her, was a pitiful singleton.

Pitiful men pity their peers and are willing to forgive one another for not being considerate.

It was not as disconcerting for the men to shit or piss in the cabin, but how was Ma Lala – a lady – supposed to unfasten her belt and remove her smalls? These travails were as hard as climbing to the heavens. Some wretches, forgetting their own bleak fortunes, were sure to make eyes at her and poke fun at Ma Lala when she couldn't hold it in. Feng Laicai reproached them for behaving rudely, though no one took him seriously. And so, Feng removed his own jacket to block the view while he stood with his back to Lala.

Even this considerate man made a mistake though. One night, he fell asleep and, perhaps in the middle of a dream, thrust out his stumpy arm and pressed it against her breast. He was unaware of this at the time but in his dream he felt a kind of softness, an ecstatic softness. On waking, he realised he had committed an inappropriate act and withdrew his arm immediately. His eyes ran into Ma's eyes. They were sparkling and wide open. She didn't blame Feng Laicai, for what was trickling out of her eyes were tears of compassion and understanding.

Feng Laicai then raised his hand and slapped his own face as punishment. Through the darkness, he could see that Ma Lala was grinning at him.

When they were released from the cabin, the poor men glanced at each other, whether intentionally or unintentionally, but none of them spoke again. Feng Laicai didn't know where Ma Lala had gone. He just hoped she was leading a better life.

Hiding away from the cadres, Feng Laicai missed Ma Lala a great deal; this woman made his heart ache.

山羊

Laicai hid in a deep ditch in front of his village.

Head-of-the-Slope Village, as its name implies, was located on the top of a slope. If you quit the village and walked upwards, you would find yourself on a boundless slope, abutting what appeared to be a bottomless ditch which leaned at a transverse angle. In the old days, this weed-occupied ditch served as a refuge for villagers who wanted to avoid wars. They selected precipitous, secluded spots and dug out cave dwellings. Over time, the ditch became peppered with caves excavated by the villagers. A number of caves had collapsed owing to a lack of maintenance. Others were still serviceable but were concealed among wild grasses, making them hard to find. On the northern tableland situated in the western portion of the Central Shaanxi Plain, huge ditches like this were a common sight. Bordering Head-of-the-Slope were Dragon's Tail Ditch and Horse's Tail Ditch. Oxtail Ditch was to the west. Feng Laicai sheltered in one of the tumbledown caves in Dragon's Tail Ditch with his dying goats. He was unwilling to drive them out onto the slope, where the cadres could easily find and capture them. That would be tantamount to suicide.

While hiding in the cave, Feng spent the days doing calculations on his fingers.

Ten days and more passed. He anchored himself inside the hollow during the day while sneaking out at night. The tasks of mowing enough grass on the slope for his old pals to eat and carrying water from the bottom of the ditch came to be his priorities. Then, under cover of darkness, he had to move stealthily back home and collect some cold food for his disabled father. Before sunrise, he quickly retreated into the cave and waited for the coming day.

The paralysed father's heart ached for his son. As he prepared things to eat in the dark he complained, with his eyes wide open: "How could it be that the Heavens have forgotten me?"

He then continued: "Please take my life, ye gods on high, and do not force this wretched existence upon my son!"

These words floated into Feng Laicai's ears. He neither replied nor felt good about them. He did everything he had to do as a son and sometimes, when he couldn't stand the way his father was cursing himself, would retort: "Stop talking nonsense. The cadres might be precious now, but the Heavens will take their lives when the time comes."

He then spoke in a softer voice: "The reason why the gods let you live is that they want you to wait for your son's golden day."

After attending to his father, Feng Laicai once again groped his way back to his cave. Tugging one goat into his arms, he started to stroke the fleece. Sensing a shadow darkening his sight, he knew that someone had followed him.

It turned out to be a white-faced cadre who was wearing white glasses and looked like a schoolmaster.

In the dim light of dawn, the cadre peered into Feng's dwelling, fixing his eyes on the goats which were living with him. His cheeks turned red; brilliant red like drops of blood.

Feng Laicai was like an already-dead swine that needn't fear the scalding water; he didn't give a damn. "Come as you please. What further damage can you and the other cadres do? I've not been living like a human being or a ghost. What about stripping me, peeling off my skin and slicing me into pieces? I very much doubt that you would. Dare you stab me?" Pondering this, Feng Laicai calmed himself down. He carefully stroked the goat for insects.

These little critters – smaller than hyacinth seeds and larger than a sesame seed – preferred to inhabit the ear channels or beneath the testicles, where there was a fecund supply of blood, rather than live in the wool. Feng Laicai was thus used to flicking back the goat's ears when he hugged them. With his penetrating sight, he had the skill to pinch out all the fleas and crush them to death on a stone which lay against his feet. The rock, which was identical in size to a goat's head, clearly bore testimony to the carnage as it had fleas' blood and skins pasted all over it.

In the mere blink of an eye, Laicai's nimble hands started to shake. He had obviously found a pitch-black louse but failed to grasp hold of it even after some poking. The appearance of that sudden intruder was too much for the goats. They were only used to having their master in the shabby cave, so they shoved themselves together closely, bleating piteously. On hearing this, Feng Laicai felt his heart was in an agony of pain like it had been mangled by a knife.

Feng Laicai considered his goats his kinsmen, just like his paralysed father who loved him deeply. They ought never to be parted. This was not that tricky to understand. As the half man of the village, where several hundred souls lived, which of them had ever acted kindly towards him? Almost everyone saw him as a joke and played him like a monkey. When he was young, Feng played with those who played him. Their tricks were so bloody humiliating, but Feng never understood that at the time. After he did come to understand it, he refused to share in the fun with the villagers but could not stop them from playing him. Sometimes they hung him up on a dirt wall and teased him: "Tell us, whose fucking made you pop out? You don't look like your father; he's not a half man." Feng Laicai knew they were bullying him, so he clenched his teeth tight without allowing a single word to leak out. Sometimes they pushed him into a hole and asked him: "Who gave birth to you? You're not one bit like your mother; she's not a half woman." Feng still refused to say anything. In most cases, Feng Laicai couldn't drag himself down from the wall or up from the hole, so he cried, painfully, as if he was vomiting up his heart and lungs. On hearing him, Feng's father and mother hurried to rescue him, and then the villagers burst out laughing and departed. In a few days, however, they would come back for more.

People still tried to play him by hanging him on the wall or by pushing him into a hole until Feng's mother began, for some reason, to spew forth white froth and died shortly thereafter. Of course, the question that had been asked a thousand times still assailed him. However, this time Feng Laicai didn't cry, nor did he beg. Instead, he cursed in a fury.

"Your father shagged me!" was the first reply. "And your mother!" came the second.

His curses actually did the trick. From then on, none of the villagers tormented him and no one ever talked to him either. He strolled along the lane in Head-of-the-Slope Village waiting for someone to speak to him, but no one did. He was so bloody lonely that he even longed for someone to hang him up on the wall or push him into a hole. He would be sure not to curse them and would, in fact, go along with it. Oh, how shameful! But shameful as his thoughts were, his thoughts were mere fantasy. It was only when his family had goats to herd and he wielded the whip that he could drive his herd into the ditch in front of the village and stay with them. This caused his loneliness to abate.

Feng Laicai grew up. He became an adult with warm blood, flesh and emotions, yet still he counted his goats as his family – as straightforward as that – and as his lovers.

Oh, lover! Who could understand the sorrow of Feng Laicai, the half man? He, too, needed to be loved, especially to have the love of a woman. This literally became the dream he never stopped dreaming. There was no woman, so he could only love his goats. He pinched fleas for them and even held them in his arms, stroking their soft wool. He kept on stroking, one nanny after another. Occasionally, he held one and gave it a sweet kiss.

When the white-faced cadre found him in the cave, he was kissing one of the goats. The white-faced cadre said nothing. He just looked at him and giggled.

Having been caught in the act, Feng Laicai panicked. He sank into a state of remorse over his covert behaviour and over the cadre who had laughed at him.

Even hiding in the cave, Feng still couldn't break away from the cadres.

Not knowing what to do, Feng Laicai, feeling depressed, thrust his fingers into the wool for fleas that had been swept away long ago. His bosom filled with resentment, he groaned: "Have them all; then I shall have relief."

The cadre wearing glasses was good-tempered with a laughing expression. Even so, Feng Laicai's expression was hostile. The face hidden by the glasses was crystal clear in Feng's eyes. It bore no falsehood or deception but was the reflection of his inner being. The goatherd was taken aback.

As expected, as soon as this cadre started talking, Feng Laicai's dead heart healed a little. "Who wants your goats?" asked the cadre. "Not I. I would like to give you specimens of a fine breed!"

Feng Laicai shrieked: "Do your words count for something?"

The blushing cadre didn't tell him who he was but told him his words did count. He added: "We raise goats out under the sun; who do we need to hide from? You live in a poor village and your family is worse off than most. According to the policy, your village has been designated a Key Poverty Alleviation Village and your family is the key to that key. You're skilled at herding; I was told that you've been herding goats since you started to walk. First you raised goats for the village, then for other villagers, and finally for yourself. You are experienced, that's a treasure. How come you are hiding your treasure away? Doing things your way, I don't think you can throw off the hat of poverty."

Feng Laicai looked blankly at the cadre and allowed his words to flow into his ears. He loved to hear this counsel and kept on nodding away.

Barely two days had passed when a farm truck loaded with five Boer goats arrived at Head-of-the-Slope Village. That cadre wearing glasses was present. He greeted Feng Laicai and drove the animals out of the truck. The Boers assimilated to Laicai's herd, making it stronger than before.

Feng Laicai was informed that the cadre who had sent him the goats was the magistrate. He appreciated how the Magistrate had fulfilled his promise and he kept on hovering about the man with embarrassment, a bashful streak suddenly suffusing his cheeks. He was agitated and felt constrained because he didn't have a clue how much the goats had cost. And he only had an empty pocket.

Magistrate Jiang saw through him. While flogging the dust from his clothes, he piped up: "Put your mind at ease and just concentrate on taking proper care of the goats; it's okay not to have any money now. As long as you feed your goats well, you'll make money."

山羊

Once the township government attached importance to the county goat competition, Head-of-the Slope Village followed suit.

Going back generations, the Village Head was somehow related to Feng Laicai. He always claimed: "We Fengs all belong to the same clan." He made out as if allowing Laicai to attend the competition was his own vanity project. After the news was first announced, he yelled hard about it to the people of his village with a goofy grin hanging on his face. It was surely the first time that had happened since the creation of the world. The villagers were happy for him and simultaneously envious. But leaving that envy aside, everyone was in rapturous spirits and expressed their sincere congratulations directly to Feng Laicai, who had earned a good reputation for Head-of-the-Slope Village. Even Feng's paralysed father, who lay on the *kang*, was more chipper than he had been. When Feng Laicai was not home, he took over as host, supporting his upper body with his arms as he greeted guests.

The disabled old chap sounded magnanimous, saying: "After the competition, let Laicai slaughter a goat for us to taste."

Then the crowd hooted: "That's right! A hand is stretching out from our longing throats to grab some goat meat!"

Presently, Magistrate Jiang came to assist Feng Laicai select a goat to enter in the competition.

But which one to choose?

A Boer goat, of course, that was a matter of principle. It would be ridiculous to choose any old white goat for the contest instead of one of the Boers promoted by Magistrate Jiang. That issue was beyond dispute. But which among those who were growing in strength was the best one? Cadre Jiang wanted to select one of the breeding nannies that Magistrate Jiang had sent. But Feng Laicai disagreed. He reasoned that while these breeding goats had given a lot to the herd by mating and whelping over these few years, they were old now and bore no comparison to what they had once been. Luckily, subsequent generations had, by contrast, surpassed them and sported the advantages of youth. Especially outstanding was a billy that was born with a pair of black eyes. It had a muscular body and smooth wool which, when it stood shoulder-to-shoulder with others of its kind, made it look like the crane among the chickens.

Feng Laicai led the black-eyed billy out for Cadre Jiang to check. He looked up and down and back and forth at it before giggling: "How come it looks like a panda?"

Laicai laughed too: "Everyone loves a panda, right?"

In this way, the black-eyed billy became the contender. It seemed the billy itself was aware of this honour, reining in its wayward and willful disposition a little and, when crowded among other goats, exhibiting its full dignity and pride. This was not difficult to comprehend. As a two-year-old, it did after all, long for love and lifted up its head to pick, with extreme caution, a nanny as a possible bride from among the herd of snowflakes. Meanwhile, it prudently guarded its status lest the other billies put up a challenge.

Cadre Jiang reported the result of his selection directly to his superiors, two of whom, Secretary Hou, the number one leader, and Township Head Gou, his second-in-command, bustled over to Head-of-the-Slope Village to inspect the black-eyed goat. When surveying the chosen billy, they could not help bursting into laughter. They guffawed hard and merrily but did not forgot to praise Feng Laicai, saying he was indeed a capable herdsman. Perhaps surprisingly, Feng Laicai acted coolly in the face of these comments, though Cadre Jiang ran back and forth between the other two cadres kissing each one's backside in turn. He pouted that tiny mouth that hung upon his greasy face, pasting it to Secretary Hou this minute and then to Township Head Gou the next, whispering on and on.

Cadre Jiang asked Secretary Hou: "How about it? Very nice indeed?"

And to Township Head Gou: "Who says it won't win the top prize? And be crowned Champion Scholar Goat? If it does win, then the village will be truly honoured!"

Secretary Hou nodded: "Yes, indeed, very nice."

Township Head Gou held out his finger, saying: "The Champion Scholar? I doubt anyone can compete with ours."

Thrilled by this encouragement, Cadre Jiang strode over to Feng Laicai and put one hand on his shoulder and instructed: "Muster up everything you have and tend well to that black-eyed one! Don't get an attack of diarrhea on the stage! This is a county level competition, so your goat won't be the only participant. There'll be goats from other towns. Will there be any goats that don't deserve to be there? No, there won't. Every last one of them is stoking up the energy to seize the Champion Scholar title. If you win, it will be your honour. More importantly, it will be the honour of our town. So, don't you slight it; don't you shit yourself. Mark that!"

After offloading this heap of a speech, Cadre Jiang paused to wipe the foam from his mouth, adding: "You've marked my words? You must mark them."

To tell the truth, who does not have a little false pride?

Feng Laicai definitely did. He had been born with a stunted body and had lived in dire poverty all these years. He had lived so piteously on the edge. Fortunately, Magistrate Jiang appeared. He found Laicai and exerted all his wits to support him and, from then on, his life improved. This time the god of fortune had prevailed on him to go to the county competition. He believed it was his turn to shine.

The observant Cadre Jiang sensed Feng Laicai's inner mind and intervened in high spirits: "Do you have the confidence to win the Champion Scholar Goat title?"

Never one to brag, Feng Laicai simply lowered his head and said nothing.

But Cadre Jiang wouldn't let it go. He incited him even more vigorously: "Show some attitude before our cadres!"

Secretary Hou and Township Head Gou went on: "Sure, you should have confidence."

Feng Laicai raised his head and stole a glance at Cadre Jiang, then fixed his eyes on the two leaders' faces and answered without delay: "Yes, I do."

The Head of the Village started to clap, then Cadre Jiang, Secretary Hou, Township Head Gou and the villagers followed. While clapping, Cadre Jiang suggested taking a cup of water at Feng's, and they all agreed. But, after entering, the two leaders did not drink water; instead they exchanged greetings with the paralysed old man on the *kang* and then left.

Cadre Jiang tailed the leaders sullenly. He watched their faces, afraid of being criticised. But things panned out in their own odd way. Whatever you fear the most will always find its way to your door. So, it is with criticism as well.

Secretary Hou started first: "We cadres must cherish and consider the masses all the time."

Township Head Gou elaborated: "Your village should think of a way to solve Feng Laicai's troubles."

These words made Feng Laicai's heart warm, and his eyes warmed too.

To ease the tension, Cadre Jiang turned to Feng Laicai: "Look, our leaders are thinking about you!" While saying this, he peeked at Secretary Hou and Township Head Gou to gauge their reactions. Receiving positive signals from the leaders' faces, he continued with his speech: "It's your fault for spending all you have on the old man's medicine. That's a bottomless pit. But you, you should have a wife, someone who can cook for your father during the day and keep your feet cosy at night."

山羊

When the day of the competition finally arrived, the magnanimous Cadre Jiang came in person to Head-of-the-Slope Village to meet Feng Laicai and his black-eyed billy. Of course, the Village Head would never be absent on such an auspicious occasion. Although Village Head Feng shared the same surname as Feng Laicai, he would have continued his old ways, never paying much attention, had not Secretary Hou and Township Head Gou criticised him. If the goatherd had not been blessed by being invited to attend the competition, he would not have given him a second thought. But things had changed. Even the township government looked up to Feng Laicai, so Village Head Feng had to amend his attitude and consider him a figure of some stature. Were he to win the big title – the Champion Scholar Goat – he would certainly feel honoured. Now, was that the wisdom that came with being Village Head or just his survival instincts kicking in?

After leaving the village, Mr Feng accompanied Feng Laicai and his black-eyed billy across a considerable distance, until Cadre Jiang blocked the way so they could have words. He then stood and took Feng Laicai by the arms, telling him solemnly: "Go compete and don't fret where your home is concerned. You have me. I will never let the old man and the goats feel they are being ill-treated."

These words had been scripted long ago by Village Head Feng and he recited them well. But Feng Laicai didn't respond with a single sound except for uttering "thanks, thanks", which left the Village Head greatly disappointed.

With Cadre Jiang pacing ahead, Feng Laicai followed behind with his black-eyed billy. After a while, they arrived at the buzzing town. The Head of the Village knew how to manage business in the proper way. He found some adept women to embroider a big flower on a piece of scarlet satin and wrapped the cloth around the billy's neck so that he would be an eye-catching competitor. As Feng Laicai and his goat walked along the street, they were met with gasps of admiration all the way. Cadre Jiang led them straight to a hair salon.

The crowd was astonished at this, and so was Feng Laicai.

This was Cadre Jiang's conspiracy. He wanted to make the black-eyed billy spick and span to win the top prize!

The black-eyed billy was not used to such an environment so it behaved in an agitated way. Had not Feng Laicai tightened its reins, who knows what trouble the lunging beast would have made. On account of the creature, the salon, which had formerly been friendly to the nose, was pervaded with an odour of urine redolent of male goat. Taken unawares, neither the hairdressers nor the customers knew how to react. The salon-keeper, who was in another cubicle, detected this whiff and began to complain. Flaring up, his outraged eyes stabbed at the impetuous billy goat and he was about to vent his anger on Feng Laicai until he saw Cadre Jiang wearing his classic smile. Instantly, the salon-keeper changed his expression. Oh, that's a skill Feng Laicai could never hope to master.

The salon-keeper greeted Cadre Jiang over-punctiliously: "Alas! It's you, what are you getting up to with a goat?"

Cadre Jiang said bluntly: "I'm here for a haircut."

The salon-keeper asked: "For you, Sir?"

Cadre Jiang replied: "Not really; for this goat. Look at it, what a fair goat. Like a nationally-treasured panda, isn't it?"

Everyone roared with laughter. Cadre Jiang waited patiently for them to regain their breath and quieten down before he declared that the goat was not a common-or-garden type. He pronounced: "This will be a contestant in the county-level goat competition and will perhaps bring home the title of Champion Scholar. If this proves to be the case, your humble salon will share in that honour." He pressed them to hurry and to deploy all the best resources they had on the goat and, of course, on its master, Feng Laicai.

Clasping his arms with both hands, the salon-keeper found it simultaneously absurd and funny. He had no choice but to give his consent.

Washing the creature was the first step, so the stylists held out their hands and touched the billy in order to give it a try. None of them had any idea where to begin. What was worse, the black-eyed goat wore a pair of horrified eyes and did not appreciate the service in the least. It dug itself into Feng Laicai's arms and refused to allow its body to become wet. The girls doubled up with laughter and winked at Cadre Jiang with giggly eyes.

As they all lived on the same street and saw each other often, the girls were well-acquainted with Cadre Jiang and didn't think much of joking around in this way. But unexpectedly, Cadre Jiang assumed a stern frown and scolded: "What's so funny? Act fast; I don't have much time!"

Although he had to maintain his proper bearing, Jiang was secretly amused by the scene. The reprimands were followed up with coaxing incentives: "Don't hold back on using what you have. There's no need for hesitation, just use the best shampoo and give our black-eyed billy a wash and wave. When the goat has been made pretty, the township government will pay the bill. Your salon-keeper will be rewarded and you girls will get a bonus for sure."

Cadre Jiang then emphasised: "The face of the black-eyed billy is the face of the township government."

Every character issued from his mouth was as hard as iron: "How can we lose face for the government? Surely we cannot!"

It was fair to say that the girls were all qualified. They mixed boiled water with cold water and filled a transparent green watering can with the resultant warm water before pouring it at a confident, unhurried pace onto the curly wool. As it was discharged, the spray had the appearance of a bright lotus seed-head and the water penetrated all the way from the felt-like hair tips down to the follicles. With one stylist pouring and another gently rubbing shampoo onto the drenched fleece, they gave the goat a professional rinse.

Animals, like humans, are in need of comfort. Despite being a little upset at the outset, the adorable black-eyed goat gradually adapted to being waited on and placed itself at the mercy of the girls, enjoying their cosseting attentions without needing to seek solace from Feng Laicai.

The black-eyed billy was indeed filthy from being secreted in Dragon's Tail Ditch. Time and again the goat turned the water black. Fully five rinses were needed. Nevertheless, Cadre Jiang, who stood fast during the whole process, was far from satisfied. He urged the girls to clean the animal with fresh water twice and to apply shampoo twice. They acted in accordance with his wishes. Finally, when the water flowing down from the goat was crystal clear, he approved of the job they had done. Still, he further indicated that they should apply conditioner to the wool and delicately blow-dry it until it was fluffy. Once everything was completed, he ordered Feng Laicai to lead out the black-eyed billy.

Cadre Jiang was delighted with the final result, but after taking a second look, he decided Feng Laicai should take the goat back into the salon because its black eyes were not glossy enough. After its hair was steamed with nutritional oil, its black eyes became even prettier, like a pair of pitch-dark sunglasses. It should be mentioned that all township government cadres, including Secretary Hou, Township Head Gou and Cadre Jiang, loved wearing sunglasses.

Naturally, Feng Laicai, the one burdened with great expectations, had his hair styled in the salon as well. He, of course, enjoyed being blow-dried and conditioned.

After a whole sequence of washing, rinsing, rubbing and blowing, the black-eyed goat seemed to epitomise the proverb "girls become prettier and prettier as they grow up". It was indeed friendlier to the eye. The animal appeared more robust. His floppy, soft wool was now piled up like a heap of snowflakes which were sure to drift away on a gust of wind. So it was with Feng Laicai too. He had undergone an amazing transformation. Although his legs were still short and his arms extended to naught, his head shone and his face was neat.

He soon realised that the ache he previously felt in his heart was down to the unprecedented act of the township government cadre, who regarded it as a pleasure to pay the bill. And he too took the advantage of his black-eyed billy by enjoying his own servicing as paid for by the government.

Cadre Jiang was more than happy. His own ingenuity made him feel excited. Rather hastily, he led Feng Laicai, who was leading his even more beautiful black-eyed billy, into the compound of the township government. Immediately, eyes were cast upon them and people started to voice acclamations, including Secretary Hou of the Township Party Committee and Township Head Gou, both of whom wore gleeful eyes. They praised the black-eyed billy and, of course, Cadre Jiang.

Cadre Jiang asked Feng Laicai to fasten the goat in the compound and then seized him by the arms to take him up to his apartment. After closing the door, he conjured up a navy blue suit and a white shirt out of nowhere. While helping Feng Laicai to change, Cadre Jiang comforted him emotionally: "Who are we? We are kinsmen! Our joints would be connected to each other even if our bones were broken. Therefore, I'm obliged to take care of you, am I not? So, we are to attend the competition in the county with our fair black-eyed goat. How could you, its master, look a disgrace? You don't have a woman to think for you; if you did, it would be none of my business. But you don't, so I must think for you. Here, I've prepared a suit; hurry up and let me see if it fits. Otherwise, I'll return it to the tailor for modifications."

Feng Laicai undressed himself, but before he had a chance to scramble into his new suit Cadre Jiang shouted in surprise: "Not yet! Look at your neck; greasy as an axle!" While his mouth was moving, he busied his hands opening a Thermos bottle and poured water into a basin. Then he drenched Feng Laicai's neck in the basin, making the water greasy. Once Feng Laicai had been wiped clean, he was allowed to wear the suit. It had been rather difficult to find a suit in his size. Nonetheless, Cadre Jiang managed to pick one. "A person has their attire; a horse has its saddle" was the right phrase to describe Feng Laicai.

山羊

The county town was trapped in a deep watercourse.

Advancing ahead to make arrangements, Secretary Hou and Township Head Gou went off separately in their own cars. "Food and fodder should go ahead of troops and horses." Feng Laicai took this for granted. Although it was nothing like marching and fighting a battle, a half man could achieve nothing in a competition without adequate preparation. Feng Laicai understood the troubles the cadres had gone to, so he consciously mounted a farm motor tricycle and caught up with them. Naturally, he was with his well-furnished black-eyed billy; one man and a goat, sticking together, covered by the earthshaking growls of the motor tricycle, springing up and down on the bumpy road to the county with high hopes.

They descended from the northern slope of the county.

Feng Laicai had never been here before. He felt like he had fallen into a huge vat. White clay cliffs encircled him and long-engraved ditches and grooves cleaved by rainwater engendered shadowy wild jujubes that did not seem to differ greatly from those in Dragon's Tail Ditch in his native Head-of-the-Slope Village. His disturbed heart was pacified by the scene. When he arrived at the basin, the farm motor tricycle climbed onto a hunched cement bridge after a further stretch. Beneath this a pitch-dark stream consisting of rolling piles of foam, both ashen grey and dirt yellow in colour, swarmed grudgingly downwards. An unpleasant smell invaded Feng Laicai's nostrils and made a sense of pride rise in his heart. Head-of-the-Slope Village, small as it was, had much clearer water than this place; the whole village was fed on mineral water, as were his goats.

The competition was to be staged somewhere over the other side of the bridge. People had long since arrived like a surging tide of water. Feng Laicai's motor tricycle was barred by Secretary Hou and Township Head Gou's drivers, who were standing on the bridgehead. They escorted Feng and the goat down from the motor vehicle once it had been parked by the bridge under their supervision. The drivers urged them: "Hurry! Hurry!" But how? The half man and his sturdy black-eyed billy immediately drew a crowd and the onlookers began to judge the two in high spirits.

"Look, the man, the goat … so funny!" was the comment of one sharp-eyed woman.

"Is this a goat? How come it looks like a panda?" a middle-aged man interposed.

"Well, here we have the Champion Scholar Goat," added another cranky woman.

A further anonymous man spoke up. "This one is certainly superior to that one."

The ruckus created by the crowd was compounded by a song broadcast through the loudspeaker. Feng Laicai knew the song, it was "Enter the New Era". He loved this song, particularly its combination of decent melody and grating criticisms, and had memorised every word.

With two lusty drivers striving ahead in the crowd, Feng Laicai and his black-eyed billy nudged their way along without a bump. Immersed in the situation, Feng Laicai felt he was simultaneously familiar with and overwhelmed by it. But how come? Oh, right, it was on TV! Only the appearance of actors, singers and stars could stir such turbulence.

The two drivers were sweating bullets as they finally sent Feng Laicai and his black-eyed goat to their pre-allocated place.

Secretary Hou, who was carrying a string of carrots, had been waiting for some time together with Township Head Gou, who held a braised pork sandwich. The moment Feng Laicai and his black-eyed billy took to the stage, Secretary Hou came up and fed the billy his carrots and Township Head Gou thrust his braised pork sandwich at Feng Laicai. Secretary Hou coaxed the black-eyed goat to graze and Township Head Gou forced Feng Laicai to gorge. Both of them appeared anxious.

They had every reason to be anxious. The black-eyed billy had consumed half of its delicacy and Feng Laicai had taken just two bites of the braised pork sandwich when, after several attempts at clearing his throat while the song was still being broadcast, the announcer declared through the loudspeaker that the first session of the county goat competition was now open.

There were many leaders standing on the temporary podium. The short Feng Laicai groped around for his beloved Magistrate Jiang among them, but failed to find him. None of the faces, however mild or bespectacled, were familiar to him. Where was he? While he was in a state of bewilderment, the loudspeaker began to introduce the goat competition committee, first among whom was Magistrate Jiang. A cluster of names followed. Feng Laicai remembered none of them except for Magistrate Jiang. Yes, he was happy and had nothing to fear as long as Magistrate Jiang was here. But he noted that the prefix "deputy" had been added before Magistrate Jiang's title.

Feng Laicai understood some bureaucracy. Having the word "deputy" before his name Magistrate Jiang was destined to take a back seat.

Magistrate Jiang mounted the platform which faced the crowd for the introduction. It was a newly-built platform, which looked like a dual dais. It was a square stage about three feet above the ground decked with dark green carpet and handrails connected with cords of the same colour. Magistrate Jiang ascended it and began to wave to the crowd. Feng Laicai started to clap with such a force it was as though he was taking out his hatred on his hands.

The goat competition was organised by the township units. Each contestant led their goat to the high platform, as instructed by the loudspeaker, where they received the judgements of the experts. The experts worked diligently and impartially. They weighed each goat, measured its height, took its temperature, inspected its teeth and checked its posture. Each animal had a detailed analysis sheet so the final result could be ascertained.

At last, the black-eyed billy was called.

It was so crowded that Feng Laicai didn't hear the announcement. Only when his name had been announced three times and he was given the heads-up sign by Secretary Hou and Township Head Gou did he lead his black-eyed charge onto the platform. Feng Laicai was undeniably special. His special quality lay in his dwarfism. The black-eyed billy was special too, though its speciality was found in its enormous stature and, of course, its black eyes. One pipsqueak and one lofty goat. The audience below the stage started to heap acclaim upon them, beginning the moment the two appeared and before the experts had started their inspection, as if a pair of admired stars were performing for them. The applause was as fierce and as relentless as a thunderstorm on a summer's day.

This was something to feel cheery about. Needless to say, Feng Laicai and his black-eyed billy had created a good impression.

The reporters from the TV station, newspapers and radio stations all stepped forward and besieged Feng Laicai and his goat on the platform. Some of them came from the provincial capital, Xi'an, some from Chencang City, and others were local. Regardless of their region of origin, they hurried to click their shutters, generating a noise like a sunny storm at the height of summer. Feng Laicai found himself almost dazzled by the lights.

Feng Laicai sensed that the reporters were more interested in him and his black-eyed billy than the others. This was not really hard to comprehend, for he and his goat were so unusual, the animal especially. The journalists had a certain shrewdness bred from their profession. They could feign interest and sincerity when confronted with the most mundane subjects. Feng Laicai, meanwhile, noticed that none of the goats was superior to his own black-eyed specimen. Indeed, his black-eyed billy was so outstanding that even before it reached the platform it was obviously a crane being made to stand among chickens. It dominated the rest of the competition like a triton of the minnows.

Like the other contestants, the goat had its weight, height, temperature and teeth measured, and then the experts requested that it do a turn on the catwalk. The black-eyed billy had not been trained for the catwalk, but it did it anyway with a style and panache that reminded people of professional models. It gave the impression that each of its hooves had been fitted with springs and the judges, who each wore an expression of satisfaction and delight, found the spectacle alluring. Suddenly, the billy held up its head and bleated to the crowd. With the momentum of a tsunami, this virtuous, melodious and esoteric piece of music caused the well-attended meeting to burst into applause.

The result was soon revealed. Feng Laicai and his black-eyed goat had, as expected, won the title of Champion Scholar Goat.

Tears coursed down Feng Laicai's cheeks.

With a gleeful smile and eyes brimming with tears, Feng and his black-eyed billy were once again invited onto the platform, where they were flashed at by countless cameras, something which caused his eyes to be more teary still.

Feng Laicai didn't know Secretary Xiong of the County Party Committee, but it was he who announced through the microphone that the black-eyed billy had won the title of Champion Scholar Goat. Feng Laicai didn't know Magistrate Niu either, but it was he who presented a gold medal to the black-eyed billy and, of course, to Feng Laicai, who had bred it. Trailing Magistrate Niu up onto the platform were two young ladies clad in *qipao* dresses. How slender were their figures! It was like being confronted by two straight white poplars. Feng Laicai warily raised his head, only to see the poplars were covered with crimson Mandarin gowns and embellished with powder and rouge. Flashing gold medals and a bunch of flowers bound with a coloured ribbon lay on the circular platter the ladies were carrying between them. After shaking hands with Feng Laicai and conveying a few compliments, Magistrate Niu draped medals around Feng and the goat's necks and passed over the bouquet.

Next came the grand parade.

The farm motor tricycle that had carried Feng here was unfit for the occasion. An over-decorated float, however, that had long since been parked nearby and was safely guarded by two fully-armed police officers, stood ready as its replacement. The officers, as martial as they were wont, thrust Feng Laicai and his black-eyed billy onto the float. The two ladies who had accompanied Magistrate Niu were already up there one step ahead of him. Feng Laicai and his goat were surrounded by the two ladies, who wore radiant faces, and by the policemen, who defended the other two. The audience, who had crowded into a circle, now made a line behind the float, spouting rapturously, as if the scholar title had actually been awarded to them.

Two huge speakers on the float broadcast songs and news items in turns. After *Enter the New Era* came news stories detailing Feng Laicai's route to prosperity and how his ram had come to win the title.

The black-eyed ram itself behaved with a jot of haughtiness, throwing its head back and turning its dark eyeballs from one side to the other to project the air of a victor. What was more, it amplified the stunning song by bleating out *baa-baa*.

山羊

Cadre Jiang, who was watching the competition on TV, sprang to his feet. It was not only he who hailed the proclamation of the black-eyed ram as Champion Scholar Goat, but all the cadres from the township government who were watching the same programme on the TV. They were simply not as cheerful as Cadre Jiang (of course they weren't). The masses had no idea how many cadres their township had, whereas Cadre Jiang, compelled as he was to muddle along with the others, knew only too well. Everyone had his own business, so they just cheered for the ram out of courtesy and support. As for those who were in the habit of calling on favours, they pestered Cadre Jiang for a treat.

They agreed in unison: let's eat that bastard scholar goat!

Cadre Jiang's response was ambiguous: "That's not my Champion Scholar Goat, don't ask me."

Jesting around with other folks, Cadre Jiang retreated from the compound to a nearby village. Although there were many cadres in the township, only a minority of them were local, with Cadre Jiang being one of the few. The village he went to was his birthplace. His failure to transfer to another town can be attributed to his background. Unlike others who became cadres as soon as they graduated, Cadre Jiang didn't have the chance to attend university in the first place. Instead, he cultivated himself through self-study and when efforts were made to implement institutional reform to the cadre system, he sat the government public entrance examination. Fortunately, he passed the exam and signed on as a so-called "contracted cadre". As the village was listed as his home on his household registration card, he had to eat grains harvested from his village, despite drawing his pay from the government. Therefore, he needed to be prudent about the people he was prepared to receive and how he dealt with affairs in the township government compound. As for those outsiders who beat a path to his door, regardless of how uncouth the manners of other cadres were and what cold shoulders buffered him, he was not entitled to act in a lordly way. How could he?

To be frank, in the light of all his endeavours on behalf of the billy goat, Cadre Jiang would have loved to have gone to watch the competition, but the appearance of Secretary Hou and Township Head Gou smothered his craving and he was forced to stay in town.

He also bore in mind his promise to Feng Laicai that he would find someone to "keep his feet warm". Yes, he had said that, and he had no plan to eat his words.

This begged the question: where was he to find the right woman?

Who would marry Feng Laicai, the half man? Still, Cadre Jiang knew the country well and his mind turned to a young widow in his neighbourhood. Cadre Jiang belonged to the same generation as her parents, so the young widow was obliged to call him "uncle". A couple of days ago, he bumped into her on the way home and made his purpose known, only to find that the young widow was more than a little hesitant.

She rebuked him, blushing, and begged: "Please, Uncle, please introduce me to someone better than that!"

Cadre Jiang provoked her: "Feng Laicai is someone better!"

"How can he be better? He's only a half man."

"He has a herd of goats!"

"That's no big deal," came the reply.

"No big deal? You want to live a life? Someone who can raise goats well ought to be able to lead his life well," Cadre Jiang said earnestly.

The young widow said nothing in reply, but her failure to speak out in denial conveyed her attitude. And now Feng Laicai and his black-eyed billy had tasted success, he was bound to talk to her again in an attempt to become privy to her innermost thoughts.

While Cadre Jiang was on his way to the young widow, Feng Laicai and his black-eyed goat were finishing the parade before retiring to a banquet staged by Magistrate Jiang.

It was Secretary Hou and Township Head Gou who informed Feng Laicai of this invitation.

Nobody knew where Secretary Hou and Township Head Gou went during the parade. They appeared from nowhere as soon as the float finished its boisterous cruise through the two main roads and parked in front of the platform. The two cadres called upon their drivers to help Feng Laicai and his black-eyed goat off the truck and relayed the invitation face-to-face.

Secretary Hou's words were tinged with envy: "The magistrate's banquet – how dignified you have become."

Township Head Gou was another jealous cove: "I can freeload on your coattails from the magistrate's table. Well, well, well."

Feng Laicai had felt as if he were in the midst of a dream all day. Everything had happened so quickly – driving his billy to the county, the competition, the parade – he felt warm in his heart and hot on his face; everything was in such a jumble and then Magistrate Jiang invited him to banquet and share a drink.

Feng Laicai followed Secretary Hou and Township Head Gou to the Guanzhong Garden restaurant to meet Magistrate Jiang.

Feng Laicai thought he was the sole invitee, only to discover that his black-eyed billy was on the guest list too. Secretary Hou and Township Head Gou strode on ahead. The red flower the ram had sported during the parade was still on its head, as was the Scholar's medal that hung about its neck. The path to the restaurant thus became another parade with some people even whistling at them. It was not until Feng Laicai sensed the emptiness in his belly that they arrived at the grand Guanzhong Garden.

Feng Laicai had heard from others that outside the county there was a courtyard-style venue for recreation. As he stepped into the garden, he found it was bigger than had been described. There was nothing novel about the layout, which followed the manner of a common-or-garden farmhouse, with the addition of newly-planted locust trees, engraved hitching posts erected in a line under the trees, carved stone lions and gate piers. Observing these items one after another, Feng Laicai noticed that each had endured a degree of wear and tear over time, which endowed them with a sense of history.

He had spent less than one day away from home and yet Feng Laicai had already started to miss his father. He wanted to tell the paralysed old man about his recent adventures to enliven his gloomy heart.

His father had shed tears more than once over his son. Like all fathers, he wished for his son to be strong and indomitable. Damn the Heavens and their blindness, he had given been a dwarf! How depressing was that? Who would have expected that the blindness of the Heavens could be healed and that, against the odds, his half son and the goat he had raised should receive the title of scholar.

What a day! What a glorious moment!

Magistrate Jiang caught Feng Laicai by the hand and said: "Congratulations!" Feng Laicai was still daydreaming about his father while the smiling Magistrate Jiang (well, "deputy", but what a vicious word that was! Feng Laicai chose to ignore the prefix) greeted him.

He blushed and murmured: "It's all because of you."

The reporters who followed Magistrate Jiang all the time now crowded the two with their weapons once again, whipping up a flashing tempest just as they had done on the platform.

The reporters then started to gabble out their questions to Feng Laicai, who did not know which ones to answer. Magistrate Jiang tried to mediate a way through the stalemate by declaring: "Let's have dinner!" But that did not work. Some reporters rejected the idea with justification: "Please show some respect. If we don't get what we want, we'd rather not have dinner." Then Feng Laicai began to speak.

He started out with a question: "Do you know who I want to express my thanks most of all to? Is it to my black-eyed billy who is now the Champion Scholar Goat?"

Speechless, the reporters looked at each other.

Feng Laicai answered his own question: "It's to Magistrate Jiang!"

Once the chatterbox had been roused, it was hard to make him settle. Laicai detailed how he had hidden from the cadres, how he'd been helpless and straitened. Then he shifted the subject to Magistrate Jiang and confided how the magistrate found him in the cave, sent him the breed, helped him to analyse the grass and water. Feng Laicai raised his voice as he spoke and again offered a question in a humorous tone: "Do you know what kind of grass my goats graze on?"

The reporters had by now become familiar with his manner of speaking, so they just waited, leaving the question up in the air.

Feng said: "It's a Chinese herbal medicine!"

Everyone was astonished.

Feng continued: "And do you know what kind of water my goats drink?"

Nobody stirred.

"Mineral water!"

Further astonishment.

Feng Laicai rambled on to the reporters about how Magistrate Jiang had followed him to Dragon's Tail Ditch to herd the goats, and how he had collected grass and water samples to be tested in the provincial capital.

The reporters, some of whom took notes and some recordings, were all intrigued by his tale. Feng Laicai answered each of their impromptu questions in a proper way.

He himself was also affected by his volubility.

When was the last time he had given such a speech? Probably never. Within the limits of his memory, he had only every been in the position of listener or of having to bear derision. Caught between the burdens of his shameful living conditions and his dwarfish figure, he had suffered jibes and humiliation.

"Why not get married?" the scoffers would always ask.

Feng Laicai was experienced enough not to be trapped by such an opening because it always served as the prelude to an even crueller prank.

But, sure enough, they usually continued: "How nice it would be for you to fling your arms around an iron hot bride! What would you do to her? Eh? Can you get it up? Need any help from us?"

Everyone burst out laughing.

That was not even the end of it: "As for the bed, how high is it off the floor? Do you need a leg-up from your honey?"

But today was different. Nobody held him up for ridicule and, being the leading player, he didn't need to hear anybody out. Those whose ears were collectively open to him today were reporters many times superior to the ones who had laughed at him. He couldn't help but be affected.

Magistrate Jiang, who stood by and listened, found a chance to join in: "Please take your seats! Our Champion Scholar Goat and its master will reside here for two days, so you have plenty of time. Now, let's fill our bellies."

The bustling interview concluded. Following Magistrate Jiang's guidance, the crowd advanced into a private dining room of the old-fashioned style. The Champion Scholar Goat, which up until now had been steered by the hands of Feng Laicai, was escorted by a waiter to enjoy its own banquet in the corner.

Through a bright windowpane, Feng Laicai saw that, without losing any of its grace, his black-eyed billy was swallowing carrots, pumpkin chips and potatoes of the type that were rarely seen back home. At intervals, enthusiastic onlookers came closer to the beast to take pictures.

Ushering Feng Laicai to the host's seat at the banqueting table, Magistrate Jiang sat beside him. Such a gesture was lauded by the reporters. Secretary Hou and Township Head Gou took their seats on the other side of Feng Laicai, forming a circle round the table with the reporters. While the reporters were still reeling at his act of abdication, Magistrate Jiang stood up with a glass of liquor clasped in his hand. He first congratulated Feng Laicai and expressed his appreciation to the reporters then, finally, he reeled off his speech to Secretary Hou and Township Head Gou, who had accompanied Feng Laicai to the county.

Magistrate Jiang sounded sincere: "These two gentlemen should be counted as what we call 'real men of merit'. Had not the Township Party Committee and the government leaders lent a hand, neither the black-eyed goat's title nor Feng Laicai's newfound prosperity would have been realised."

Shrewd as they both were, neither Secretary Hou nor Township Head Gou interrupted, but when he was finished, they said: "That's too much, we're so embarrassed by your praise, it's all because of your resolution, Magistrate."

Their response aroused a question that lay buried in Feng Laicai's heart: was it true that Magistrate Jiang had spent his own money importing the fine breed?

Magistrate Jiang threw back his head and drank deeply, giving a bottoms-up sign. He then displayed his cup upside down, as a sign of absolute courtesy. On seeing this, all the others followed likewise.

Feng Laicai, who had never drunk before, tossed back his cup in the name of infinite gratitude.

山羊

The young widow was none other than Ma Lala, who was known to Feng Laicai from his days in the township government's black detention cabin. For years, she had been unemployed and wept on account of this predicament from time to time.

Borne along by his meteoric paces, Cadre Jiang reached Ma Lala's threshold ahead of schedule. Ma Lala was mucking-out the goat pen. Later, she would shift the waste to the field to guarantee next year's harvest. Ma Lala was a diligent and thrifty woman and would always apply her know-how. With this in mind, she summoned up all her courage and attention to turn the dirt and so didn't sense Cadre Jiang's presence outside the fold.

Cadre Jiang started with a sigh: "Ah! Your lot is so bitter!"

His greeting, however, coincided with Ma Lala lifting a spade of goat manure and he recoiled back from within the waist-high wall of the enclosure. Pellets of dung and dirt landed on Cadre Jiang's shoes, causing him to stamp his feet as he bounced away from the fold. Stunned by this brouhaha, Ma Lala looked on the verge of making an awkward apology that never came.

Wiping the sweat from her brow, Ma Lala said: "Oh, it's you. Still thinking about my bitterness?"

Cadre Jiang seized upon her words and stepped forward: "Me thinking about you? About another marriage? I do know someone who's thinking of you for sure."

Removing herself from the goat pen, Ma Lala welcomed Cadre Jiang into the front yard for a talk. In the front yard there stood a jujube tree, covered with light green fruit that reflected a jade radiance beneath the sun. In its shade lay a verdigris flagstone that had previously been used for drying out quilts. It was supported by four stout bricks at each corner and was flanked by two matching piers. The piers served as benches for guests and had long ago been bruised into the colour of jade as well. Living in the same village as Ma Lala, Cadre Jiang was acquainted with her household. He was aware of Ma Lala's prudence and orderliness, which whether she was acting as a wife or a widow, had been engraved onto her disposition. Of course, her household had a more lethargic air than before. Once the cadre had planted his posterior on the pier, he started to talk.

"Do you want to know who's thinking about you all the time?"

Clutching a bowl of water in her hands, Ma Lala said to Cadre Jiang, who appeared in a high mood: "Have some water and give your throat a rest."

Cadre Jiang took the bowl. Instead of drinking, he fixed his eyes on Ma Lala: "Don't you want to know?"

Rendered bashful by his passionate eyes, she said: "You told me last time. Why bother asking again?"

Cadre Jiang was pleased with her reply and declared: "Yes, I did. But do you know what's up with him now? In a trice, he's become famous and everyone knows him. His black-eyed billy won the county competition and the title of Champion Scholar Goat! How about that? His goat has garnered a reputation and so has he. Didn't you watch it on TV? I did. I saw him. He was wearing a red flower and a colourful sash and leading his ram through the township government to have his photograph taken with the magistrate. And they joined a parade, like a carnival, cruising all around the county. What a day! You'd be jealous if you'd seen the show. What's more, there were handsome ladies in *qipao* next to him on the float. Their long legs, their bare white thighs … alongside Feng Laicai. The whole county saw it. Feng Laicai was so blessed."

Cadre Jiang's speech was simmering away. He kept on boasting until, all of a sudden, he found Ma Lala's face had clouded over. Bridling his tongue, he washed the words down with some water.

What Cadre Jiang didn't know was that Ma Lala had kept his words in mind ever since the last time they met. Since then, her heart had become attached to the one who went over to the county town. Since she didn't have a TV set at home, she went to her neighbour's to watch Feng Laicai. How happy she was for the man who had once been her cellmate in the black cabin. She was so elated that she forgot herself. Even the neighbour whose house she was visiting became suspicious that she was taking drugs. After returning home, she had paced up and down in the yard, pondering Cadre Jiang's words. Her face flared in a fiery way and she couldn't calm herself down. Finally, she was brought back to herself by the sight of the fold, which needed mucking out. So, she scurried in and stuck her shovel fiercely into the dirt. All the while, she was awaiting Cadre Jiang's visit, longing to hear his enquiries. Now, Cadre Jiang was here, enquiring after her, but she was struggling.

Seeing through her, Cadre Jiang put down the bowl and asked: "This is strange. You don't want to hear from him?"

Ma Lala quibbled: "Hearing about his affairs won't do me any good."

Cadre Jiang laughed, knowing a result was in sight. "Hear me out, if you will. Lead your goat to his. He'll be the herdsman and you the housewife. Then his affairs will be your affairs."

Her clouded face turned coy, yet she still refused to give way. "Sure, that half man's something now, but how can he look up to me? Young ladies, perhaps, are out of his league."

Cadre Jiang raised his bowl, quaffed a mouthful of water, then stood up and enjoined Ma Lala: "Wait for my message. I'm a cadre; cadres never lie."

On the other hand, Feng Laicai was still in the county and had no idea about the changes ahead. According to Magistrate Jiang's arrangements, he, together with the newly-crowned black-eyed billy, would go to several up-and-coming country towns to make speeches, inciting others to get on board with this business like him so that everyone might shake off poverty and strive for a comfortable life.

Feng Laicai was already tired of this gallivanting around, and so was his black-eyed goat. After the rigmarole was over, Secretary

Hou and Township Head Gou accompanied him back to Head-of-the-Slope Village.

A gong and drum band hired by the Village Head was waiting for Laicai at the entrance to the village. Feng Laicai was thus received by the band and was caught among the deafening maelstrom as it heaved towards his home. The whole of Head-of-the-Slope Village was stirred by this boisterousness and the red silks tied to the drumsticks danced in the hands of the drummers.

Having weathered the events of the last few days, Feng Laicai wasn't at all surprised. He'd grown accustomed to it, for all the prior festivities had been on a larger scale than this one at home. On his return home, he could not, however, ignore the celebrations but had to stand in a daze with his eyes wide open and his heart fully occupied.

That once messy yard was now clean and orderly.

The scattered bits of rubble and broken tiles had been sorted into a corner, everything had been trimmed into shipshape fashion, and every scrap of firewood and hay had been carried to another corner and piled up carefully. As for the weeds, someone had uprooted them one blade after another before drenching the bare ground and stamping on it, one foot after another, until it was flat and smooth. Feng Laicai saw dense footprints. Those were the footprints of a woman! His heart was drumming but he couldn't hazard a guess at who this buddha might be. In his wildest imagination he could conceive of the seven heavenly fairies, a fox fairy and some evil spirits, but who could this be?

Standing close to Feng Laicai, Cadre Jiang announced loudly to the smoky kitchen: "Ma Lala, come out and receive your man!"

An eye-scorching red entity blazed out from behind the fog and flame. The colour of her clothing seemed to directly reflect the hue of the fog and flame.

Ma Lala? Who's she? His thoughts, like a train in reverse, shunted back to the township government's black cabin. Were they one and the same person?

That eye-scorching red entity stepped gaily towards Feng Laicai, transferring the cloth bag that had been on his shoulder onto hers. She said: "You must be tired. Come on in and rest. Lunch will be ready soon."

Her voice and her figure assured Feng Laicai that she was the Ma Lala who had spent days with him in the black cabin.

Thinking he must have slipped into a dream, Feng Laicai mumbled: "Is it you?"

Ma Lala replied with a coy smile. Her glossy face was as rosy as the garments she was wearing.

Feng Laicai was still caught in confusion: "It really is you?"

Of the three people in the room, Cadre Jiang was momentarily ignored by the other two. Clearly he was also oblivious to their inner thoughts. He just looked at them, relieved to have made their acquaintance and believing that his efforts were worthy. Cadre Jiang had told Feng Laicai's father what was going on and had introduced Ma Lala to her future father-in-law in advance of meeting her husband. Her would-be father-in-law was so excited about it that he nearly recovered from his paralysis and sat up.

Brimming with tears, the old man snuffled: "Fine, fine, my son will have a bride. Now I can die in peace."

Ma Lala was not only an observant woman, but a diligent hand. Two days before Feng Laicai's arrival, she followed Cadre Jiang to Feng's house and met with his kindhearted, paralysed old man. At once she felt pity in her heart. Without any prompting, she stayed of her own volition. She first laundered the old man's bedding and garments then she boiled a pot of hot water to wash the plates and bowls before finally cleaning up the yard.

The scene Feng Laicai observed upon returning home that morning was the product of Ma Lala's labour. She started cooking the moment the band struck up at the entrance under the baton of the Village Head.

Cadre Jiang was elated. With a smile on his face and in high spirits, he improvised a speech to the Head-of-the-Slope villagers who crowded into Feng's house, announcing: "I have a pair of shoes to wear."

It was a custom in the Western Plain that a couple expressed their thanks to a matchmaker with a pair of shoes.

"Hang out the red satin! Hurry!" Someone yelled.

"Slaughter a goat! Hurry!"

The gong and drum band that had been about to bring their performance to an end suddenly stirred up again. Streaks of red silk were flying up and down in the bandsmen's hands and Feng Laicai's house was drowning in a sea of scarlet.

Ma Lala had been shoved upon Feng Laicai, but these two – one tall and one short – forged an unexpected harmony between their discordant figures.

山羊

The seasons ran in sympathy with Feng Laicai's fortune, advancing from a sweltering summer through a fully-fledged autumn before eventually entering a lengthy winter. A deputy was needed from Head-of-the-Slope Village to participate in the general election for the township government. What should have been a solemn event went awry in Head-of-the-Slope Village for the villagers, in the main, pledged their sacred ballots to Feng Laicai's black-eyed billy.

Their reasoning was simple: it had to be the Champion Scholar Goat. Who could boast a bigger name than the goat? Who had a better reputation? They plumped for the Champion Scholar Goat.

Although it was only early winter, the northwesterly wind blowing in from Dragon's Tail Ditch still brought a nip to the air, chilling the atmosphere at the voter mobilisation meeting staged in Head-of-the-Slope Village.

The Village Head, the host of the meeting, was black in the face. In the past, several sessions of deputies had been elected from the village and he, the Village Head, was re-elected every single time, but now the voting came to an inevitable deadlock. Before the session began, he had thought it through and judged that there was nobody in the village who could defeat him. That's why he appeared relaxed before the vote. He neither canvassed for the unanimous backing of influential voters nor demanded that they persuade the villagers to support him. Instead, assuming an informal manner, he merely encouraged everyone to carry forward the spirit of democracy and not be afraid and indecisive. He further – blithely – asked them to vote for whomever they trusted (even a goat would be fine).

To discuss their choice of the goat, some villagers split off into small huddles and although they tried to keep to a low mutter, they still could not help letting out the occasional audible sneer.

The Village Head could not smell trouble brewing, but continued to simmer in the smugness of his oratory, which, in his opinion, resonated with his fellow villagers.

Voting commenced. The ballot consisted of a soybean clutched in the hand of each voter and cast into one of three bowls on a long table. Each bowl bore the name card of the candidate, one of these being the Village Head. To begin with, everyone just copied the Village Head, who led the line and put the soybean in his own bowl. The Village Head was so confident about his re-election that he went over to one side with a winner's smile to chat with other people. At this moment, someone put another bowl on the table beside the other three and threw his soybean in it. "The Champion Scholar Goat", someone gently read out loud with a smirk. This proved to be the start of the disaster. The voters who followed on behind each successively threw their soybeans into the fourth bowl.

Two inspectors realised the gravity of the situation and left to tell the Village Head. But the outcome was irreversible.

There was no need to count. Even a child could tell that the black-eyed billy had the most soybeans in his bowl. The Village Head swapped his smug face for a gloomy leer. He could hear sly giggles among the crowd, and some even hooted. "The Champion Scholar Goat," some muffled voice let out as though it was carefully planned. "The black-eyed billy," piped up another.

Feng Laicai was not there at the time, so he did not know how astounded his wife was. Ma Lala stared blankly at the fervent crowd and felt an odd sense of gaiety. The type of blushes that normally only appear after drinking sprang up on her cheeks and resembled two amorous flowers in full bloom.

As a bride married to a Head-of-the-Slope villager, Ma Lala had long ago made two resolutions for herself: never volunteer for anything; never speak out on behalf of anyone. But facing something as gravid as this, she had no choice but to speak.

"How could a goat get in?" She mumbled.

Though this was meant as a soliloquy, she was overheard by the villagers and they settled down.

"A goat is not a man," she uttered again.

It was her words that prompted Cadre Jiang, who had come from the township government to oversee the election. Just now, he had been puzzled by the voters. His chubby, round face, wrung out by such an awkward predicament, effused strings of greasy sweat. He was groaning in his heart: "Oh! Oh! What to do?" Having been a capable cadre, Jiang felt himself pinned down this time. But Ma Lala's appearance, like an eye-flashing torch, made him exuberant again. He reverted back to being that capable Cadre Jiang.

From where he was seated behind the bowls of soybeans, Cadre Jiang stood up in an imposing manner. He cleared his throat with affectation, placed one hand on the table and through bulging eyes scanned around the gathered villagers.

His opening speech praised the Head-of-the-Slope villagers for their sense of propriety and responsibility before outlining what he had experienced and how he had been toughened as a cadre. He said: "Very good! In the course of our development, it would be absolutely unwise to abandon our sense of propriety and our sense of responsibility as long as we hope to live happy and comfortable lives. Today, our election for a township NPC member rightly gave expression to these two senses. We voted for the Champion Scholar Goat because the goat – that black-eyed billy – best represented our interests!"

The previously silent crowd became a little agitated.

Cadre Jiang then paused for a while. He lifted his hands and turned his palms downwards, as if he wanted to squash something down, and the crowd returned to silence.

"Of course, the black-eyed goat is not a man," Cadre Jiang's voice was loud and his gestures potent. Under the guidance of his hands, he hastened onto to say: "This is a fact; a fact we cannot deny; a fact we cannot argue with. The Champion Scholar Goat is no man, but I would like to ask: was the goat blown over here on the wind or did it fall down from the Heavens? I doubt it. Then, where did it come from? In other words, how was it reared? Reared to be a Champion Scholar Goat? It's because of a man, my dear fellows. You should see that more clearly than I do. The goat was raised by Feng Laicai! It was Feng Laicai who fed it up to be a Champion Scholar Goat!"

The speech was followed by great gusts of applause.

Cadre Jiang wiped the sweat from his forehead and waited for the applause to stop.

"The Champion Scholar Goat is no man, but Feng Laicai is a man. Voting for the goat was tantamount to voting for Feng Laicai. You tell me, is that not so?" He added.

"Yes!" came the perfectly synchronised answer.

Everybody was squinting around looking for Feng Laicai, the newly-elected representative. Unfortunately, he was not there. They only found his newly-married wife Ma Lala. It was no strange thing for Feng Laicai to be absent. No one had ever seen him in any meeting of the village. Before today, Feng Laicai was a forgotten cog in the political life of Head-of-the-Slope Village.

Little talks were taking place stealthily among the huddles. Others overheard things only vaguely and so no one could relay them lucidly. Meanwhile, someone yelled at the joyful Ma Lala: "Ma Lala, say something! Slaughter a goat and cook some soup for us!"

Then others joined in: "You promised to slaughter a goat once you got married. Since we were all prepared to eat your goat, you kept quiet. This time we won't let you off the hook!"

Ma Lala, who had once been detained in the black cabin, started to cry among the wrangle and laughter of the villagers. She was happy for her half man husband, especially as he had once endured the same sufferings as her in the cabin. What were they back then? Worse than hogs! But now, the half man was her man and she his woman. Her servile half man had the chance to be a real man; he had been elected the representative! How could she not be happy? The tears that simmered out tasted sweet and delightful. They were tears of joy.

The clamour still reverberated in everybody's ears: "Kill a goat! Make us soup!"

Ma Lala stood with her chest out and her head raised. She had decided to comply with the villagers. When she was marrying Feng Laicai, she had stood in the way of her man, who was ready to slaughter a goat for the wedding banquet. She asked him in a plain way: "Do we just mean to live for this one day? Tomorrow must we tie up our mouths and have nothing to eat?" Feng Laicai wasn't at all persuaded. She continued: "I'm no spring chicken anymore, not a first-time bride. If you aren't afraid of gossip, hold a swish wedding party, but please be considerate. I'm worried that others will criticise me behind my back." So, the goat survived and she let the villagers down. But this time was different. Feng Laicai had been elected the representative; that once despised thing was now qualified to attend people's congress as a "person" and could express his views and stand like a "person". There was now good reason to slaughter the goat.

Sunlight landed on the villagers and made them warm. Head-of-the-Slope villagers, whether old or young, all heard the promise emanating from Ma Lala: "Slaughter a goat. Make soup!"

山羊

One, two … seven, eight … eighteen, nineteen … the half man Feng Laicai was completely unaware of his election as the people's deputy. Like every other day, he ran to the goat pen in Dragon's Tail Ditch to drive his animals. While letting the black-eyed billy lead the herd to the slope to eat, he, having a shiny shovel at hand, dived straight into the cote to collect manure. He scooped up the droppings onto a wooden cart and promptly wheeled it out to a nearby heap. In time, the pile turned into a dunghill. As a base for wheat, nothing could beat it; for an autumn harvest, nothing could beat it. Compared with other people's fields which relied on expensive chemical fertiliser, his allocated field was not as carefully tended, but his goat manure gave it a better yield. Goats were the bedrock upon which everything that happened to him was built. He loved his goats as if they were his life. Not only the black-eyed billy, but every animal he owned. He spent most of his time with his goats and he never ignored a single one of them, let alone slaughtered them. After finishing his work in the pen, he would scurry to catch up with his goats and count them as a matter of routine.

Every time he counted the herd, his emotions deepened and he found something novel in the process. For example, the one upon which his eyes now fell had become his intimate friend. He even gave it a lovely name: Blessed Maid.

Feng Laicai couldn't recall when exactly their intimacy had begun, nor could he remember whether he or Blessed Maid initiated the relationship. But that was not the point. Whenever he saw her, his eyes assumed a genial look. Although he was genial to every last one of his goats, there were still crevices that only he comprehended.

It seemed Blessed Maid could read his mind. A sturdy, pasture-dwelling specimen, she was the most handsome one among the flock and had given birth to three kids in her prime and weaned them singlehandedly. Her sons, daughters and grandchildren were part of the herd. In other words, Blessed Maid was a merciful grandma with a large family around her.

Blessed Maid seemed aware of Feng Laicai's partiality for her and responded in no time to her master whenever he yelled randomly or roared a little ditty. She did so with her perpetual refrain: *baa!* This monotonous echo was not pleasant but it would attract Feng Laicai's attention. How tender his eyes were! Leapfrogging over all the other goats, his sight locked on the snow-white Blessed Maid and caressed her. Then, utterly satisfied, Blessed Maid would gorge herself on the grass in preparation for her next conception.

Alas, Blessed Maid was old. Within four or five years she would grow too old to conceive. Yet she still grazed as much as she could and stuffed her tummy. If possible, she even found her way to Feng

Laicai and snuggled against him to ruminate. Feng Laicai noticed that she was ruminating much less frequently than in the past.

Today, as usual, Blessed Maid followed the flock into the depths of Dragon's Tail Ditch. Arriving at what had been a fertile meadow, the herd abandoned their procession, dispersing instead to enjoy the yellow autumn grass. Everybody knows that the green grass of spring adds flesh to goats, but few know that the withered grass of late autumn functions in the same way. The former is prized for its juice while the latter has its seeds. As always, after she had stuffed herself with grass, Blessed Maid strolled to Feng Laicai and crouched by his side to ruminate. Feng Laicai fondled her curled wool, bit by bit. Then he gave a heavy sigh, over Blessed Maid of course. Once barren, a goat had nothing ahead of it except slaughter.

Blessed Maid, her eyes suddenly moist, seemed to understand Feng Laicai's sigh.

As a herdsman, Feng Laicai was kept busy from dawn to dusk, his only company the animals and the slope. A herdsman was also a man, and how could a man not communicate with others all day long. But apart from Laicai himself, there was no other person in the wild Dragon's Tail Ditch. It was true that he had married his Ma Lala and she already had a son of her own, but they could only talk after he had returned home. And even then, all Feng Laicai spoke about whenever he ate the dinner cooked by Ma Lala, stroked his stepson's glossy black hair or fed his paralysed but jolly father was his goats. That Blessed Maid of his, his most bellicose goat, the most yappy goat and, of course, the illustriously-named and meritorious one: the black-eyed billy.

With regard to the black-eyed billy, Feng Laicai was again about to consult his beloved Magistrate Jiang. Since his return from the county with this great honour, he hadn't caught sight of the man. Feng Laicai was, however, thinking about him a lot: "Magistrate Jiang took a risk when loaning me money for my Boer goats, so I won't let him take any more risks. I'll save some money to pay him back."

Feng Laicai repeated his vow many times in the house until he was made aware that it was annoying. Then he started to nag his goats out on the slope. Among such a herd, only the gaunt goat that could not digest loved to be his audience and preferred that he restate his story ad nauseum.

It was so amusing that the goat bleated out one sound after another without ever shutting its mouth. It wanted to speak out and even pounded its hooves to make Feng Laicai understand what she wanted.

Feng Laicai's patience was on full display now. He would wave to the yappy goat and stamp, like it did, at the grass and shout loudly: "Speak less! Eat more! Eat until you put on some weight."

While counting the goats, his gaze fell upon the aggressive one.

Even though this one loved to quarrel, Feng Laicai was still fond of it. One of the reasons was that it bore a close resemblance to the Champion Scholar Goat. It, like the Champion Scholar Goat, had snow-white wool and two oddly black circles around its eyes, which looked as if they were painted on by some eminent artist with a saturated brush. It was so beautiful.

It sported a pair of bulky, sharp horns as well.

It was eager to fight like a martial hero because it knew that the glory of life rested on its pair of horns. It stuck out its sharp horns to fight. At first, it challenged whoever crossed its path with bare-faced contact. After some moments of rampage, it started to direct its attention to the black-eyed billy and, within days of observing it, the turbid eyes of the goat were fully focused on the Champion Scholar Goat.

It was not so strange, for both the billies were full of pride.

Only one male had the honour of being dominant over the others. Presently, the black-eyed billy was king of the herd and did not fear competitors, even tolerating its reckless kin with a regal spirit. Obviously, the black-eyed billy underestimated its mate, for it hadn't anticipated that the duel that was brewing would break out the selfsame day when, without bloodshed, Feng Laicai defeated his Village Head in the election for the people's deputy.

The young should never be fearful in the face of grey age. But in a duel that rested on muscle power alone, the black-eyed billy was trounced by its opponent in the first round. Meanwhile, the Head-of-the-Slope villagers were throwing their soybeans in the bowl that belonged to the black-eyed billy.

Feng Laicai had missed his opportunity to witness the defeat of the Village Head, but he was present to view the duel between the two male goats in its entirety. At first, Feng Laicai was displeased over his black-eyed billy and rushed to the battlefield in the hope of intervening. Instead of interfering in the fight, however, he bellowed with laughter over his moronic behaviour. After years of being a goatherd and from his own personal experiences, he knew that it was perfectly natural for the younger party to defy the senior. So it was with the black-eyed billy; it couldn't escape. Lost in thought, Feng Laicai stood aloof from the duel, his eyes fixed on the action and unable to stop himself applauding.

The two beasts kept on fighting for such a long time that even the onlooker became exhausted. At last, the two worn out antagonists backed down at the same time and called it a day. Now, Feng Laicai sat down on the slope and started to count his goats. When he came to the last one that tailed the herd, his heart ached immediately.

It was an ache that couldn't be alleviated. The last one left behind was up for the cull. Since Ma Lala moved in with him, his father had rallied under her attention. According to Ma Lala's plan, every two weeks she'd pull the old man on a handcart to the hospital. The cart was lined with straw and bedding and the paralysed father on top of it was well-wrapped in a warm quilt. Acupuncture, cupping and prescriptions of all kinds were employed, so their expenditure rocketed. When short of cash, she took over a goat as compensation. And so it was, Ma Lala pulled the cart with her paralysed father on it, dragging a goat behind. Thanks to the reputation of the black-eyed billy, people felt it would be a lucky gourmet who took a bite of the beast that had been fed on Chinese herbs and mineral water. As a result, being short of money was not a big deal because goat meat made up the balance for the medical expenses.

Over the course of many days, a total of six stragglers joined the line to the hospital kitchen.

Then the teachers to whom Feng Laicai's stepson would be assigned after the summer politely demanded two goats fed on herbs and mineral water as a guarantee of enrollment. Goat lover that he was, Feng Laicai couldn't think of any reason to decline, so on the day term began he led another two goats to the school along with his son and handed them over to the teachers.

Driving goats carelessly on the slope of Dragon's Tail Ditch, Feng Laicai listened carefully for the sound of reading to waft into his ears and, unexpectedly, heard the plaintive whine of his dying animals floating over.

Lamentable yet curiously optimistic, Feng Laicai stopped counting and simply closed his eyes. Again, he raised his head to feel the sunshine, which enveloped the world around him and left he and his goats both shrouded in its illusion.

Ma Lala, who was by now in a rush, sidled up to Feng Laicai. She was in such a hurry that Feng Laicai was startled by her presence.

"You … what's going on?" Feng Laicai's heart was racing.

"I can't wait." Ma Lala was breathless.

"What happened?" Feng Laicai was in a daze.

"Something good!"

"Are you pregnant?" Feng Laicai asked, laughing.

Regaining her breath, Ma Lala stopped teasing her man and told him directly: "You've been elected as the deputy."

山羊

Instead of celebrating with his wife, Feng Laicai turned his head to the herd and grumbled: "People's Deputy? Me? Sounds like they elected my goat!"

It felt rather good to be a People's Deputy.

Before experiencing it for himself, Feng Laicai already knew that the repast was fairly good at the People's Congress, but its true magnitude was beyond his imagination. Chargers drenched with wine and engulfed with meat were in every corner. Even though he was full-flush with all kinds of fantastic thoughts, he still found himself staggered by the banquet table and had no idea which plate he should start with. During meetings, the town's high-grade restaurants were all booked up by the township government and every meal was prepared à la carte. To avoid any possible disorderliness, all the people's deputies were split into groups and each group was led by one township cadre. Coincidentally, Feng Laicai was dispatched to the group led by Cadre Jiang.

If asked, Feng Laicai probably would not remember what he had consumed during those days because there were tons of delicacies that he had never seen or heard of before. Trepang, soft-shelled turtle and river crab were among those he had heard of but never clapped eyes on; sashimi, squid, clams and mouse-fish were dishes he had never even heard of. As delicacies landed like bombs, Feng Laicai and his fellow deputies stuffed themselves to the accompaniment of furious burping. Everyone was elated with the arrangements. In addition, all kinds of beverages were served to the deputies: white wine, red wine, beer, yoghurt, fruit juices and fruit vinegar. None of these were familiar to Feng Laicai and he was embarrassed when the waiter asked him which one he would like. Not knowing what to request, he just ordered what others were ordering, which meant he basically tasted everything that was going.

So did Cadre Jiang, who, in a heroic manner, stood at the table and toasted the deputies one by one. He raised three rounds to each man: a shot of Chinese liquor, a shot of red wine and a shot of beer. Every time he came to Feng Laicai's table he would stop for a while to chat. "How's your family?" Cadre Jiang patted Feng on the shoulder and asked. "Fine, fine," Feng Laicai swiftly replied and nodded his head tacitly. He understood that Cadre Jiang was talking about his wife Ma Lala and he gave the same answer three times regardless of whether Cadre Jiang's hand contained Chinese liquor, red wine or beer. However, the deputies at the same table, who were not familiar with the background, all sensed that this was odd. Sure enough, the news of the happy event did become known to those around the table and they howled at Feng Laicai, saying that he shouldn't forget the matchmaker once he had got married and should thank him no matter what.

Deputies at the next table were affected by the mood and joined in as well. They argued that Feng Laicai should bring two goats to the session as an acknowledgement to the matchmaker, and of course, to everyone else.

One after another there were howls of: "Kill a goat, we want the soup!"

Having been driven into a corner, Feng Laicai had no other choice but to consent. He believed that Cadre Jiang had treated him well and regarded the promotion of the black-eyed billy to Champion Scholar Goat as his own business. The same could be said of fixing him up with a good wife. He should thank Cadre Jiang.

The noise had not yet calmed down: "Feng Laicai, kill the goat! We support Cadre Jiang!"

Drowning in such a scrum, Feng Laicai stood up (although he was the same height as he was when sitting down, the gesture showed his determination). He raised a glass of beer and forced it down. He then mopped his mouth with both hands and shrieked: "I'm going home to fetch the goat!"

The rumbustious deputies were silenced at last by Feng Laicai's announcement. In fact, they were so silent that even the movement of the hands on their watches sounded noisy. Cadre Jiang, as always, stood up to mediate by pulling Feng Laicai to his seat. "Why are you crying out? I showed compassion for him. It was my duty as a cadre. How can I accept gifts? Save your mouths for food!"

Everyone complied with Cadre Jiang's instruction except for Feng Laicai, who, shaking his stubborn head, tried to stand up and threatened to go home right away for the goat.

Cadre Jiang pressed his hand on Feng's shoulder: "Do you want me to slip-up, eh? The township government can afford to stage the meeting, so we can cover the catering. This is out of our respect for the deputies as well as the popular will."

Finally, Feng Laicai stopped struggling but still said: "Wait for me, I'll bring two goats for sure; I won't make empty promises."

The feast continued. Cadre Jiang told Feng Laicai all about Magistrate Jiang's promotion from deputy to acting magistrate.

Feng Laicai was overjoyed and asked for confirmation: "That is true, isn't it?"

The reply from Cadre Jiang was affirmative. Then Feng Laicai answered in relief: "That's the way it should be!"

Cadre Jiang further disclosed to him the news about Township Secretary Hou, saying that he had achieved what he longed for by being transferred to the county and thus reunited with his family.

Feng Laicai was happy for him: "That's great, really great."

In between these snippets of conversation, they did not forgot to toast to one another. With greasy lips and wine-tasting mouths, the group did not give up their bingeing until the table was a mess.

Feng Laicai returned to Head-of-the-Slope Village alone on the second night of the meeting. He led two goats from the herd and returned to town that very night. While delivering his goats to the restaurant, he confided in the kitchen staff that they should slaughter them and make broth for the deputies the next morning.

Feng Laicai could not bear the nightmarish wails and brays of his goats going under the cleaver. So, after handing them over, he ducked away to find Cadre Jiang.

Feng Laicai met Cadre Jiang in his dormitory. That night, a young man like him, who never even tried a cigarette, had been transformed into a chain smoker. As he opened the door, Feng Laicai thought the room had caught fire, only to find Cadre Jiang sitting next to his three-drawer table smoking in a pall of choking fog. A bowl stuffed with butts served as a makeshift ashtray.

Slipping in, Feng Laicai startled Cadre Jiang.

Feng Laicai affected an innocent smile and told him all about the goats.

Then came the wails of the goats again. Feng Laicai instinctively cricked his neck and started shivering. He shivered hard, as if it were he rather than the goat that was being slaughtered. Cadre Jiang had, of course, heard the sound but, being much less bothered by it, crushed out the stub in the bowl and turned to Feng Laicai, who was still trembling: "Not necessary, it wasn't worth it."

A puzzled Feng Laicai asked: "Why?"

Cadre Jiang smiled bitterly: "You wouldn't understand even if I told you."

"I don't need to know," Feng Laicai retorted. "All I need to do is support whoever serves the people."

Cadre Jiang said nothing in reply but caught Feng Laicai by the arm and shook it vigorously.

The next morning mutton soup was served and, while breakfast was being taken, word circulated among the deputies that it was Feng Laicai who had offered up the goat.

The voting for the post of supplementary Deputy Head of the Township began and, surprisingly, apart from some ballots cast for the favoured parachuted-in candidate, most of the deputies voted for Cadre Jiang. The announcement of the winner resulted in a ripple of applause, to which Feng Laicai contributed the fiercest clapping. What he didn't know while celebrating Cadre Jiang's win was that something pitiful and yet irreversible had occurred in Head-of-the-Slope primary school.

山羊

Ma Lala's son was asked by the teacher to pick nuts from a walnut tree. Unfortunately, he stamped on an unstable branch and fell to the ground, ending up in a coma.

The moment Feng Laicai stepped out of the meeting room, his way was blocked by a messenger from the village. Still immersed in the thrill of victory, he responded to the man with a broken smile: "*Who* fell from the tree?"

The messenger was too impatient to retell the story and dragged Feng Laicai away and hit the road.

While haring home, Feng Laicai, now clearly filled in on the situation, asked the man in a total panic: "How's my son now? Where is he?"

The messenger told him that his son had been taken to hospital.

They ran in the direction of the township hospital on West Street. Feng Laicai was running so fast that his legs caved in upon reaching the hospital gate and he crashed to the ground like a man who has had his muscles removed and his bones smashed. He struggled and struggled but still failed to stand up. It was the messenger who, by tugging and carrying, brought him to the emergency room. Seeing his son lying on a door plank, Feng Laicai at once threw himself down on him and dissolved into a storm of weeping: "Son! My poor son!"

Ma Lala, to his side, was reduced to sobs too.

Feng Laicai could not stop wailing and, as he raised his voice still further, was joined in his lament by Ma Lala.

The doctor, who was by now done with her examination, shook her head as she cleared away the instruments. She told the battered parents to transfer the boy as soon as possible because the limited resources on the ward could do nothing for such a grievously injured patient.

In his despair, Feng Laicai turned to the doctor, grabbing her hands and imploring with broken words: "Doctor, master, you check over my son. I'll go fetch my goats. However many you want, I can bring them all."

As a woman, and a young woman at that, the doctor was not altogether comfortable with Feng Laicai's reaction. Working in the hospital, she had endured all kinds of uneasy experiences. Kowtowing and rolling about on the ground, hugging her legs, she accepted it all. Instead of making a scene, she smothered her anger and soothed Feng Laicai: "We don't want your goats."

Laicai was a stubborn-headed soul. "I have goats. I insist."

The doctor interrupted him: "It's not about your goats. Your boy is too badly hurt. If you delay transferring him for even one minute he will be put at greater risk. Is that what you want?"

On hearing this, Ma Lala, who was choking back her own tears, fell to the floor.

The doctor shook off Feng Laicai's hand and dashed over to Ma Lala. With the help of the kind-hearted doctor, an ambulance from the county hospital was called and the trio was transferred.

The child was saved in the county hospital. After a series of remedies, the boy was able to swallow and empty his bowels and bladder, but could not speak. His eyes darted all around without a word.

Ma Lala, guarding the bed, wiped away her tears and nagged all day long: "Say something, son, say that you ache, that your body aches, please!"

Feng Laicai echoed: "Yes, say one word: ache."

The consultant's conclusions were devastating. Feng Laicai and Ma Lala were informed by the hospital that their son was in a persistent vegetative state.

山羊

At first, the couple was not clear what this meant and conferred with the doctor, who impatiently tossed out a reply: "Call out your son's name and see if he responds. If not, there's your answer."

Feng Laicai and Ma Lala still declined to acknowledge the facts. Instead they murmured: "He can eat, he can drink and his eyes are open. How can it be so?"

Some doctors who knew Feng Laicai from the media mocked him: "Who might you be, the master of the black-eyed billy? How dare we fool you? Eh? How dare we?"

Feeling discouraged, the couple still wouldn't surrender to fate, so they stationed themselves in the county hospital, waiting for a miracle. Unfortunately, the medical costs, which would prove a bottomless pit to the rich, were all the more grave to a humble family like Feng's. Even if their banknotes were bundled up as bricks it would be impossible to plug the hole.

Boundless misery and everlasting sorrow seared their brows like the freezing winter. Seeing their plight and observing their determination, the doctor in attendance, whose intentions were benevolent, stepped onto their ward one snowy morning. Making a routine round, the physician said with a heavy sigh: "I won't make excuses for myself, nor will I blame you as parents; we all tried our best. I'm a doctor. I don't give the sick a wide berth, yet there are some sick people who cannot be cured. You're the parents, that's true, and all your efforts are for your child. Your hearts must ache over his illness. But all you can do is ache in vain because you can't replace your son. So, where's the way out? Unless you want to wear the whole family down, it is unwise to let him suffer in the hospital. I can write some prescriptions and you can complete the discharge procedure and go home. Have a good rest at home in case a miracle does come along."

While enduring this agony in the hospital, Ma Lala found that even her rough swarthy hands had become bleached. She stroked her son's forehead again and again without responding to the doctor, and without even raising her head. Tears shimmered in her eyes and fell down in strings like cold rain onto her fair hand and her child's face.

"Never!" Laicai stuck out his chest. "We won't go home, we'll stay till there is a cure."

Feng Laicai's voice assumed a volume that it had never possessed before. In fact, he was so loud that even Ma Lala was startled. She lifted her head and glanced at her man, then turned to the doctor. It was hard to imagine that Ma Lala, at this juncture, would break into a smile. What a beautiful smile! It had been a long time since she had worn such a smile. What a weeping beauty! She made Feng Laicai – the father – and the dutiful doctor feel like they had been stabbed in the heart with a dagger.

Ma Lala eventually relented: "Thank you doctor. Thank you for your kindness. You did your best. We will follow your suggestion."

Tipping himself onto his feet, Feng Laicai dabbed the melting snowflakes from the doctor's shoulder and formed a contrary plan: "We put our child in your hands. We're not afraid of spending money. As long as our son is cured, spending cash is no big deal. Right?" Feng sounded simultaneously masculine and tender in tone; being a father, how could he carry a child who had not been cured out of the hospital?

What more could the doctor say? Struggling in his heart, he turned to the door. Ma Lala, however, called him back and said: "I'm the child's next of kin and I've decided to accept your advice and leave right away." Hearing this, Feng Laicai stepped forward and herded the doctor out of the room: "Listen, doctor, my words count. I'll go home now and fetch a goat. Just like the Champion Scholar Goat, it's been fed on traditional Chinese herbs and mineral water. It'll make a delicious mutton broth!"

Despite the doctor's reluctance, Feng Laicai fulfilled his promise by bringing a goat, a black-eyed one, the kindred of the Champion Scholar Goat, from his fold back in Head-of-the-Slope Village.

Instead of picking the "drop out" goat as he usually did, this time Feng Laicai broke the rule he insisted on. To show the doctor his sincerity, he purposely chose the lively one that had challenged the Champion Scholar Goat. He thought in this way the doctor would be sure to cure his son.

Bearing some of the joint liability, the school gave a sum in compensation to the family. But how much money could a rural school offer? A tiny piece of expenditure like this was already enough to crush it. Feng Laicai was clear on this point. He knew that were the school pushed to the wall it would face dissolution or be put under the hammer. He could not ruin the school.

Cadre Jiang, who had been elected Deputy Head of the Township, planned to promote Feng Laicai's experience of gaining prosperity. Upon learning of this accident, he, in the first instance, arranged for volunteers to mind Feng's goats, and, in the second, donated half his monthly salary to fund the son's treatment. Following his example, all the school teachers donated likewise. Nonetheless, when dealing with acute situations like this, such charity often proves utterly inadequate.

Even a hero can be defeated by money.

Feng Laicai the half man was not a hero, but he must act like one for the sake of his son. Collaring the goat, he glanced at his father and scuttled all the way to the county hospital. He felt estranged from his village, but couldn't put his finger on why. It was just that the villagers' attitude towards him seemed to have slipped back to how it had been when he was a nobody. Nevertheless, the Village Head, who Feng Laicai had replaced as a deputy, seemed to be acting in a conciliatory manner. His overzealous greetings raised Laicai's suspicions, making him probe whether he was being considerate or sneering.

Passing the township government made Feng Laicai think of Cadre Jiang, so he decided to step inside. Knocking on the door of Cadre Jiang's dormitory, Feng Laicai didn't expect that some other cadres would open it. They refused to divulge more when questioned. Disappointed by this failed visit, Feng Laicai had no choice but to lead his goat out. "What a bloody weird day!" he mused. "The atmosphere here is the same as at Head-of-the-Slope Village."

Some idlers, seeing Feng Laicai towing a goat in a gloomy mood, crowded over, calling: "Is that the Champion Scholar Goat?"

"Not really," was Feng Laicai's honest answer.

"Don't try and fool us," the idlers continued. "Nobody will rob you of your goat even it is the Champion Scholar Goat."

The crowd was bemused by him. Then one thing led to another. Some of them mentioned the deputy election at Head-of-the-Slope Village, in which Cadre Jiang was involved. One said: "Filled with the pride he borrowed from the Champion Scholar Goat, Cadre Jiang didn't take the candidate chosen by his superiors seriously. Well, wielding his power, he managed to get himself elected. But guess what? Nobody told him the truth until his seat was already warm. Let's wait and see what fallout he might have to deal with."

The gang dispersed.

The crowd was far away, yet Laicai could still hear them: "What scholar?"; "Isn't that just one of Cadre Jiang's tricks?"; "They not only washed the goat at that salon but lacquered it and gave it a blow-dry. Everybody knows the stories."; "What a plot!"

Feng Laicai could not remember how he had ended up on that rowdy street and how he had made his way to the county. Not until he ran full tilt into the missing Cadre Jiang at the gate of the hospital was he roused to full consciousness. He felt his cheeks were burning as if he had done something that Cadre Jiang would never forgive. Originally, Laicai planned to confide his misfortunes to Jiang, but now he couldn't utter a word.

In contrast, Cadre Jiang had depression sketched over his face. It seemed like he had a thousand replies for Feng Laicai but could not muster one solitary word.

The goatherd could not help but ask: "Tell me, are you under investigation?"

Cadre Jiang simply nodded: "It's best that you know. Then you can prepare yourself in case they ask you for information."

Before he could finish, Feng Laicai interposed: "Then I shall tell them that you're a clean cadre! A cadre who people welcome!"

Feeling a little relieved, Cadre Jiang admitted: "Yes, I want to be that type of cadre. But it's not up to me; it's beyond my reach."

Trying to lift his spirits, Feng Laicai said: "I'll visit Magistrate Jiang. He told me to call on him whenever I have troubles. I'll go to him and tell him."

Cadre Jiang smiled.

Then Feng Laicai added, sounding confident: "You take care. Just let them conduct their investigation. After I've met with Magistrate Jiang, let's see what happens then."

山羊

Two streets separated the county government from the hospital.

A humming market cleaved a passageway between the county government on the old street and the hospital on the new street. Ever since it was established, the market had been crammed with people. The second they entered the market, some sharp-eyed individuals recognised Feng Laicai and the goat behind him. The animal, despite not being the renowned Champion Scholar Goat, was taken by everyone as the black-eyed one.

"Wow! The Champion Scholar Goat!"

"For sale? How much? I'll take it!"

"For sure, this goat will prove a delicacy."

All this gabbling awoke Feng Laicai to the fact that he still had the goat while on his way to see Magistrate Jiang. Embarrassed and shamefaced, he turned to the county hospital and went directly to the staff canteen. Explaining himself to the chief cook, he fastened his goat to the pillar of the coal bunker and went off. Unfortunately, he didn't meet Magistrate Jiang. In fact, he didn't even enter the gate. He was barred by two uniformed young men at the gatehouse who, with a word, tossed out the news that Magistrate Jiang had a meeting in the provincial capital.

Deciding not to make himself tiresome, Feng Laicai turned and left. But then he turned back again after two further steps and said to the young men: "If Magistrate Jiang comes back, tell him that Feng Laicai's here. I want to express my thanks to him for helping me win with the Champion Scholar Goat."

Back at the hospital, the day was growing dark.

Before entering the ward, Feng Laicai heard his wife calling their son gently by his name. This made his heart shudder and he felt that every word that passed from his beloved Ma Lala's throat conveyed the taste of warm blood. Slipping into the ward, Feng touched his child's forehead and stroked his wife on the head as well. Saying nothing, he withdrew from the ward and went to the canteen in the backyard.

The cooks knew Feng Laicai well for he had long been stationed in the hospital and, more importantly, Feng and his Champion Scholar Goat were celebrities. The cooks also knew that he had sent his goat for the doctors to feast on. So, some of the cooks thrust steamed breads crammed with pickles and porridge his way as soon as they saw him entering the canteen. They wanted him to fill his own belly before slaughtering the goat.

Feng Laicai was deeply uneasy over dinner and even choked on it several times.

Laicai would rather die than slaughter the goat. It was his goat. He raised his goats, and every last one of them was his treasure. How could he pick up a blade and slit its throat? For the sake of his son and his wife, he had no choice but to do the deed.

His dinner hardly ingested, Feng Laicai took a blade from the cook and went off to his dear goat. To the accompaniment of a baleful squeaking, the black-eyed animal collapsed in a pool of blood. Dropping the blade, Laicai turned his head without glancing at the goat and went straight to the ward in the front yard.

"How delicious! This is a true delicacy!"

Waking up from his nightmare, Feng Laicai sensed a whiff of exotic fragrance. He scrambled up from his stool and followed his nose to the staff canteen. A dense crowd was descending for the soup. The chief cook had already ladled out a bowl in preparation for Feng Laicai. Carrying the vessel in both his hands, Feng Laicai swallowed several times, his gaunt neck moving up and down. The rim had already touched his lips, but still he didn't take his share.

It was his dear goat and he could never swallow it down.

Feng Laicai left the canteen holding the bowl. He exited the hospital, slid through the lonely market and reached the gate of the county government. The two uniformed young men he met yesterday had been replaced by another pair.

Feng Laicai asked: "Has Magistrate Jiang come back?"

The two looked blankly at one other and it dawned on him that he had been gulled yesterday. They had fabricated a story because they didn't want him to see Magistrate Jiang. Pretending to be audacious and without seeking the sentries' consent, Feng Laicai strode in through the gate. Sobering up from their consternation, the two men caught up with Feng Laicai and collared him.

"What's your business here?" they demanded.

Laicai pushed the soup towards them and answered: "Nothing serious; I came to bring Magistrate Jiang this mutton soup."

The two sentries pulled at his clothes and retorted: "Keep it for yourself, Magistrate Jiang has no shortage of soup to drink."

"Sure, sure. I tell you what though, he hasn't tasted my mutton soup. Hear me out; do you know who I am? I am master of the Champion Scholar Goat. Magistrate Jiang supported me, so I owe him the guarantee for my loan. It would be nothing for me to send him a bowl of soup. It wouldn't be enough to pay back his favour if I sent him one goat. No, ten!"

Laicai became more and more emotional, but in spite of how he yelled and growled, the two young men still tried to shoo him out of the gate. Time elapsed and the press of people thickened. The once steaming bowl turned cold and was covered with a layer of oil as white as wax.

Beep, beep sounded the horn of a shiny black car from the depths of the yard. It stopped at the gate, against which the young sentries hailed Feng Laicai to the side and saluted, watching the car go off to the other end of the street. Simmering with grievances in his heart, Feng Laicai watched the car as it passed him by. Suddenly, he realised that the man sitting in the back seat receiving the salutation was the one he was looking for. Breaking away from the sentries, he ran after the accelerating car.

"Magistrate Jiang, mutton soup! Magistrate Jiang, soup!" Feng Laicai wailed.

山羊

The following days saw him shuttling to and fro from the hospital to the government building. At first, he was able to keep count of the number of times he made the journey, but later on he slipped into confusion. It was as though he was revising school work and could see no end to it all. Ultimately, he did not once get permission to enter the compound, let alone see Magistrate Jiang.

Feng Laicai had to foot his son's medical expenses, which had already exhausted his pathetic savings along with Ma Lala's dowry. He began to sell his goats and, however fine the breed was, they all had to be converted into cash. Feng Laicai seized one goat after another from Head-of-the-Slope Village and sold them in the town or county. What meagre paper money he earned, Feng Laicai spent it all on his son. But, just as the doctor had told them, there was no sign of recovery in spite of the money that flowed in. Days went by and only the renowned Champion Scholar Goat was left.

As the proverb states: "Misfortune never comes along alone." On the third snowy day in succession, the paralysed old man became stiff upon the clay *kang* to which he had been confined for life.

Feng Laicai returned to Head-of-the-Slope Village to take care of his father's funeral. Harbouring immense grief, he erected a memorial tablet and waited for Ma Lala who, carrying their son on her back, arrived in no time. She simply set down the boy on the other end of the *kang* and burst into moans before the tablet. But weeping would not help cover the cost of the old man's burial.

Feng Laicai led his Scholar Goat to the Village Head and knelt down, hoarsely begging: "Please Village Head, I have nothing else to show my appreciation with. Just this Champion Scholar Goat, fed with herbs and mineral water. Kill it. Make a broth for the villagers."

Cold-faced – colder than ever – the Village Head squinted at the kneeling Feng Laicai, took a cigarette from his pocket and lit it. Not until the stub had burnt up to his lips did he spit it out. Finally, he opened his mouth and every word smashed into Feng Laicai's face as cold as ice.

"Still so proud? Proud of your herd? Even now?"

"Don't kowtow to me. I can't bury your father. Kowtow from door to door in front of every villager until they agree."

As well as detecting Village Head's resentment, Feng Laicai sensed his fellow villagers' resentment too. But he couldn't figure out why they had changed so fast, as fast as a baby's bottom, which was clean yesterday and filthy today. Who had he offended? Nobody. He had just fallen foul of the fickleness of fate, which was responsible for shattering his son, killing his father and then abruptly making the villagers angry with him. Feng Laicai couldn't get over it, for he believed there must be other reasons. Could it stem from his lone moment of glory with his goat? If so, he was still puzzled. Why couldn't he be afforded decency for once? He had his rights but knew that it was useless to try and reason with the others. Begging for help was what needed to be done right now. Nothing could be more important than burying his father in peace. For that reason, Feng Laicai dared not answer back.

Feng Laicai turned to the fold and hugged the Champion Scholar Goat in his arms before thrusting it away and stabbing its throat.

The Champion Scholar Goat bayed.

That night, Feng Laicai set up an iron cauldron and stewed the skinned goat until it was tender. He jointed the carcass and ladled the pieces into bowls of soup. Before dawn, he delivered the broth to every door in turn. He believed they all must have heard the slaughter and, having drunk his Scholar soup, would come and chip in.

As expected, the villagers who had hitherto been underground all reappeared.

Looking into the distance, Cadre Jiang had to wipe away tears again and again as the bier made its descent into the grave.

Feng Laicai did not know that Cadre Jiang had already been dismissed from his post as Deputy Township Head.

山羊

The pan was cold; so too was the *kang*.

Leaning close to each other, the poor couple couldn't feel one bit of warmth. Partitioned off by loess walls, this pathetic pair could only sniff the aroma of steamed buns and boiled meat drifting in from others' kitchens. New Year was coming and some repeat-snapping firecrackers would occasionally leap up into the sky and then make the ground blossom with red paper. Through the window pane, which was one hand's width, Feng Laicai spied the goatskin nailed to the wall. Oh, his glorious Champion Scholar Goat, pegged flat with some splinters of wood. The only valuable thing owned by this utterly destitute family was this pelt.

Off-loading the drowsy and weary Ma Lala from his arms, Feng Laicai whispered into her ear: "Tough as the New Year may be, we have to face it anyway." He then dismounted the *kang* and strode to the goatskin, his head feeling heavy. He pulled out the splinters and rolled the hide under his arm. Coming out of the village, the day was dark, so he groped his way towards the gate of the township government.

To tell the truth, Feng Laicai had not wanted to come here again.

He was no fool and he knew that Magistrate Jiang was hiding from him.

Feng Laicai was about to sell the skin for some lean meat to make dumplings. Without knowing the reason though, his feet betrayed his heart and nudged him to the county government once again. There could be no doubt he wanted to see Magistrate Jiang. He wanted to tell him about Cadre Jiang, who had been elected as Deputy Head of the township and then removed from office. Was he unqualified for the job? As for the charge of bribery, hadn't it been his own intention to sacrifice his goat for the deputies? How then did it concern Cadre Jiang? Of course, he wanted to apologise to him as well. Apologise for having lost all the Boer goats and for not paying off the loan he had made as guarantee. But he could only brazen it out and wait for his day to come.

He also wanted to ask: "Why have you gone so far as to hide from me?" This time, instead of arguing with the sentries, declaring that he belonged to the specialist households sponsored by Magistrate Jiang and that his goat had won the title of Champion Scholar Goat, Feng Laicai ducked into the darkness outside the gate and watched people and cars go in and out. Maybe Magistrate Jiang would once again be as amiable and considerate as the first time they met. Feng Laicai waited, rapt in his dreams, but Magistrate Jiang never appeared.

Had he forgotten him? He was puzzled and perplexed.

The day was still completely dark. Snowflakes fell from the sky and kissed the ground for the second time. Feng Laicai was too drowsy to stand still. Strolling to another corner near the gate for shelter, he kept on staring at the entrance. He noticed that everyone looked busy as they paced along and everybody was carrying or shouldering bags of different shapes and sizes, almost as if the space before the gate was a trading market for New Year gifts. Finally, all returned to silence. Feng Laicai felt cold. It started first in his skin then penetrated into his blood and, finally, his bones. Before freezing to death, Feng Laicai realised that the goatskin was under his arm. He shook out the fleece and wrapped it about his person. How warm the skin was! His body shrank little by little into the skin and, at last, merged with it. Snow kept falling on the curly wool, one layer after another, eventually transforming Feng Laicai into the black-eyed Champion Scholar Goat.

That's right. Feng Laicai would rather be a goat. He told himself: "It's fair enough that my beloved Magistrate Jiang has forgotten me, but how could he forget the Champion Scholar Goat?"

Notes on the text

Various traditional Chinese units of measurement are used in the text:
1 *sheng* = approximately 1 litre
1 *zhang* = approximately 3 1/3 metres
1 *li* = approximately 0.5 kilometres
1 *mu* = approximately 663 2/3 square metres

The counties of Shaanxi Province in which the stories of Wu Kejing are set all fall under the jurisdiction of present-day Baoji City. Since ancient times, this region has been referred to as *Xifu*, meaning the "Western Prefecture". Owing to the cumbersome nature of this expression, *Xifu* is here translated as "Western Plain" in further reference to how Baoji lies in the westerly portion of the Guanzhong Plain (alternatively known as the Central Shaanxi Plain).

As demonstrated in 'The Qiyang Widow', *Xifu* people traditionally pride themselves on their hospitality and banqueting follows a set etiquette derived mostly from *The Rites of Zhou* (*Zhou Li*), attributed to Duke Wen of Zhou (11th century BC), though probably not of such remote antiquity. The host should be modest about the quality of their spread, toasts should be given in rounds of three and the cook may add coins to the filling of boiled dumplings, rather like British people putting silver sixpences in a Christmas pudding. As a counterpoint, the author mentions two famous examples of feasts thrown with ulterior motives. Liu Bang (256 BC-195 BC), who was later enthroned as the Emperor Gaozu of Han, sat and ate with his sworn enemy Xiang Yu at Hongmen, not knowing if he was about to be assassinated. On ascending the throne as Emperor Taizu of Song, Zhao Kuangyin (927-76 AD) threw a banquet at which, during the drinking stage, he convinced his leading generals to retire from their posts.

The life of cultured retreat initially led by the Qiyang Widow and her husband is also strongly redolent of the pre-Communist era, when every village and small town had its own scholars, aspiring to perfect their pastimes. In seeking to emulate Yan's sinews and Liu's bones in their calligraphy, they are harking back to Yan Zhengqin (709-85 AD) and Liu Gongquan (778-865 AD), two masters of the regular script style.

The ten stories in this volume are arranged in broadly chronological order, according to the historical events referred to in the text. In 'The Bloodstained Dress', Madame Spots is a graduate of the all-female Ginling College, set up in 1913 in Nanjing (capital of the Republic of China from 1927-37 and 1940-5). She and her husband return to Shaanxi following the Fall of Shanghai late in 1937 and there are several allusions to local notables of the day, including her purchasing a sign by the Sanyuan-born calligrapher and statesman Yu Youren (1879-1964). By living past 1947, the Qiyang Widow has the misfortune of losing her property in the first round of land redistribution enacted locally by the Communists. Like Madame Spots, she has her grave desecrated under the Tomb Planning Movement. In some instances, local authorities would insist on the levelling of burial grounds to maximise the amount of land available for agricultural cultivation.

Similarly, the protagonist in 'Red Lantern' finds herself caught between tradition and progress to her cost. Uneducated as she is, she is still familiar with the stories of how the Han Dynasty beauty Wang Zhaojuan was married off to appease the Hunnish tribes, how the royal concubine Yang Guifei (719-56 AD) drowned her sorrows all too easily when she felt the Emperor had spurned her and how the female warrior Mulan enlisted in the army disguised as a man. The poetess Su Hui (4th and 5th centuries AD) is perhaps included by way of a kindred spirit for she too plied her hands to curry favour. In her case, she embroidered a self-composed palindrome poem to win back her errant husband.

'The Blood Red Sun' reaches its climax at the height of The Great Leap Forward (1958-62), when meals were taken communally with co-workers in the Production Brigade. The hair-raising displays of Date Stone's father and grandfather highlight how, at the time, beggars extorted money through threats of mutilation and self-harm rather than spinning tales of woe.

Other stories including 'Cliff-slide', 'Tile', 'The Well Head' and 'The Champion Scholar Goat' are set more or less contemporaneous to their time of composition. Here, the rural economy had undergone another significant reform, not least in the disbanding of Production Brigades and the redistribution of communal land back to villagers in 1982-5. Coming full circle, when Feng Laicai's billy goat wins the county level competition he is dubbed, somewhat satirically, a "Champion Scholar". In pre-revolutionary days, residents of provincial areas sat an imperial entrance examination as a ticket to securing government employment at a higher level. The top scorer in each round gained the much-coveted title of "Champion Scholar" (*Zhuangyuan*).

Endnotes

a These lines are quoted from the *Three Character Classic (Sanzijing)* and the *Hundred Family Surnames (Baijiaxing)*.

b **The Three Principles of the People** *(Sanmin Zhuyi)* refer to the democratic concepts formulated by Sun Yat-sen (1866-1925), the early leader of the Republic of China. They are: People's Rule *(Minzu Zhuyi)*, People's Democracy *(Minquan Zhuyi)* and People's Livelihood *(Minsheng Zhuyi)*.

c **Xiezhi** is a legendary beast in the ancient times which can tell right from wrong and use its horn to butt an evildoer whenever there is a fight.

d **Hou** is a legendary doglike man-eating creature.

e In China, willow twigs are commonly inserted into the soil of a grave. The practice emerged out of the belief that this plant has the power to ward off evil spirits and ghosts and protect the living from malign supernatural forces.

Acknowledgements

The stories in this collection were translated by the following: 'The Bloodstained Dress' by Professor Zhang Yating (Shaanxi Normal University); 'The Phoenix Widow' Dr Su Rui (Northwest University); 'The Qiyang Widow' He Longping (Changsha Normal University); 'Red Lantern' Dr Wan Bing (Hunan Normal University); 'The Blood Red Sun' Liu Xiaofeng (Civil Aviation University of China, Tianjin); 'The Black Bean Field' Ai Fuqi (Xidian University); 'Tile' Jin Huaifang (Northwest University); 'The Well Head' Gao Minna (Northwest University); 'Cliff-slide' Xu Lin (Northwest University); and 'The Champion Scholar Goat' Zhang Hongrui (doctoral candidate at Beijing Foreign Studies University). Dr Robin Gilbank co-operated closely in the editing and preparation of the text. An earlier version of 'The Bloodstained Dress' appeared in *Old Land, New Tales* (China Commercial Press, 2011).

The authors and translators wish to thank Jamie McGarry and Valley Press for bringing this publication to fruition. Financial support was provided by the Centre for Chinese Literary Criticism at Northwest University. Thanks are also due to Dr J Graham Jones for his assistance in proofreading.

Lightning Source UK Ltd.
Milton Keynes UK
UKHW041228300719
347088UK00001B/22/P